THE DEFENDANTS

THADDEUS MURFEE SERIES LEGAL THRILLER

JOHN ELLSWORTH

SUBJUDICA HOUSE

ISBN: 0615953778

ISBN-13: 978-0615953779

1

S he was standing at the ancient desk in his law office when she unbuttoned her blouse. She was wearing a white button-down Ralph Lauren, paisley tie, khaki slacks, penny loafers, and a red barrette to keep the pageboy cut off her face.

Ermeline Ransom was thirty-two, the mother of Jaime, authentic blond, pale blue eyes. Like most cocktail waitresses she was a little taller than average, had clear skin and full lips, and was proud of her work and proud of her ability to support her little boy by honest work. Until last night she had no tattoos, but now she had a mess.

Ermeline began by loosening the tie and raising it over her head like a noose. Next, the blouse was unbuttoned, top to bottom. She was wearing what could only be a Victoria's Secret bra, with its trademark structural engineering, icy red, that featured a green butterfly where the bra clasped in front. The butterfly held everything together and it separated, wings to the left, thorax to the right. The girl clicked the butterfly and her breasts spilled forward, freed at last, and pointed at Attorney Thaddeus Murfee like two pears, separate but equal. She shivered and looked away.

Thaddeus Murfee's eyes bulged. "Good grief—who did this to you! Let me grab our camera!"

Thaddeus Murfee was twenty-five, unmarried, a member of Orbit's Rotary and Moose, and a lawyer of eighteen months. He was tall enough to play point guard—which he had, on the Arizona Wildcats team that went to the Sweet Sixteen. A bowl cut kept his dark brown hair naturally in place, and the wire spectacles with their round frames gave him the look of a friendly owl. Or so his last girlfriend had said. They had broken up after he chose the Midwest over Los Angeles. She had opted for L.A., where her visual arts career could take root.

Thaddeus couldn't believe his own eyes. Someone had taken a ballpoint and tattooed V-I-C-T-O-R into her breasts. Three letters per breast, each letter maybe two inches tall. The ballpoint had broken the skin and the cuts were deep and angry. There was matted blood around the wounds.

Thaddeus was stunned. "Who did this?"

"Victor Harrow did this. While I was passed out."

"You're certain it was Victor?"

"That's who I was drinking with. We were at his portable office."

"The purple bus."

"That's the one."

He knew it well. The bus said *"Harrow and Sons"* along the side. If Victor Harrow was in fact the one who had mutilated Ermeline Ransom, then Victor was going to end up owing the woman a busload of money. The County would erupt over news like this. He would finally become known. A twinge of excitement thumped through his chest.

"Why would Victor do this?" Thaddeus said, coming back to reality.

"I think he did it because he knew he could get away with it. Some men are like that."

Thaddeus frowned. It was more than a little difficult imagining Victor carving his name in anyone's breasts. After all, Victor was a deacon at First Christian, the president of Orbit Rotary, and a Silver Star from Vietnam. He was a lot of things, but an assailant of women? Thaddeus' frown deepened. It was all very hard to imagine.

"I don't know any men like that."

"Then you don't know men. Trust me. Victor Harrow *is* like that, especially when he's three sheets."

"Wait right here." Thaddeus went around to the office door and swung it wide open. "Come in here, please," he called to Christine, "and bring the firm camera with you."

Christine complied, and in minutes had made her way to Thaddeus' side. She was unclicking the camera case when she looked up. "Damn!" she cried. "What happened to you, girl?"

"Victor Harrow happened to me. Isn't it lovely?" She wiggled her breasts side to side.

Against his will, Thaddeus found himself growing aroused. "Now Christine, I'm going to go in the other room and get some coffee while you take a dozen pictures of Ermeline's breasts. Shoot from across the desk, then side view, and then close ups. When I come back let's everyone be buttoned up and ready to talk. Okay?"

"Got it," said Christine.

Thaddeus was passing through Christine's office/waiting room when the phone beeped. He quickly retraced his steps and picked up. "Thaddeus Murfee here. How can I help?"

"Thad, did she come over?" said Quentin Erwin, Jr., the Hickam County District Attorney and Thaddeus Murfee's best friend. "I sent her to see you because I sure as hell didn't know what to do with her. Great tits, though, huh?" Quentin loved raunchy cases like Ermeline's.

"She came over. Thanks, I guess. Christine's getting pictures right now."

"Are you watching the show?"

"No, I'm here in Christine's office, talking to you."

"Oh, man, you should be in on taking the pictures."

"No, chain-of-evidence. I want to be able to put Christine on the stand and ask her about the photos and establish chain-of-evidence."

"So you're thinking court?"

"I guess. Any ideas?"

"File suit against Victor Harrow, I guess. He's got the bucks."

"Are you going to prosecute him?"

"For what? He'll just say she consented to it. How else does he get his whole damn name there? I mean if she was resisting he wouldn't have gotten anywhere."

"She says she was passed out."

"That's what she told me too. I've been to a lot of parties with Ermeline. That girl can hold her booze. I can't see her passed out. My guess is it was Vic who was passed out and Ermeline did it to herself to get into his bank account."

"Damn, you're sick."

"Why?"

"I'll be over at the Dome for coffee around ten-fifteen. We can talk then. I don't want them to hear me, out here. Bye."

Thaddeus hung up and peeked into his office. From the backside, Ermeline Ransom looked like a bat about to take flight. Her hands and arms were outstretched and her shirt was held wide open while the camera clicked and whirred. He poured a cup of coffee. He slowly counted to 200 and noisily went back inside. By now, Christine and Ermeline were seated in the two client chairs side by side.

"Okay, Chris, you got them?"

Christine nodded. "I hope they're okay. Front, side, top-down."

Ermeline pulled a tissue from the box on Thaddeus' desk. She dabbed at her eyes. "I showed Dr. Ahmad this morning. He tried alcohol but he said it's too deep. Alcohol didn't touch it."

"Did he have any other suggestions?"

"Not really. He had a mom call in for labor and had to leave anyway. But his nurse gave me a tetanus shot. He left a prescription for pain pills. I haven't filled it yet."

Thaddeus gulped his coffee. "Did Christine offer you coffee or a drink when you came in?"

"I told her I was too upset to have anything. Look at my hands shake!"

"I can see that. You should be upset. But we'll find someone who can do something about this. A dermatology doctor. Maybe it's just a matter of some kind of skin peel or dermabrasion."

"Dr. Ahmad said it's too deep for that. I already asked." Ermeline's eyes welled up with tears again. She instinctively placed her hand across her breasts, which were protected once again by bra and shirt.

The young lawyer knew Ermeline Ransom was a good soul, a hard worker and a dedicated single mom. But, just now, her look was of grave confusion. Something had gone terribly wrong in her life, and she didn't know where to start to unravel it. She dabbed at the tears.

"Look, Ermeline, why don't you take us through what happened. What was it Saturday night or last night?"

"Last night. Amateur night. I worked from two until ten at the Silver Dome. Lounge side." Thaddeus nodded and scribbled a mental note. "You got off at ten on Sunday night?"

"Right. Bronco Groski comes on duty then, because Bruce wants someone there who's tough enough to handle the rowdies. I'm only five-seven and 120 pounds, so I don't scare anyone."

"Got it." Thaddeus pulled out a yellow pad and scribbled his first notes.

"Ermeline, here's a thought. I'm pretty new at lawyering. Which you know. You might want to have someone with more experience than me handle this. Like Jeremy down the street, or his partner Elvin, although Elvin really only wants to do estates. Jeremy used to be District Attorney and might really have a feel for this kind of case, where I'm still learning how to patty-cake."

"I thought of that already. Trouble with everyone in town is they're all in bed with Victor Harrow. Or they want to be. I bet having him for a client is every lawyer's dream. He's always getting someone hurt on a highway job, or not paying his subs, like he did to my dad, or making new investments and needing more legal papers drawn up. I'm even surprised you're talking to me. You must want him for a client too."

"I might at that. But he would never come to me, I'm too green."

Victor Harrow was the richest, and thus the most respected, man in town. He did *this*? To this poor girl? Thaddeus felt the indignation rising.

"Now, let's back up. What time did you get to work yesterday?"

"1:45 in the afternoon. Bruce was changing out the till and making a deposit before the bank deposit box closed."

"What were you wearing?"

"What I always wear. Black mini and white peasant blouse. My hair was blown dry, held by a barrette, and I was wearing pretty heavy lip gloss. Smiles mean tips."

"How'd you wind up at Vic Harrow's office?"

She turned to the window. "Vic had been buying rounds for everyone. He always does. Some of the guys from his crews were there, and they were kidding around, and Vic was getting them drunk. A benefit of working for him."

"Sure."

"So, around nine o'clock, he's in the hallway by the restrooms. I came out of the Ladies', and he's hitting the cigarette machine. He's cursing. I told him I'd get Bruce to unlock it. He said okay. Then he said, Ermeline, I need your help tonight. I asked how. He said he had just heard his bid was accepted on a new State job, and he was going to become a millionaire—again."

"So he was trying to impress you. Was he trying to get in your pants?"

"That's just Vic. He's always saying what's on his mind, and he doesn't mind who he's saying it to. Maybe, maybe not."

"But you left with him after you got off?"

"Over the next little while he kept buying rounds and asking me would I tag along to his office. He wanted to share a glass of champagne. He got pretty insistent. He said Betty Anne Harrow was out of town, so he had no one to share the good news with. Honestly, he sounded very lonely."

"So you volunteered."

"Color me stupid. I guess you could say I volunteered. Vic leaves huge tips for all the girls. What's not to love about Vic and his money? We want him to keep coming back."

"So you volunteered, but you were also feathering your nest a little?"

"A little, yes. I call my babysitter, and she calls her folks to ask if it's okay for her to stay an extra half hour. She's fifteen and it's past curfew, but her parents have no objection. So I tell Victor I'll follow him out to the bus but only for a half hour, one drink, and then I was off."

"Was that okay with him?"

"His eyes lit up. He smiled that huge smile of his. I felt like I had made his night."

"You followed him in your car?"

She turned away from the window and looked Thaddeus in the eye. "I followed in my car. I had no intention of staying a minute past ten-thirty, and I wanted my own ride out of there. Swear to God."

"I'm sure that's true. So what happened once you got to the bus?"

"We went inside. He turned on some lights. He had me wait on the sofa while he poured us a tumbler of champagne. He brought it to me, we toasted. That's when someone knocked on the door. It sounded like the rear door of the bus. Vic went over to the window and looked out. 'Be right back,' he said. He disappeared down the hall.

"I heard talking but muffled. Then there was brief shouting, angry sounding. Then a man I've never seen before. He came in with Vic close behind. 'Meet Johnny Bladanni,' Vic says, and I stand up and stick out my hand. He takes my hand. Then—of all things—he kisses my hand. I was mortified, that's not how we do things in Orbit."

"What did you find out about Johnny Bladanni?"

"He was down from Chicago on business with Victor. He was only staying ten or fifteen minutes. Victor told him to help himself to some champagne. Mr. Bladanni asked if I needed a refill, I said 'No,' but he insisted and almost yanked it out of my hand. Still smiling all the time. He was very smooth, very oily, very Chicago."

"Got it. So he got you a drink?"

"He did. Then we had a three-way toast to Victor's new business."

Thaddeus looked up from his scribbling. His notes covered two pages of the yellow pad. "What happened next? Give all the details you can remember."

"Next? I woke up, it was black outside, and my breasts were, like, on fire."

"And you did what?"

"I switched on the light over the couch. My blouse was pulled down and my bra was around my neck all tangled up. I saw my chest and screamed."

"Did Vic come when you screamed?"

"No. In fact, I never did see Vic again. He might have left me there alone, for all I know."

"How do you know it was Vic who did this to you and not Johnny Oily Guy?"

"Why would anyone carve someone else's name in a girl's breasts? Just doesn't make sense, does it?"

"Not that I have that kind of experience, but no, I guess it doesn't. So we're pretty sure it was Vic."

"When I left there were no other cars. Just Vic's truck and my car. Johnny Bladanni wasn't around. Besides, I was too terrified to pay much attention. All I wanted to do was get the hell out of there and get home and check on Jaime."

"You needed to see Jaime."

"That was my only thought. I wasn't thinking about what had happened to me or why. I could only think about my little boy who I'd abandoned. My watch said a little after four a.m. As soon as I got on Washington, I tore home."

"You had been there maybe six and a half hours."

"Something like that."

"What happened next?"

"Got home, found the babysitter asleep on the couch—with her mom, God bless her. Went tearing into Jaime's room. Sound asleep, hugging his teddy bear. I felt horrible and couldn't explain what had happened. The mom was insanely angry with me and thought I'd been out on an all-night hoot. I started crying and trying to explain, but she wasn't listening by then. She shoved her daughter out the door. 'Never again,' she said as the door slammed. 'Never again.'"

"Which only made you feel worse."

She nodded and tears rolled down her cheeks. "I felt like the world's worst mother! I had no idea what happened to me."

"What did you do next?"

"I found some cigarettes in the back of the kitchen drawer. Salems. I don't smoke, but that didn't stop me. I lit up and stood at the kitchen sink. I was smoking and crying. I had to keep it soft for Jaime's sake."

"Did you call anyone?"

"Who's there to call?"

"The cops?"

"No."

"Why not."

"My first idea, once I put out the cigarette, was get in the shower and see if the ink would come off. I also needed to see if I had been raped."

"Were you?"

"I don't think so. If I was, he used a condom. The ink didn't come off."

"What did you do?"

"Believe it or not, I took my tooth brush in the shower with me. I scraped some soap on it and scrubbed the letters on my breasts."

"Did it help?"

"Not a bit. It just made it hurt more. Some of the scratches were so deep they started bleeding."

"Just a minute. Christine," she was still sitting beside Ermeline, "how about some more coffee? I'll bet Ermeline would like one now."

"Ermeline?"

"Black," said Ermeline. She put a hand on her chest and held it there.

"Okay, so you probably weren't raped, and you took a shower."

"Then I went to bed and couldn't sleep. Around seven I called my mom, and she came over. I left her with Jaime, and I went up to my doctor's, then to the Sheriff's office. I talked to Sheriff Altiman, and he said I should come see District Attorney Quentin Erwin. I drove back home, got Jaime off to school, and drove back to the courthouse and parked next to Quentin's space. I sat out front until Quentin arrived."

Christine returned with two coffees and set one on the desk before Ermeline. She passed the second one to Thaddeus and excused herself. "I'm going back out to get the phones. Don't want to miss any exciting calls."

"Thanks," said Thaddeus.

"So what comes next?" Ermeline asked after swallowing a gulp of coffee. "Can you help me?"

"I think so. I need to talk to Quentin and Sheriff Altiman and see whether they plan to prosecute. Then I'll call you, and we'll make some plans, is that okay?"

"Did you want to get any more pictures?"

"I think we've got enough," he said. "Chris was trained to take pictures in the Army and does a very fine job for me."

"I'm going to go call a skin doctor in Quincy. I want to know if they can get this stuff off."

"Unknown. It might depend on the type of ink, but I'm just guessing, and I don't like to guess," he said.

"No more peasant blouses at work, not for a while anyway."

"It would show?"

"Yes, I already tried. Sad to say. Thaddeus, can I ask one thing?"

"Sure."

"Would you sue Victor Harrow for me?"

"I would, if the facts pan out. Right now, it looks very promising. But I still need to talk to some people and read some law."

She placed her coffee cup back in its saucer. "Well, then, I guess we're done here?"

"For now. Remember the rule: don't discuss this matter with anyone. Not even your mom. Everyone is a potential witness if you discuss the case with them."

"I'll be quiet."

They shook hands and their eyes met like conspirators. Thaddeus walked Ermeline to the front door. They said their goodbyes, and

Thaddeus returned to his office and checked his watch. 10:15. Time to catch Quentin at the Silver Dome. They had a lot to discuss.

THAT MORNING, Thaddeus had begun his day at 5:45 a.m. like he did every day except for Sunday. He flew out of bed wearing nothing but boxers, and mounted the Lifecycle, which he pedaled like a jackhammer for the next thirty minutes, working up a glistening sweat and matted hair.

He dismounted the Lifecycle and went to the junior fridge in his studio. A new gallon of OJ awaited him. He spun the cap and drank half straight down and topped it off with a protein bar, the wrapper of which guaranteed increased muscle mass.

At 6:25 he was in the shower, listening to Sirius on the waterproof pink radio, and flossing.

Dressed in his gray pinstripes and black wingtips and fresh from the shower, Thaddeus had checked his briefcase that morning and counted files. Everything looked fine. Satisfied that the previous night's work was accounted for, he stepped onto the small porch outside his front door. Thaddeus lived only four blocks off the Orbit County Square, where all the lawyers spun their webs.

His porch faced Madison Street, to the south. The sun was still hiding behind the buildings on the town square off to his left, but its orange glow could be seen above the rooflines and trees. As quickly as the sun was coming up, the clouds from last night's rainstorm were burning off, and large patches of blue sky could be seen. The air was clear, the mourning doves were calling, and two small boys came blasting by on skateboards, probably headed uptown to the best skating around the courthouse.

He paused on the red brick porch, flipped the Oakley's over his eyes, inhaled a huge breath of the clear Illinois morning air, and reached the southwest corner of the square at exactly 7 a.m.

He strolled past a few stores and took a right into the Silver Dome

Inn, part of Bruce Blongeir's spread. Here, Thaddeus drank his morning coffee and caught up with the latest.

His coffee group consisted mostly of Orbit County farmers who came to town and had coffee with their gossip every day just like Thaddeus. And there was also one other lawyer in attendance, 89-year-old D.B. Leinager.

Cece Seymour, came around with coffee, cup, and saucer for Thaddeus. She presided over the room, filling cups and taking breakfast orders, laughing and back-slapping and keeping the place happy and loud.

One farmer, Jonas Meiling, was offering his two cents worth when Thaddeus' coffee was poured.

"From what I hear, some very funny business went down in Victor Harrow's bus last night," Meiling said. He raised a white eyebrow and waited to see if anyone else wanted to chime in. Not a nibble. "Harrow's funny business involved a certain young lady we all know, I might add."

"Vic Harrow throws some wild parties in that bus," Thaddeus offered.

"Pure hearsay," interjected D.B. Leinager, the emeritus lawyer in his loud, boisterous, German voice. "Victor Harrow is my client and a good and decent man. I don't know where you people come up with such rubbish as that. No such thing as wild parties at his bus. For your information, that bus is his office. I've been there, and I've never seen a single bottle of beer or jug of whiskey."

"Which means old Vic didn't care enough to offer you a drink," laughed Jonas Meiling. Both white eyebrows shot up in anticipation of D.B.'s comeback. But D.B. only snorted and forked a glob of scrambled eggs in his mouth.

"So what did you hear, Jonas," Thaddeus asked. "What kind of funny business went down last night in the bus?"

Jonas Meiling snidely remarked, "Sheriff Altiman was paid a visit early this a.m. by a very distraught young woman who our fine sheriff referred over to the District Attorney. Seems she had been attacked by Victor Harrow—now this is just gossip, and I'm the first to admit it. But I heard this from a deputy sheriff who shall remain anonymous."

"That wouldn't be your son-in-law Deputy Mike Hermes, would it?" D.B. Leinager shot down the table. "This anonymous source a close family member?"

Jonas Meiling spread his hands and shook his head, a smile playing around his mouth. "Can't say."

"What about you, Thaddeus," Frances Dorman asked, moving all eyes to Thaddeus. "Tell us what you've heard about last night."

Thaddeus took a sip of his coffee and shook his head. "Last night I watched my two shows on HBO and was fast asleep by eleven. I haven't heard jack."

"Isn't Harrow a client of yours?" Dorman persisted.

Thaddeus smiled. "You know I couldn't confess to that even if it was true. A lawyer can't tell who his clients are and aren't."

Dorman looked around the table. He cut off a half sausage and poked it in his mouth, which didn't stop him from coming after Thaddeus. "From what I hear, you're the one lawyer in town he doesn't do business with. At least not yet. Victor Harrow likes to keep all you lawyers busy so none of you is free to sue him ever. Conflict of interest or some such thing." Dorman smirked, letting everyone know he knew more than they might think.

Thaddeus knew Vic Harrow's money came from the strategic relationships he maintained with politicos in Springfield, people who helped him file lowball bids on state highway jobs, especially the never-ending saga of the freeway between Springfield and Chicago. Like all Illinois highway boondoggles, this particular freeway had been under construction for forty years, and no less than eight general contractors had made enough to retire forever, thanks to this concrete plum. In return for getting hired as the general contractor on the freeway, Victor kicked back to the pols and the mob in Chicago. This way everyone remained happy—with the exception of the traveling public, who, in planning to journey between Springfield and Chicago, always allowed extra time for the twenty miles of construction zone that perpetually plagued the four-lane, like a flesh-eating pox that was always tearing-down and hauling away truck-loads of dirt and concrete, which it later replaced with dirt and concrete that looked remarkably like what had just been removed.

"You might be right about Victor's choice in lawyers," Thaddeus finally said. "But I don't know enough to be much help there, sorry."

Cece came wheeling around with the coffee pots and a tray of desserts. "Anyone?" she asked the table.

Thaddeus covered his cup with his hand. "Nothing more for me, Cece. Gotta go make a buck."

"Knowing the lawyers in this town, you'll make more today than most farmers make in a month!" Jonas Meiling shot at Thaddeus as he climbed to his feet.

"That's because I'm such a hard worker, Jonas," Thaddeus replied, resting a hand on Jonas' shoulder. "Unlike you, I don't have hours to burn in the coffee shops around our little town. Later, Gents."

They all nodded goodbye, and he paid his check at 7:50 and left the Silver Dome.

The sky was flaming red in the east as the early morning yawned over the City of Orbit. Last night's rain was gone, and the air was clear and cool.

As he did every weekday, Thaddeus scampered across Washington Street when he saw a break, and jumped up on the sidewalk on the east side of the square along Monroe Street.

He was headed toward his office and kept a brisk step in his stride as if he had important business waiting at the office. In fact, he knew he had no appointments this morning, and the best he could hope for was a DWI from Saturday night or a domestic dispute over the weekend that was continuing today with divorce lawyers.

On his left, was the courthouse, a magnificent structure built in 1890, according to its inscribed cornerstone, when so much of the rest of America was built in what must have been a gigantic building boom.

Thaddeus crossed the street on the north side of the square, edged left two doors, and inserted his key. His office was directly above a Western Auto catalog store.

At 8 a.m., on schedule, he sat behind his wide oak table and took a sip of coffee. He looked at his calendar for the day and sighed. He admitted to himself that it looked neither promising nor profitable. Yet, here he was, ahead of the crowd, and ready to rule it all across the street. Just biding my time, he thought. It will happen, sooner or later, the great case will walk in that door, and I'll be on my way.

PARALEGAL CHRISTINE SUSMANN had received her professional training in the U.S. Army. Following Basic Training, she had begun her career working as an M.P. and had served two years at a Black Ops detention center in Baghdad. She was under lifetime orders to never discuss what she had seen or done on that post, which was fine, she never wanted to discuss it anyway. Following two successful years working hand-in-glove with the CIA field officers, she had her choice of Army schools and selected paralegal school. She had seen all she ever wanted to see of detention centers, prisons, jails, or any other institution where people were held against their will. Paralegal training had dragged on for almost a year, but when she finished she was assigned to a JAG unit of busy lawyers in Germany.

Christine was five-five and average weight, but that's where "average" ended for her. For one thing, she was beautiful and had won Miss Hickam County in the summer of her senior year, right before enlisting. For another thing she was built like an NFL safety: broad, heavily muscled shoulders and upper arms, muscular thighs and calves, and she could still press 275 while she only weighed 135. She worked out religiously at the East Orbit Athletic Club with her husband, Sonny. Christine found working for Thaddeus to be pleasant yet difficult, mainly because Thaddeus knew so little about the practicalities of law practice, which drove Christine to the phones, where she was constantly calling her friends in other law offices with questions about how to do this and that, the nuts and bolts that pay the bills.

Chris's day began at 8:30. At 8:25 she came up the stairs two-at-a-time and bounced into the office. She called out good morning, made sure Thaddeus had coffee, checked the voice mails, and went over the day's diary.

Today, she was wearing the outfit that always made it to the office at least one day a week: long gray skirt, embroidered top, and navy blazer with gold buttons. She kept the nails short and clear of polish; they would only be traumatized at the athletic club anyway.

Following the scan of the calendar, Christine called into Thaddeus, "Got another hot chick for you next Saturday night!"

Thaddeus winced. He answered her over their intercom system which consisted of the two of them shouting back and forth from their desks, down the short hallway separating them. "No thanks. I'll do my own recruiting. Besides, my ideal woman is getting her Ph.D. in English lit. I doubt you know her."

"No, this is different. Her name's Lila and she went through Basic with me. She's coming for a visit."

"She's too old for me if she went through Basic with you. I don't date older women, I told you that."

"Thad, I'm five years older than you. So's Lila. That's not an 'older woman,' as you so hatefully put it."

"Not hatefully, not scornfully, just cautiously."

"We need to get you matched up with someone."

"Why is that again?"

"So you can be truly happy. Like Sonny."

He knew better than to say anything about her husband.

"Quentin Erwin, Junior just called from the DA's office. He's sending over a young woman for you to talk to."

"Probably a divorce client. Here's hoping she's got fifteen hundred bucks."

"I'll second that!"

While Christine was busy in her office, Thaddeus went back to updating his Facebook page. Status: Single. But looking.

Ten minutes later Ermeline Ransom was standing on the other side of his desk, unbuttoning her blouse, while Thaddeus, for once, was speechless.

2

The governor's mansion was located in Springfield. But, because of the huge number of state employees—not to mention registered voters—in Chicago, most governors maintained a residence there, too. On the taxpayers' dime, of course. And Governor Cleman L. Walker was no different. He kept a beautiful 1920 tri-level on the Gold Coast.

The Governor himself was short in stature but long on mythology: it was said, while he was a Chicago precinct committeeman, he had seen more than one uncooperative political crony chained and dumped in nearby Lake Michigan, and that, while he was quick to pull the trigger on politicians of the opposite political party, he was equally as quick to head up a dozen charitable drives a year.

His favorite charities were the ones that got the big headlines: veterans and orphans and dying children without insurance. He was known to have a huge heart, it was true, but he was just as well known for having a heavy hand when it came to running his state. He was red-faced from his booze and cigars and high stress levels.

A week before the Ermeline Ransom incident, the governor was in his private study, reclined in a leather chair, whiskey and water in hand, a Cuban cigar burning nearby, enjoying the trouncing the Bears were handing to the Cowboys.

Occasionally, he would check his Rolex. Bang Bang Moltinari was already a half hour late and Cleman L. Walker was beginning to wonder if the man was late simply because something unexpected had come up, or was his late arrival aimed at proving a point about his sovereignty from the Governor?

He took another deep drag off the rolled Cuban tobacco leaves. "The best," he murmured and rolled the cigar in his fingers admiringly. He closed his pale blue eyes, savoring what few Americans got to savor anymore, Cuban smoke. Within two minutes, one of his three cellphones rang. It was Robert K. Amistaggio, the Illinois Attorney General.

"Bob?" the Governor said. "I'm going to need to talk to you for about ten minutes tomorrow. Confidential, my office."

"Done. What time?"

"Noon. We'll have lunch brought in. You still like the oysters?"

"I do. Should I bring any files along?"

"Bring what you have on Victor Harrow."

"Who?"

"Victor Harrow of Harrow and Sons. He's a two-bit contractor out of Orbit. He has the contract on the Springfield-Chicago run."

"Name doesn't ring a bell. We need to control him?"

"We do. And if we can't do it through your office I'll have to go to the mat with him."

"Anything I should look for?" said the AG.

"We need to figure out where he's vulnerable. He's stiffing us."

"How far behind?"

"The contract is seventy-five percent paid out. We're in for half. He's paid us less than one-fourth. Word is, he's done and refuses to pay another dime. This cannot continue. Either the AG's office or Bang Bang is going to have to enforce."

"Another cowboy."

"Yes, he's got a wild hair from somewhere; you know what I always say."

"A wild hair from somewhere."

"See you at noon, then."

RICARDO "BANG BANG" Moltinari was the namesake and head of the Moltinari mob. This was the mob that controlled Chicago, operating primarily out of Skokie, where the key labor unions and building trades offices were located.

Like the Governor, Bang Bang also lived on the Gold Coast, except while the Governor's residence was English Countryside and consisted of a home and attached three-car, Moltinari's spread was a Historic Register enclave walled in by indigenous rock and mortar, and consisted of a 10,000 square foot home and four outbuildings, including a guest house where his bodyguards passed their off-time with high-stakes poker, craps, and a steady stream of Michigan Avenue hookers whose arrivals and departures spanned about one hour apiece.

Bang Bang left home that day handcuffed to a Halliburton aluminum briefcase. He exited the gates in a bullet-proof Cadillac sedan. He was backed up by a Cadillac SUV bristling with guns behind black-out windows. The windows were illegal, but the cops knew better than to hassle one of the Governor's key friends. In short, Bang Bang was immune. He enforced the Governor's state contracts. In return, the Governor protected Bang Bang's crime syndicate. That's the way it had been done for 100 years in Chicago, and it wasn't ever going to change. Not as long as the Chicago politicians and the Chicago mob were in charge and running things.

Bang Bang's entourage headed southeast, toward Lake Michigan. As they clipped along at twenty over and careened around corners, a lookout was kept for other cars that might try to cut them off or follow too close. Those idiots were menaced with a gun barrel or a killer stare-down from one of the vehicles. Mostly, though, the people of Chicago knew that there were certain cars and certain neighbors one simply did not approach. To do so was to risk life and limb.

At 3:45 Bang Bang's procession screeched into the Governor's lot and proceeded to park. A small army of Illinois State Policemen, all burly and scowling, peered inside the cars and cautiously allowed the visitors to exit their vehicles. They were prudently searched but allowed to retain their firearms unless going inside to meet with the governor.

Bang Bang was first out. The briefcase dangled from his wrist while his hands went on top of the car. He was frisked by an angry looking sergeant. A state trooper escorted him to a side door of the Governor's house, and knocked twice. An interior state trooper took him from there. The leftover police and mobsters lolled around the two black vehicles. They smoked. They engaged in stare-downs. Nobody minded; everybody stared right back. Here were nature's natural enemies come together on solemn ground, where the outside rules didn't apply, where the lions let the lions alone. There was a high degree of mutual respect and mutual distaste. Each group had its orders. You better damn well get along with the other side if you want to keep working this easy duty. Everyone obeyed. At the end of the day, it was easy and safe duty. No one would ever be insane enough to make an attempt on either the Governor or on Bang Bang.

Bang Bang Moltinari followed the state trooper into the Governor's office. "Morning, Your Honor," he snarled at the Governor, upset that he had been called away from family on a Sunday. His son was home for mid-term break from Harvard where he was pre-law, and his twin daughters were home from the University of Illinois in Urbana.

"You're looking old today," the Governor said, and choked on laughter.

Bang Bang was in his early fifties and had come up in the mob the hard way. He had started out running numbers and girls on Chicago's West Side, and then he caught the eye of Jimmy Novalici, a Lieutenant in the mob who was expert at cargo hijacking from O'Hare International.

Bang Bang had become wealthy exploiting interstate freight and gunning down those who interfered. He was tall, wore his black hair combed straight back and his teeth were perfect. His smile stopped the ladies cold. He had never had a love problem; they all adored and worshipped him and he was very generous with the gifts ladies like. Cartier, Australian Pink Diamonds (a lady's best friend), Rolex—all of the good names found their ways onto his ladies' fingers, necks, and wrists.

"Hello, Bangman," the Governor said, using his pet name for the mob boss.

"We got problems to get me out this cold Sunday?"

"We do. We got some customers who are neglecting their payments to our little fund."

"What, we couldn't do this Monday?"

"I'm leaving for a governors' conference in San Francisco after lunch tomorrow. Too late. Don't worry, I've only got three names for you."

"I'm listening. Who's first?"

The Governor pulled a page from the back of the legal pad on his desk. "Great Lakes Underpass and Overpass, LLC. Late as always."

"GLUO again? I warned that son of a bitch to keep up with his contracts. How much?"

"Well, I'm down $150K for the month, and GLUO's portion is thirty-five."

"Got it," said Bang Bang. "A call from me will jar this guy loose. Next."

"Midland Freeway and Secondary. They have four paving jobs open east of Springfield, and the management has changed due to a shareholders' restructure. The new owner is playing dumb, like he's never heard of us."

"We'll visit him first thing in the morning. We'll make sure he understands the program. How much we light?"

"Fifty grand, give or take, five. Fifty makes me happy at this point."

"Done. Who's the third?"

"A nobody out of Orbit. Name of Victor Harrow, Harrow and Sons Construction."

"Poor Victor. He picked a damn poor time to stop paying if he's the reason I'm over here on Sunday."

"He's a large part of the reason. He's into me for one-ten."

"110 G's?"

"That's right."

Bang Bang spread his hands. "Look, you gotta tell me these things right away. This guy's way over on the skim. He'll cry like a pig when we demand the whole play up front."

"Let him cry. My people tell me he's been paid three-fourths on his bid contract, there's only about a fourth left, and he says 'Enough,' he says 'he's done with us.' We're in for half, he's paid less than a fourth."

"Stupid SOB. What do you want from me here?"

"Just put the fear in him. He's a nobody. But he's high profile in his crapola little town."

"Johnny Blades?"

"Johnny's perfect. Just don't break anything on the guy. We only need him scared. And tell Johnny not to come back without at least fifty grand on him. Persistence is what this is going to take. Johnny might be down there a couple days."

Bang Bang smiled. "You don't know Johnny. He can say more to a man in thirty seconds than anyone I've ever known. And I've known plenty."

"I don't doubt that, Bangman. I don't doubt that."

"So what else we got?"

"Like I say, I'm $150K light this month. Make it a happy holiday for me, yes?"

"Done. Until next time."

The Governor's eyes narrowed. He gave Bang Bang his coldest look. "Aren't you forgetting something," he said, holding up his hand while his face glowed red. "Don't you have a little something for me?"

Bang Bang smiled and opened the briefcase. He pulled out a

stack of banded $100 bills and bounced them against his knee. "It's all there. $75K, all from yesterday, all from Michigan Avenue."

"Bless those merchants. They are going to be very happy when we allow them to open for Black Friday on Thanksgiving Day. They deserve no less."

"Black Friday, Pink Tuesday, who gives a big damn?"

"I do, Bangman, I do."

3

J ohnny "The Blade" Bladanni pulled the cell from his inside
coat pocket. He hit speed dial and Bang Bang Moltinari
immediately answered, "Go, Blade."

"This guy got a bus for an office?"

"Could be."

"Why didn't no one tell me it was a bus? I've never broke in a bus before."

"Don't break in. Get invited. Goodbye."

Johnny frowned at the disconnection. He was a swarthy man, early thirties, who looked early twenties, with his baby face and baby blues. But there, everything baby about him, ended. He was wearing a silver sharkskin suit with $2000 Gucci's, silver shades hiding his eyes, and a Sixties style pompadour such as the East Coast crooners wore.

The car was one of Bang Bang's Escalade SUV's, black in color, with plates that were protected by the State of Illinois DMV in case Johnny got pulled over. The designation meant to any law enforcement officer: Hands Off, The Driver is Connected. He was sitting across the street from Victor Harrow's construction yard in Orbit, where the purple bus sat just outside the gate, ready to roar off to a troubled job site on a moment's notice.

Johnny was parked westbound, headed toward Orbit, and he had no flashers blinking. The lane he was in was a traffic lane, but he really didn't give a damn. Let the fools figure it out, he thought. Besides, he'd only be a minute or two.

He felt around in his shirt pocket and produced a driver's license photo of Victor Harrow. "Ugly bastard," he commented. "Bet you ain't gettin' much action."

An 18-wheeler came up behind and blew out its air brakes sliding to a stop behind Johnny.

Johnny flipped the guy off, which wasn't seen by anyone due to the black windows. He laid down rubber and wheeled the Caddy from the right lane across three lanes of traffic, up and across the driveway, and nosed in beside Victor's bus. "Now eat it and die," he muttered to the trucker.

He checked his hair in the rearview and went inside.

"I'm here to meet with Victor Harrow," Johnny said to the gum smacker behind the first desk.

The girl looked up from her screen. "Is he expecting you?"

"He oughta be, you get my drift."

"Who shall I tell him is calling?"

"Just tell him I'm here from the Governor's office. He'll understand."

"Don't you have a name, Sir?" The gum smacking increased in speed along with the woman's frustration. "Mister Harrow is very busy, and it's my job to screen all drop-ins."

"Tell him it's Johnny Bladanni from Chicago. That name opens lotsa doors."

"Very well." She buzzed Victor on the telephone and waited. No answer. She buzzed again. Still no answer. "I'm sorry, Mr. Bladna—"

"Bladanni. B-L-A-D-A-N-N-I."

"I'm sorry, but it looks like Mister Harrow might have slipped out for lunch."

"And what time does he get back?"

"Probably late tonight. He has stops to make at job sites."

"What's he driving?"

"Why, you plan on pulling him over?"

"No, you know, just in case I happen to see him."

"Company truck, purple top, cream bottom. Says 'Harrow'—"

"I get it 'Harrow and Sons' down the side. Am I close?"

The gum smacker sniffed. "Will that be all, Mister Bladanni?"

"For now. Just for now."

"Do you have a card you'd like to leave for Mister Harrow?"

"Lady, you don't want to see my card," Johnny smiled, patting his inside pocket where he kept his ten-inch switchblade. "Ain't nobody lookin' to see my card. Later."

"All right, I'll tell him you stopped by."

"No, let's make it a surprise when I come back tonight."

"Goodbye, Sir. Have a nice afternoon."

"In this town? What, you know somethin' fun to do here that I ain't figured out already?"

"Thanks again."

"Later."

VICTOR HARROW WAS LUNCHING on short ribs and noodles, the noon special at the Red Bird Inn, a mile west of Orbit. It was a low-slung whitewashed restaurant from the 'Forties,' with a sign out front in the shape of a ten-foot-high cardinal. At night the sign blinked red and white. The joint was known locally as the Red Bird Inn. It was a favorite hangout of farmers and truckers who had done business at the sale barn across the road, where pigs and cows were sold off to the local slaughterhouse, another mile further west.

Victor Harrow's lunch guest was Bud Leinager, attorney at law, who nested in a Victorian office one block west of the Orbit town square. His office was in a section of town where several of the buildings on the formerly residential street were being reformulated as professionals' offices: dentists, lawyers, and a family medical practice, plus two CPA firms. Plus, a stockbroker who was always desperate for sales, as rural Illinoisans will invest in land much more quickly than they will consider intangibles such as stocks and bonds.

Bud was the son of D.B. Leinager, the 89-year-old lawyer who drank coffee with Thaddeus. Bud was known around Orbit as a ne'er-do-well who'd rather tell a lie than the truth even when the truth would win him a gold star for the day. He was a natural born prevaricator and fabricator: in short, he had found the perfect job in the practice of law, where things are never what they're said to be.

It was the afternoon before the night when Ermeline Ransom was drugged and tattooed at Victor Harrow's bus. Victor didn't know yet that Johnny the Blade Bladanni was in town to see him, and so he was dining in relative peace. In fact, Victor had never even heard of Johnny the Blade.

Victor's face was broad and pitted on the front. He'd started his career as a pipeline welder, working as an Ironworker on the Alaska Pipeline, before hanging up his helmet and gloves and returning home to Orbit, where he established Harrow and Sons Construction in 1982. As a welder in Alaska there were days he just wore goggles and the constant sparks and hot metal had burned his face repeatedly. He wasn't disfigured, but anyone who knew construction would have guessed his line of work just by looking upon his face. He was clinically obese at 275, for he had never grown to be six feet, and the charts at his doctor's office were all in red and screamed that he needed to lose 85 pounds. Victor ignored that advice, of course, and went right on eating and drinking like he always had. Everyone in Orbit joined him in that; food was a key solace for people whose lives were paid for at an hourly rate, too often minimum wage, and who had too many kids and not enough joy.

"Bud, I've got a problem" Victor said, and forked a load of rib meat and noodles into his mouth.

"Mmm," Bud muttered and went back to carefully slicing away the gristle from the meat. "Somebody needs to talk to the cook. This ain't meat, it's fat."

"I say I've got a problem."

"What happened? You stiff some sub? Hey, it's going around, Vic. Try not to lose any sleep over it."

"It's not that."

"Then what?"

Victor slurped his iced tea. He wiped his mouth with the back of his hand. "I haven't been paying my kickbacks."

"You *what*? Have you gone nuts, Victor? You always pay upstairs," he hissed across the table. "That's playing with fire to stiff the upstairs."

"I know, I know that. It's just—I don't know, with Marleen and Bruce doing so well, I started thinking. 'What the hell am I doing?' I asked myself. 'Why am I paying off the Governor?' After all, Bruce isn't and he's doing gangbusters. I wanted to flip them off. I wanted to yell 'Hey, screw you!' one time. It just got to me."

"How much you behind?"

"It's the Springfield-Chicago job. Probably a hundred."

"A hundred as in *thou*sand? Are you serious, man?" Bud paused, his fork halfway to his mouth. He wasn't sure he heard right. "You've held out a hundred grand on the Governor and his boys?"

"'Fraid so."

Bud looked around and ducked his head. "Hey, you don't mind I move to a different table, do you? You're like radioactive, my friend."

Victor picked apart a slab of rib. "So, what do I do?"

"Pay up. Now, like yesterday."

"And if I haven't got it?"

"Borrow it. Sell something. Sell some of Betty Anne Harrow's diamonds."

"C'mon."

"Hey, I am coming on. You're about to go up in flames. Sorry, Vic, but I can't help you with this one. This is *way* outside my league."

"Who can?"

"Help you? Moses, Adam, and the First National Bank. Go see Brody Mathewson this afternoon over at First National. Go in hock if you have to, but call your bag man and let him know you have the dough before closing time today. *Capisce*?"

"Yeah."

"And call me tonight. Let me know you've paid up. If something happens to you I'm a witness that way."

"Lot of good that does me."

At just that moment, Johnny Bladanni entered the Red Bird Inn. All eyes turned to him as one because, first, he was a stranger and therefore suspect but even more, two, in his sharkskin and Gucci's and silver shades he was light-years out of place. Everyone gave him the "New Guy Stare" for fifteen seconds, and then returned to stuffing their faces and talking with their mouths full. Johnny, meantime, compared the photo in his hand to the man sitting across from Bud Leinager, and he instantly knew he had located Victor Harrow.

He brushed the hostess aside and glided coolly back to Victor's table.

Johnny didn't bother with an introduction. Instead announced, "I need to talk to you."

"And you are?" Victor asked, eyeing the man with all due suspicion.

"Let's just say the Governor sent me."

At this, Bud Leinager shrank even lower in his chair. He looked off to the side. He was neither hearing any of this nor participating in it. Without a word he suddenly lurched upright, sliding his wooden captain's chair back with a loud "Squawk!" He grabbed the lunch bill and headed for the cash register.

"Nice," said Johnny admiringly. "I like a man who knows when to get back to work."

"You still haven't told me your name, Mister."

"Bladanni. My friends call me The Blade."

"Look, I don't have it. It's all been spent on overhead. It's all gone. Sorry."

"No, friend, that's where you're wrong. You see the Governor's share is solid as gold. It's never gone. It's always around somewhere. Now we just have to find it."

"Well, my attorney—who you just jack rabbited the hell out of here—he was advising me to drop by the bank this afternoon and see how much I can get my hands on."

Johnny smiled. He walked around and sat down in Bud's chair. He scooted up to the table. "I like the sound of that. 'See how much I can get my hands on'—yes, that has a nice sound."

"So I'll be in touch. Right now I have to get out to several job sites, Mister Baldano."

"Bladanni—B-L-A-D-A-N-N-I. Why do I gotta spell everything out to you people down here?"

"Well, sir, my name is Victor, V-I-C-T-O-R and you can tell the Governor I'm working on it. I'll know something by the end of the week."

"No, no, no, no, no," said Johnny. "You'll know something by five today. I'll be at the office waiting for you. I'll be waiting for a nice fat bag of $100K."

"I won't be back by five. I've got two hundred miles to drive."

"Then what time? I ain't leaving 'til we meet."

Victor sighed. "I could be back at ten-ten-thirty tonight."

"You going to bring me a present?"

"If the bank will loan it, I'll have it."

"And if the bank won't? What then?"

"See you then."

"Victor, let me be clear about this. You will see me again, tonight. But you won't see me the next time. So don't make there be a next time after tonight, understand?"

"I understand. I'm doing everything I can."

"Mister, you don't even begin to know what you can do," Johnny laughed.

THAT NIGHT VICTOR returned from his stops.

First he had gone to the bank and met with Brody Mathewson. He told Brody he needed $100,000 in his account by five o'clock.

Brody had touched his fingertips together and then started

scrolling documents on his screen.

He looked up Victor's general business account. He reviewed Victor's balance sheet. He checked out his last twelve months of P&Ls. He studied his asset-liability ratio to see if such a loan was even feasible.

Finally, Brody had frowned and clasped his hands behind his head. He was thoughtful for a full minute, then abruptly sat up and asked Victor what the money was for, was it going into hard assets the bank could lien?

Victor said No, the money was to be used for current expenses.

He explained they were having a month where outgo had outpaced income, and they were meeting payroll and materials on three lucrative jobs. Brody nodded. He knew that enough of Victor's money flowed into the bank that Victor was a Top Ten customer. Brody and First National were, he told Victor, *damn* glad to have his business. But right now, with the recession and all, one hundred thousand unsecured was asking a lot. He wasn't sure the bank was prepared to go *that* far. He would have to check with the branch manager, who was out the rest of the afternoon.

Victor had become animated and said that wasn't good enough, that he needed the money today, *now*.

Several minutes passed while Brody again studied his computer screen and made repeated mouse clicks. He wasn't through looking and that was a good sign.

At long last, he broke away from his study and spread his hands. He said we're just going to have to wait and talk to Mr. Edwards in the morning and see if the bank will cover Victor's paper, *unsecured* as it was.

Finally, Victor had given in and stood.

He shook Brody's hand energetically to let him know he wasn't upset, and told him he'd be by in the morning for the money. For the money? Brody had asked. Yes, said Victor, I need the total amount in cash.

Brody had done a funny thing then, he had laughed, 100% certain Victor had been kidding about the cash. Nobody wanted cash.

After the bank, Victor had climbed in his truck and driven down Baker to the Dari-Ripple. A double scoop waffle cone was called for. Food always helped, especially when it was still too early for a highball.

He left the drive-thru and that was when he first noticed the black SUV falling in behind him.

Racing the cone against its melt, slurping and licking at the soft custard, Victor then drove southwest to Macomb, where a paving job was in trouble over a local union dispute. He agreed to the re-write on the local bargaining agreement and the reps declared they would have the workers back on the job tomorrow. Easy enough, but it took no less than Victor himself to do the deal.

Then he was off to Springfield, where he had to meet with a marketing group he was toying with the idea of hiring. General contractors in Illinois had such a bad name, and Victor was no different, that he was looking into hiring Media Specials SW to improve the image of Harrow & Sons Contracting. His rationale was simple: he didn't really give a damn about the construction company. But secretly—something he'd never discussed with anyone—Victor was considering a run for the Illinois House of Representatives. How great it would be, he thought, to represent the people of his district and, at the same time, be contracting with their government! The possibilities were staggering: the State could throw jobs his way, his company could bid, and his Illinois House seat would be instrumental in voting to approve all such bids. It was 100% win-win and a no-brainer. His only regret was that he hadn't thought of it before.

So at 4:30 p.m. he was pulling into the Windsor Office Park in North Springfield, parking to go inside and hear MSSW's pitch, when he noticed the black Escalade in the rearview. It had turned into the lot right behind him. It had followed him from the freeway, he was sure of it, and now it was making no secret of the fact it was following him.

Victor climbed down out of his purple-over-cream truck and walked back to the Escalade. The windows were blacked out, and he couldn't see the driver.

He took a deep breath, hitched himself to his full 5-11, and knocked on the glass. Rather, he rapped on the glass, with his own ignition key. The window immediately lowered. There sat the man who had visited him at lunch at the Red Bird, Johnny Something. Victor put his hands on the window frame.

"You lose something, friend?" Victor asked.

"You mean me? Did I lose something? No, I ain't lost nothin'."

"Well...it looks like you're following me."

"You're the guy with $100,000 belongs to me. I gotta protect you."

"I won't have the money until in the morning."

"Oh, I saw you go inside the bank and everything, don't worry."

Victor frowned. "You followed me to the bank?"

"Mister Harrow, you ain't been outta my sight since you left that dump you was eatin' at. You're far too valuable to lose sight of."

"Come by in the morning. I'll have it then."

Johnny Bladanni raised an index finger. He waggled it under Victor's pitted nose. "No, no, no, no, no. That ain't the deal. The deal is I get my money tonight. Ten o'clock, your place. The full $100,000."

"That might have been *your* deal," said Victor. He stood upright. "But that wasn't my deal. My deal was, I said I'd go by the bank and make whatever arrangements I could."

"Say what you will, Mister Harrow. The deal is tonight, one hundred and not a dime less. Your place. I'll be waiting there for you."

"And if I don't show?"

"Then I'll come by your home and kick the frigging door down. Then I'll cut your throat, rape your wife, and stab your dog. We ain't messin' here, Mr. Harrow. Do we understand each other?"

Johnny's outburst had backed Victor off a full step. He'd never been talked to like that, at least not since the Alaska pipeline and some of the outlaws working those crews, guys who carried guns and weren't afraid of anybody.

Right now, he wished he had a gun—something—or someone to protect him. This was getting out of hand. What if he called Sheriff Altiman? Would that help? Johnny Bladanni was glaring at him. He curled his finger at Victor. Victor again closed the distance between them. Johnny held up a finger and reached inside his jacket pocket.

As if it had a life of its own, the ten-inch switchblade sprung open not an inch from Victor's nose. "See this? This is why they call me The Blade. Not for nothin', but I'm gonna slice your fat throat open tonight, you don't get my money. Now see where you've got us to?"

Victor knew then and there that the cops weren't the answer. Chicago hoodlums far outnumbered all the law enforcement in southern Illinois. That was a fact. He could run to the cops all he wanted and have Johnny arrested for threatening him. The mob would just send another, and then another, and then they'd get tired of the routine and simply blow his house up with him and Betty Anne Harrow inside. He was trapped and he knew it. "I don't want us there...honestly," Victor managed to say. "No need for that. I've got a meeting."

"I'll be right here. I ain't goin' nowhere."

~

ON THE DRIVE back to Orbit, Victor's first call was to Brody Mathewson at First National. He asked Brody-- could he call Mister Edwards at home about the loan? He was desperate and stood to look a great deal of money if the loan funds weren't available today. Brody said he would try, call him back in ten.

Victor drove on, exceeding the speed limit now, while the black Caddy hung on his tail. After several minutes but probably less than ten, he redialed Brody. Brody was sorry, but Mister Edwards was out of town until tomorrow morning. Victor would just have to wait until then. Victor managed a weak "thanks" to Brody and ended the call. Now what?

Just after dark Victor wheeled the purple-over-cream truck into the lot beside the Silver Dome, on Monroe Street. He turned off the ignition and waited while the black SUV pulled in beside him. Several minutes ticked by. It became clear to Victor that Johnny Bladanni wasn't going to be the first to get out of his vehicle.

Victor opened his door and went around the tailgate of his truck and went into the front door of the Silver Dome. The front entrance was actually a short hall parallel to the street, and if you went through the door to the left, you would enter the restaurant, and if you went to the right, you would enter the lounge. Victor went into the lounge.

He was immediately assailed by loud "Hellos!" and "There he is!" calls from the West Town crew. He called back to his workers and indicated he had to hit the restroom, which he did.

When he came back out, he slid into the booth as his men made room.

Ermeline Ransom came right over and asked what he was having. They bantered back and forth while Victor scanned the room for Johnny Bladanni. He was nowhere to be seen, so Victor ordered a round for his men, a Bud for himself, and a burger and fries—make that a cheeseburger and fries. Without making a note, Ermeline nodded, touched the side of her head, smiled at the gathering, and headed for the kitchen to place the order.

Victor stayed late—for him, anyway—at the Silver Dome that night and when he left at ten it was with Ermeline Ransom following in her aging Impala. Victor noted, with huge relief, that the black SUV was nowhere to be seen. Looked like they had decided to give him until morning, after all, he thought and smiled. Damn but he was charming and, after all, he did intend to pay them. He really wasn't stalling; it was all just a matter of making the paperwork fit together at the bank. Ermeline had agreed to a single glass of champagne to celebrate Victor's new contract with the State. Or so she had been told. Truth of the matter was, Victor needed her at the office with him in case Johnny Bladanni showed up while Victor was passing out tomorrow's crew assignments to his crew chief's cells. Ermeline suspected nothing, wanted only to have a drink and go home to her son, and promised herself she'd be long gone by ten-thirty. Victor was, after all, a helluva good customer and someone she would go out of her way to make happy. At least within reason.

4

Johnny Bladanni left the Silver Dome after Victor went inside. Next d
oor, he went into Bruce's Juices and picked up a pint of Chivas and two packs of smokes. He also bought two jerky whips and had one halfway down before the door dinged on his Caddy.

He tossed the items on the passenger seat and climbed inside. He opened the Chivas and took a huge swallow. And another. Holding the pint, he rested his hand over the steering wheel. The Caddy SUV only had 14,500 on the odometer, and it still smelled like leather and new car. He loved that smell. Maybe after this pickup from Victor he would please Bang Bang and get a nice enough bonus to put down fifteen or twenty on a new Caddy or Lincoln of his own. He preferred Caddy's, but some of the older guys were being toured around town in Lincolns, so that was always a possibility.

He started the engine and listened while it made no sound whatsoever. "Cadillac," he said with a smile, "there is no other." Cadillac or Lincoln—it really made no difference; either was better than the Chevrolet Caprice he was driving now. His car had over a hundred grand, and the tires were on their third version and pretty much to the point where they were unreliable. He needed the Victor money because Bang Bang would love him and bonus him, and that would take care of the car problem like that—he snapped his fingers. Just as he did, the cellphone played "Volare" by Dean Martin and Johnny Bladanni answered.

"Blade Runner. Hello, Bangs."

"Got it? Got my money with you?"

"Not yet. He won't know if the bank will loan until in the morning."

"Then we got a problem. I told His Honor we'd have the money to him by ten tonight, latest."

"We're not done yet. I'm seein' him at ten. We'll know more then."

"And if he ain't got it at ten?"

"Bangs, that's your call. Just say the word, man."

"If he ain't got it at ten I want you to scare the hell out of him. No broken bones, no cuts that's gonna show. But scare him bad."

"Done."

"Johnny, we're counting on you. It means a lot to the Big Guy."

"I'll have your money in your hands by noon tomorrow. This guy will never short us again. That is my solemn promise to you, Bangs."

"Attaboy, Johnny. Well, look. I'll call His Honor, tell him there's an unavoidable delay. I'll tell him we'll have his funds by noon. That should loosen him up."

Johnny laughed over the cell connection. He needed to be in good with his superior. "Bangs, I gotta get outta here. There's no women in this town, no clubs, no decent food, no strippers, no game—nothin' for a guy to do. I mean, I take care of this guy, then what? Where do I go?"

"Same place you stayed last night."

"That's some dive in Springfield. That's an hour away."

"The drive will do you good after you're done with him tonight. Give you a chance to think about the bonus I'm layin' on you for all your troubles."

"Jeez, you wouldn't mind tellin' me how much—"

"But you gotta produce! None of this comin' back empty-handed.

No comin' back short. This guy has it. You make damn sure you get it. That's our money he's glommed onto!"

"You got it, Bangs. I'm your main play here."

"Remember, no breaks, no visible cuts. That's my boy."

"I'm your boy, Bangs."

They hung up, and Johnny slipped the cell in his pocket.

He pulled out of the Silver Dome lot and headed back east. He would find a quiet street and music down while he waited. It was already nine, give or take. Wouldn't be long now.

Johnny drove farther out east until he was almost to Victor's bus, then he found the closest cross-street, Mason Street, and hung a left onto it, drove to the end, spun a U, then came back and parked so he could see the bus. He now had a clear view of the front door with its little metal step. It wouldn't be long until Victor showed, he'd get the haps, then head back to his hotel. Tomorrow would be a new day.

EXACTLY AT 10:05 Victor flew past Johnny's spot, and moments later came a woman following in an old Impala.

"Gotta love them old cars," Johnny muttered.

The woman was going half the speed of Victor, and he was waiting for her at the bus when she nosed in and put it in park. Johnny saw her brake lights flare red when she shoved the tranny into park, and he saw her door swing open. "Now who's this?" he said to himself. "Some road dog or something nice?" He watched Victor insert his key in the lock, whereupon the overhead exterior light blinked on, and Victor ushered the woman up the two low steps and on inside the bus. The door closed and within minutes the exterior light blinked out, only to be followed by the sudden glare of a night security light hanging from a pole at the end of the bus. Victor must have activated that light from the bus, he thought, but why isn't it always on? He had no explanation, so he just waited, giving them time to settle in and drop their guard, with Victor thinking he was safe. Johnny wanted his guard down on purpose; that's why he had disappeared after Victor went inside the Silver Dome. He had driven around, scouting the bullcrap town with its rolled up sidewalks, killing time, killing more time, until he went back to Bruce's Juices and loaded up on refreshments. He closed his eyes and waited. After five minutes he punched his cell phone. 10:17. Perfect.

Without headlights Johnny started up and swung a left. He crept down Washington until he came to Victor's, where he nosed in. He reached and switched off the Caddy's interior auto light.

He opened the door as quietly as he could.

He crept to the back door of the bus. He wanted Victor alone, away from the girl—or woman, whatever—so he could get right down to it about the money. No sense in her seeing his face, not if it could be helped.

In gliding past the bus's center window, he saw Victor look down at him and move toward the rear of the bus all in one motion. All right, he knew he was there.

Johnny knocked, and the door immediately swung open. There was no backlight; Victor hadn't switched on the overhead, so Johnny didn't know if Victor was armed or not. "Can I come inside?" he asked. "Just to talk. Then I'm gone." He made a slick motion with his hand, a Chicago indication of "gone." Victor took a step back and opened the door.

"I told you I wouldn't have it until morning. Maybe not all of it even then."

Johnny's eyes quickly adjusted to the dark room. "Why you live like this?" He complained, "No lights?"

"There, that better?" Victor said, and reached behind for the switch. Wrap-around fluorescents bathed the room and Johnny could see that Victor looked scared and old under the harsh light. He won't be getting any tonight, Johnny laughed to himself, not looking like that. Does this guy never manicure? Never pick that crap out of his face? The blackheads across Victor's nose were emphasized under the glare, and Johnny was suddenly repulsed by the man.

"Why you got me down here in bumtown the middle of the night, hey, Victor?"

"I don't got you anyplace. You could've called me from Chicago, and I would have made things right."

"No, no, no, no, no. That ain't the way business gets done. No calls to you. You could be wired, you could be tapped, who knows? My people, we like to do our business eyeball to eyeball. That way everything gets done nice and tidy. You ain't wired, are you Victor?"

"No way! Look." Without being asked, Victor pulled up his sweater and shirt. His belly protruded, and his obese physique further sickened Johnny. It made him hate the man even more.

"Victor, how about I join you and the lady for a drink? We can talk and get some things settled. Who knows, I might even get lucky with her."

"No, no, she's not that kind of girl. She's just a friend, a waitress who dropped in for one drink, then she's gone."

"A waitress. That's even better. I'll say when she's gone, Vic. *Capisce?*"

"*Capisce.*"

"Now, go get your bottle and bring it to me. I'm going to sweeten it up."

"I don't think so. I think you should leave now."

In one sleight-of-hand move Johnny displayed the flashing switchblade and pressed the steel point directly under Victor's chin. "We ain't negotiatin' friend. This ain't no sit-down. You don't have my money, you gotta pay. You gotta see how bad it is to screw your friends in Chicago." The knife pressed in and pierced the skin. It touched the jaw bone and Victor's head involuntarily snapped back. "Easy, Vic. You don't want me to slip. Now, get that bottle and get your fat ass back in here."

Victor returned with an open champagne bottle in minutes. Johnny was ready with a capsule of dry power. Victor asked what the hell he thought he was doing. Johnny told him it's a roofy, the date rape drug. Roofy is a benzo-something drug used in Mexico as an anesthetic, Johnny said while he powdered the bottle. It's legal in Mexico. We get it FedEx from Sinaloa. Why anesthetic? Victor wanted to know. Then Victor was pleading. Don't do this, he begged, don't. Johnny smiled and shook a second capsule's contents into the bottle.

"Now, let's go refresh your guest's drink. She must be thirsty and feeling so lonely."

Which is when Ermeline first laid eyes on Johnny Bladanni.

He strode into the room, flashed her the great smile nature gave him, and swiped her drink out of her hand. He said he would refresh it for her.

She started to object, started to say she'd had all she agreed to have, but Johnny brushed her aside. Just one more—with me, this time—he said. You'll make me a happy man, and then you can go. She thought he was attractive in a kind of city way, and maybe she even liked his dark quality, maybe even liked that he seemed a little bit dangerous around the edges. She'd been known to be attracted to certain types. She agreed. One more and then—gone.

She came to five hours later. Her chest—her breasts—were on fire and she struggled to understand where she was. Victor was nowhere to be seen, and the other man was gone. She screamed.

5

Following Ermeline's visit, Thaddeus met Quentin Erwin at the Silver Dome. They entered on the restaurant side and took the last remaining booth, one nobody wanted, at the very rear of the restaurant where the bus boys crashed in and out of the kitchen with their tubs of dirty dishes.

It was loud back there, and the heat from the kitchen made it very warm.

Cece Seymour commanded one of the bus boys to clear the table, and she followed up with a quick wipe down, table top and booths.

Quentin took the far side. "I like my back against the wall," he was fond of saying, which left Thaddeus staring at a blank wall and a constant stream of bus boys and two waitresses miraculously missing each other and avoiding head-ons as they came and went through the double doors.

Quentin brought Thaddeus up on the day's events. He smoked Marlboros endlessly and put them out on his saucer. He loved to expound on the law. His family owned the Orbit Motel on the west end of town, and, a mile beyond, was Quentin's eighty acre spread complete with horse barns and training rings. His family was horsey and Quentin had inherited the equine disease from his dad, Ed

Erwin, who everyone assumed was associated with the mob because he kept slot machines all over southern Illinois in bars and clubs and the police left him alone, even though gambling was illegal. The natural conclusion reached by all was that Ed Erwin was paying everybody off in order to keep his slots running, which was, in fact, true. So heads were turned, and the one-arm bandits continued to spin out their profits, and Ed bought a big spread on the edge of town and raised Quarter Horses just for the hell of it.

Quentin had inherited his father's competitive streak and, just about every weekend in the summer, he would load up a trailer of a half dozen horses, hitch up to his one-ton Ford, and head off across the state to a show or a county fair, where his animals would race. Sometimes Thaddeus went along on these ventures but usually not, as the breeders and trainers were a hard drinking lot and Thaddeus thought himself much too busy for that kind of stuff.

"Coffee and a cheese Danish," Quentin told Cece. "Half and half, not that plastic creamer."

"Okay," said Cece. "Thaddeus?"

"I'm hungry. How about two scrambled and three links. Coffee and OJ. And water."

"You're thirsty," said Quentin after Cece had turned away with their order. "Get drunk last night or something?"

"No, I didn't get drunk last night. You know I rarely touch the crap."

"One of your key failings," said Quentin. "Drink and come to know your fellow man's inner thoughts."

"You mean everyone spills their guts when loaded."

"Exactly."

"Listen, thanks for sending over Ermeline."

"Has she got the tits or what?"

"She's hurt, Quentin, really messed up. Dr. Ahmad already told her it's going to be very difficult to get the ink out of her skin."

"You think Victor Harrow lettered her tits like that?"

"Who else would have done it?"

"She said there was another guy there. Some greaseball."

"Problem is, guys usually don't carve other guy's names in girls' breasts. Just doesn't figure."

"True. Ouch, that must've hurt like hell!"

"She was drugged. I've got her going by the hospital for a blood draw. I want to know what kind of drug Vic slipped her."

"So you're thinking it all comes down to Victor Harrow?"

"You know what, it doesn't matter what I think. What matters is whether she has enough facts to sue Victor Harrow. I believe she does."

"Probably right. What will be the grounds of the lawsuit?"

Just then their orders arrived. Cece slung the plates and cups on the table and raised an eyebrow. "Gentlemen?"

"We're good," Quentin smiled at her. "Thank you."

"I'll check back with coffee in ten."

"What's the grounds?" Quentin asked again.

"I'm still thinking about that. Assault, for one."

"No good. Don't sue him for assault." He pushed the heavy glasses back up on his nose.

"Really? Why not?" Thaddeus was all ears. His fork was forgotten on the plate.

"Because his insurance won't pay. His insurance will pay up only if it's an unintentional act, negligence. If you sue him for assault there's no insurance money to grab, because assault is an intentional act, and insurance doesn't cover it."

"So like I was saying, I've ruled out assault."

"Atta boy. How about negligent supervision of his workplace?"

"How's that work?"

"Here's what you do. You find out who the greaseball was. Then you sue Victor for failing to maintain a safe workplace for a business invitee. Or even just a social invitee. Let's say Ermeline was there just for a drink, nothing else. She wasn't looking for a job; she wasn't there for any business purpose. Which makes her a pure social invitee. Victor owed her a legal duty of supervision of the premises he had invited her to. Meaning, he owed her the duty of a safe place. Letting some Chicago greaseball into the bus is what led to the assault. I'm thinking it wasn't Victor at all. I'm thinking it was the greaseball."

"One problem with that."

"Okay?"

"I don't know who the greaseball is. Ermeline doesn't remember his name. Johnny Something—Baloney or some such"

"That's no problem at all. File suit against Victor, and allege negligence based on the wrongful acts of a John Doe. Then during discovery, you take Victor's deposition and get the guy's name. You then go back and amend your complaint by adding John Doe's correct name. George Greaseball—or whatever."

"This is beautiful. Beautiful. Thanks, Quentin."

"No need to thank me. I just wish I could prosecute the guy."

"Why can't you?"

"Simple. Each guy is going to point the finger at the other guy. I can't prove beyond a reasonable doubt which one did the cut-and-ink job. Your civil case is a much better case. That's why I sent it over to you."

"Thanks again. Tell the truth, I'm pretty revved up about it."

"You should be. She's been intolerably damaged, all kidding aside. Ermeline is a good kid and a damn hard worker. She waits on me every night. She's got that hard-times loser ex-husband creeping around sometimes, but she pays her bills, does a good job with Jaime, and provides her kid with a pretty good standard of living. No thanks to Craphead. She came to see me two years ago. Ex won't pay child support."

"What did you do?"

"I told her it would take the FBI to keep up with the guy. He moves every Saturday morning, new town, new job. A wage levy would be impossible to get."

"Course you could just lock his ass up."

"Yes, and I might do that, next time he shows his face in Hickam County. I just might, wouldn't surprise me."

Thaddeus forked up egg and sausage. He crammed a huge bite in his mouth and sat chewing, making his mental notes. This was only going to get better and better, he was thinking. We'll file suit ASAP.

They both sat quietly. Quentin broke the silence, asking, "Hey, you want to go to Springfield with me this weekend?"

"Might. What's up?"

"Sangamon County Fair, Dude. Just the biggest horse show of the year. Outside of the Arlington season, of course."

"Yes, I think I can do that. Maybe we can talk some more about the case on the ride over."

"Definitely. So here's the plan. Be at my place at seven. We'll clean out the trailer, stock it up, and hit the road no later than nine. Also, got a couple of stalls to clean, but you're great at that."

Thaddeus laughed. "It's the least I can do. You're keeping me in clients with all your great referrals. I'd be up the creek without them."

"No, you'd be out in the bars at night passing out business cards, like Franey."

"Fletcher Franey? I thought he had a pretty good practice built up by now."

"Hell no, he loses everything he takes on. No repeat business there. So he's out hustling DWIs and divorces all over the county. Every night. He must pass out twenty cards a night—let's see, which would be 100 cards per week. Bring in two or three suckers, that's pretty good advertising. Good ROI, as they say at Wharton."

"Damn good. Maybe I should give that a try."

"Hell no. Drunks can't pay. No money, they drink it all up. Franey's always suing some client or other for non-payment. Stay away from that kind of bullcrap."

"So who will Vic hire when I sue him?"

"Nobody. His insurance company will do the hiring. They'll probably retain Bill Johansson III over in Polk. They fall all over themselves over Dick."

"He's really a great lawyer."

"He's all right. But don't worry about it. You've got the facts on your side. The facts always make the case, not the lawyer. Don't get me wrong, a guy like Franey can screw up even a good fact presentation, but you're not Franey, Thad. You're like a racehorse: you're going to be fast, Dude. Even D.B. says so. Which is something."

"Don't embarrass me. I still can't find my butt with both hands, most of the time. Most of the time I'm clueless. Like today. I would have sued Vic for assault if you hadn't wised me up."

"You're welcome. Gotta get back."

"Let's do it," Thaddeus said. Quentin went on ahead, Thaddeus finished up his eggs and sausage, paid the check and headed back to the office.

VICTOR AWOKE that morning at half past seven, with absolutely no recall of the night before. Roofies were good at that, erasing the victim's memory of the night before.

He had spent the night in his clothes, on the queen size at the rear of the bus. Luckily, Betty Anne Harrow was out of town and hadn't gone ape over him missing.

Victor found himself with muddled thinking and increasing panic as he realized his memory had been wiped. Parts of it slowly came back to him as he showered. He began to remember Johnny Bladanni coming to the back door and coming inside. Anything beyond that, however, was wiped out of his memory banks. And, oh yes, Ermeline was here for a drink, he remembered—and his panic shot up. Where did she go? Was she all right? Earlier parts of the day before were firmly attached in memory. Brody Mathewson at First National had to be contacted as soon as they opened at nine. He needed to have the payoff money ready for the gangster from Chicago before they cut his throat—or worse.

He went into the bedroom and selected a pair of yellow Sans-A-Belt slacks to accommodate his large abdominal overhang, and a plain white shirt, button-down, XL. He slipped on Roper boots, ran a brush through his hair, and studied himself in the tiny bathroom mirror. There was a deep puncture wound under his chin. It was caked in blood. "What the hell?" he muttered. He unwrapped a Band-

Aid and covered the spot. Then he smiled at himself in the small glass. All in all, none the worse for wear. He hoped the same was true for Ermeline. He pointed at himself in the mirror. "You're *way* out of your league."

Victor drove west on Washington, beyond the town square, until he came to an office in the middle of a block that was once occupied by a motel, now defunct. The sign said it was the First National Bank, though it still had more a motel feel to it. Victor parked and went inside.

Brody Mathewson was back by the third teller, refilling his coffee cup, when he spotted Victor. He immediately came out from behind the teller cages and walked Victor over to his desk. On his desk was a simple gold—plastic—sign that said, "Brody Mathewson, New Accounts." He asked Victor to please sit, and he would get his paperwork on screen. Several minutes passed and finally Brody broke the silence.

"I've spoken to Mister Edwards. He feels—I feel too—that if we were loaning on tangible assets we could go the full one hundred. But we're not. We're loaning open-ended, and we have no security. Mister Edwards has authorized a credit line of twenty-five thousand, but that's the best he'll do right now, Victor."

"But I— "

"I know what you're gonna say. You need the full one hundred, and I get that. But with the recession still hanging around and given how you're mortgaged to the hilt on all the machines and equipment and trucks, we're stuck on twenty-five. I'm sorry."

"You're sure?"

Brody waved a hand expansively. "We've all decided. Now. Do you want me to open this as a credit line or do you want it as a check guarantee up to the full twenty-five—you tell me."

Victor was at a loss for words. He had no idea what he was going to tell Johnny Bladanni. And there was no way he could tell First National about his jam or about the fact he'd been paying off Chicago. He knew they would call every note he had with them if he told them the truth. So would the other two banks he had accounts with. It wouldn't be pretty.

"Neither. I need it as cash."

"Come again?"

"That's it," Victor said, and smoothed his sleeve as if he was slightly indifferent to the whole issue. "I need cash. Twenty-five thousand dollars."

"I don't know that we even have that in the bank. Be right back."

Brody jumped up and strode back to the vault, where he inserted a key in the skeleton door and ducked inside. Within minutes he returned. "Yes," he said, "the Fed was here late last night. We can cover you. You're sure you want cash? That's not safe, you know, Victor."

"I have a gun in the truck."

"Well, sure you do. But still— "

"Look, don't make me wait. Just give it to me. Please."

"Sure enough, Victor. We will prepare it and give it to you in a check box. Okay? Do you want to count it?"

"No. I trust you."

"Thank you. But you should at least count it."

"I trust you."

"So how much can you get for this bus?" Johnny Bladanni said, waving his hand at the wall of Victor's office. They were in the rear office of the bus; the office manager and gum smacker were up front, managing the constant flow of paperwork of Victor's three State construction jobs.

"I told you," Victor moaned. "The bus has a lien. Do you understand what that means?"

"I don't give a damn what that means. What time today can you get this bus sold? You owe me another 75K."

"I can't sell the bus, Mister Bladanni. I don't have any other freed-up assets. I'm mortgaged to the hilt on my home and this construction yard. The bank gave me twenty-five, but that's it. I'm tapped out."

Johnny's face twisted. A malicious sneer. "You just don't get it. I got orders not to leave here without the money you owe us."

"You can't get blood out of a rock."

"Let's think about that. By about noon today you're going to hear from the cops. They're going to want to take your statement. There will be an investigation."

"What the hell are you talking about?"

"Gimme that," Johnny said, pointing at a Chivas bottle behind Victor, snugged toward the rear of a two-drawer filing cabinet. "Right, that."

Victor passed him the bottle. Johnny popped the plastic lid on Victor's coffee. He poured two fingers of the scotch into the coffee. "Drink that."

"I don't start this early. It's only ten-thirty."

"Don't matter. Drink it."

With a long sigh and shrug Victor took a drink of the coffee. The scotch definitely didn't mix well. The taste was bitter and acid. "Crap."

"Now the rest of it. All of it."

Victor shut his eyes and lifted the cup. In one long pull he drank down the coffee and scotch. "Happy now?"

"You're the one needs to get happy. You're going to get a call from your Sheriff and he's going to be asking you about your work last night. You're going to be stinking of whiskey."

Victor frowned. "My work last night?"

"You tuned up Miss Priss, the girl you had out here last night."

"I didn't touch her."

"Oh, it was after you was knocked out. You was sleepwalking. You took your knife, carved your name in her tits, and traced it with a Magic Marker. She ain't happy with you, Victor."

"What! You hurt that girl, and I'll— "

Johnny stood up and leaned across the small desk. "You'll what? You'll go to jail for it? Is that what you'll do?"

"Damn! Why would you do something like that?"

"Victor, you was warned. We told you to have our money yesterday. You blew us off, so you had to be seriously warned. Now you cut up that poor girl."

Victor held up his hands. "Mr. Bladanni, if you would get your boss on the phone, we could straighten this out in three minutes. I'm a reasonable man."

"No. I gotta run. You got to explain things to the police. But I'll be back, I promise, and I want the title to this bus. Free and clear of any lien. Got it?"

"I can't believe you hurt Ermeline. I swear, I'll— "

Johnny flourished the switchblade and suddenly it was at Victor's chin again. There was already one bandage there; Victor Harrow didn't want another. "You'll what?" Johnny menaced.

"Please. Just go."

"I will. But I'll be back. And next time you ain't got our money I'm gonna kick down your door, cut your throat, rape your wife, and stab your dog. You've been warned twice."

6

F letcher T. Franey was medium frame and height, bald with a yellow fringe, wore tortoise shell glasses, had a black mole on his cheek near the right eye socket, and dressed in ten-year-old sport coats and shiny slacks from the men's store downstairs. Franey was a lawyer, not a well-thought-of one, but he was also the Chairman of the Hickam County Democrat Party. The party position gave him all the power anyone could want—in a small county. He possessed the ability to get political favors for friends, steer small state contracts among the loyalists, have a direct line to the movers and shakers in Chicago and Springfield, and get your driver's license reinstated if you got yourself nailed for drunk driving. In fact, drunk driving and divorce cases were his mainstay.

He had gone to a third tier law school, drank himself silly all three years, got a D in wills and trusts, which meant he wasn't going to graduate, then, at the last minute, wrangled an A in commercial paper, which gave him a 2.0, exactly what he needed to graduate. By a hair. Still, it was the old joke: What do you call the guy at the bottom of his law school class? Attorney.

His office was on the west side of the Orbit town square, the entranceway squeezed in between a men's store, Bertham's Haberdashery, and an office supply, Grant's Paper and Pens Office Supply.

The law office was up an old flight of battleship gray stairs, and opened on a bleak, dark waiting room and law office all rolled into one. His secretary was there three afternoons a week, and the rest of the time he answered the phone. "No, Mary Ellen is busy, that's why I'm answering," he would lie. "But can I help?" His manners were impeccable, and that's how he got along with the city fathers and merchants.

He had very little local business as he wasn't possessed of much legal wisdom, and the people of Orbit knew that, so he became the city attorney for Marlin Township, an incorporated village ten miles northwest of Orbit. Marlin Township was home to fewer than 1000 souls, most of whom got a government check, and most of whom couldn't afford legal advice, not even for a simple will. Yet, Franey managed to pick up enough hours at the council meetings to pay his rent back in Orbit, so it worked well for him. He kept a Mr. Coffee burning behind his desk, poured himself cup after cup during the day, allowed them to get cold, and most often could be found drinking cold coffee out of a mug he had purchased in Nogales, Sonora, on a trip last summer with Nemecia, his wife.

Today, he was sitting with his booted feet up on his desk, puffing on a pipe he had just bought at Haines drug store, and wondering if the pipe satisfied the image of himself he wanted to portray—when the phone rang.

"Franey Law. This is Fletcher."

"Mister Franey, please hold for the Attorney General."

Franey swallowed hard. Had he heard right? The Attorney General of Illinois—calling *him*? Hell, it wasn't even an election year.

A strong voice reached out to him. "Fletcher? Robert K. Amistaggio, Attorney General here. Got a few minutes?"

"Yes, Mister Attorney General. Anything you want."

"Well, we've got a little situation with one of your locals over there."

"Who's that?" Franey puffed the pipe. It had gone out. Again. He flicked the yellow plastic lighter and sucked the flame down into the bowl. Smoke exploded and swirled.

"Gentleman by the name of Victor Harrow. You know Mister Harrow?"

"Victor? Everyone knows Victor."

"He a client?"

"Sad to say, no. He's always in trouble of some sort and would make anyone a great client."

"Well, not now he wouldn't. He's upside down on some money he owes the State."

"How much?"

"Not much. About seventy-five thousand."

Franey bit the pipe stem. Not much? Seventy-five thousand *dollars* and that's "not much?"

The AG continued. "He's got a contract, and he's light on the service fee."

Franey's heart skipped. "Service Fee" was monkey talk for "payoff."

"Who's he owe it to," Franey said, his voice weak.

"His Honor, the Governor."

"Holy crap."

"Exactly. Now here's what we need you to do. We want you to keep this under wraps, but scooch on over to the courthouse and find out everything you can about old Vic's assets. We might have to sue and sell to get paid, you get my drift."

"Yessir." Franey wrote on the pink message pad: "Find out about assets."

"And get his tax return. We need to know about his depreciation schedule. That will tell us what property he has."

"Excuse me, tax return? That won't be at the court house."

"No, course not. That you'll have to get from the IRS."

"IRS, okay. Anything else?"

"Let me give you my direct line. Call this number when you've got the dope on this guy."

"Will do."

They said goodbye and hung up. The damn pipe was out, and Franey felt the narrow ridge of sweat already forming on his forehead. How in the world would he get tax returns from the IRS? They don't just give those away to anyone who asks. He brought up Internet Explorer on his screen and browsed over to irs.gov.

He spent the next half hour learning all about obtaining taxpayer documents from the IRS. It looked like he was going to have to dummy up a power of attorney and sign Victor's name to it. He was also going to need Victor's social security number.

The sweat was flowing freely now. That was a crime, a serious one. Fletcher T. Franey knew if he committed a crime he would likely get caught; he just wasn't smart enough to get away with it. Still, the AG had spoken, and that was like hearing from the Archangel Michael. Direct from God's mouth to your ears, he told himself. You have to do this.

Then it occurred to him that maybe if he performed this task simply and well, why, he would have his foot in the AG's office. Who knew what kind of local legal work the AG might then feel predisposed to send his way? The payoff here could be huge; the potential was unlimited. If only he had the AG recorded while he was asking for Victor's tax returns. Then he'd *really* have some leverage, the AG promoting a criminal act. That had conspiracy and other federal crimes written all over it! The opportunities were unlimited here!

He again sucked flame into the pipe bowl. It was time to move ahead fearlessly, and they had their man. He would do it. Definitely, he would do it.

Attorney Franey punched in the AG's direct line. He was shocked that the AG, himself, answered. He told him about Victor's social security number being a must-have, the AG said he would have someone call him from the Secretary of State's office with the information he needed, and Franey said thanks. This time when he hung up he switched off the tape recorder he used to take telephone statements. He hit rewind/playback.

"Mister Attorney General? Attorney Fletcher T. Franey here again."

"Okay."

"I'm going to need the subject's social security number in order to get his tax return. Can you help?"

"I'll have someone call you from the Secretary of State's office with that information. Will that be all?"

"Well—I just wanted to say thanks for trusting me with this. I won't let you down."

"Thank you, Mister Franey. Goodbye now."

"Goodbye."

Recorded: busted! He had the Attorney General of the State of Illinois combining with him in a conspiracy to defraud the federal government out of a private citizens' tax return. He was giddy, and he stood and raised his arms overhead. "Yippee!" he exhorted, then immediately sat down. He hoped to high heavens they hadn't heard him downstairs in the haberdashery and office supply. Still, he was elated.

He jumped back to his feet and began pacing behind his desk.

Smoke billowed from the pipe as he puffed madly.

Now how, he asked himself, are you going to parlay this arrow in the AG's heart into some real money? What the hell, maybe he could come out of this with a State contract for legal work of some kind. Of course, he would go for the usual payoff—State money. And the title of Special Assistant Attorney General. He had seen that used before, and it never failed to scare hell out of folks. Why not him? Indeed, why not? In the energy of the moment, Franey neglected to think about the AG's muscle. No, not the appointment of special prosecutors or special investigators out of the AG's office. He forgot to think about the AG's *real* muscle, the mob. They wouldn't let a nobody like Fletcher T. Franey get within ten feet of their Attorney General. Heads would roll before that would ever happen.

7

Thaddeus and Christine were gathered around his desk like wolves at a carcass. They were hungry. Money hungry, and they were tired of being poor, tired of always having to hustle every month to get the office bills paid, the salary paid, the Buick paid. At last, something good had come their way with Ermeline's case. They had talked it over and they had both agreed. They were going to sue the hell out of Victor Harrow.

Their tools were books, open and stacked on top each other, multiple legal pads with blue and black ink, several Styrofoam coffee cups empty and half-full, and pens, paperclips, binders, pencils, erasers and documents everywhere, and the dozen photographs of Ermeline Ransom's tattooed breasts in a neat stack. There was a brainstorm underway, the attorney and his paralegal.

Christine stood up to stretch. Her muscular shoulders flexed beneath her gray lamb's wool sweater. Her features were fine and sized just right, so that she looked very feminine at first glance, until you realized those shoulders were probably more muscled than yours, and that those biceps, forearms, splayed hands, torso and stout legs would probably own you in a fight. But deep down hers was a gentle soul, and she only wanted peace in her life and for her husband and little girl. She was not an angry person; she was mellow enough, which was one of the key features of her personality that had told Thaddeus to hire her after her interview. She would be a cool head in the middle of a storm and he had known, eighteen months ago, that he would definitely need that, the practice of law being as uproarious as it is.

Thaddeus took a long pull at his coffee and frowned. "This is icy," he said. She offered to get the refill, but he waved her off. "My turn. Let me get you one," he said.

It was 4:15 on a cloudy Tuesday, and they were going back over their tracks, making sure they had left no stone unturned in their quest to prepare and file the most complete and legal complaint for negligence and assault against another person ever filed in Hickam County Circuit Court.

Victor Harrow better, damn well, duck. They had finally laughed when they had finished drafting the complaint and traded high-fives. This lawsuit was going to take him down. All that remained now was for Christine to prepare the cover sheet and summons, and Thaddeus could walk the papers across the street, file them in the clerk's office, and send them out for service by Sheriff Altiman's deputy.

THE NEXT MORNING at 9:30 Thaddeus left the office with the filing. Inside the red file folder, he had the signed and dated complaint, the filled-in cover sheet, and the summons ready for signing and stamping by the Circuit Clerk. He would file in the next fifteen minutes, and by noon, the entire square would be talking about the lawsuit. By tonight, the entire county. Thursday noon the *Hickam Press* would roll off the presses onto the mail trucks for distribution to every rural inhabitant in a thirty-mile radius. The story would be page one—they had already interviewed Thaddeus and taken several shots of him at his desk. The story would light up the telephone lines. No one had ever heard of a man carving his name in a woman's breasts. Much less a respected businessman, one with everything to

lose and nothing to gain, a deacon at his church, a Silver Star in Vietnam, a member of Rotary and Moose, and Sergeant-at-Arms at the
Orbit VFW Post.

Thaddeus' step quickened, and he made it across Adams Street,
hopping up on the courthouse sidewalk, walking west 100 steps, then
taking a left and on up the courthouse steps into the atrium. He took
a deep breath and turned the handle to the Circuit Clerk's Office.

8

L unch hour—11:30-1:30 at the Silver Dome was packed. The merchants all filed out of their stores around the square and dutifully reported to the large dining room where they would join their usual lunch bunch. It was duck hunting season and football season, so first, they all swapped tales about who got his limit and whether Ducks Unlimited was going to have a record annual meeting/dinner in the basement of the Red Bird Inn. Then came football; although the State was Illinois and the Chicago Bears ruled upstate, Orbit was downstate and all hope and attention was focused on the season of the Saint Louis Rams and their record. Would they at long last return to the playoffs? And what of Geoff Gentry, their great quarterback out of Syracuse: would he play after being knocked unconscious and carried off the field last Sunday?

Once football and ducks were settled, the merchants compared notes on sales so far from this day to sales from a year ago, five years ago, and even ten years ago. It was true: many of the merchants kept journals, detailing sales as far back as when they had first acquired their businesses, from Junior Grant at Grant's Pen and Pencil Office Store to Rich Tatinger at Schnizzle's Shoes, the grand record-keeper of them all, whose records (thanks, in part, to his predecessor father) went all the way back to 1976. Shoe sales were pegged to climatic changes, and Rich could tell you what would happen with waterproofs and high tops when the temperatures plunged, as well as what would happen with Nikes and Adidas when basketball season rolled around. True, he wasn't prescient, but he was a great judge of his customers' spending habits.

As plates were ferried out of the kitchen by the wait staff and as earnest eating began, Junior Grant suddenly, in a buckle in the conversation, said loudly, "Say, I hear Thaddeus Murfee sued Vic Harrow this morning. They say Vic really got his foot stuck in the mud this time."

"It wasn't Thaddeus who sued," one of the minor clerks from the Clerk's Office replied. "It was Ermeline Ransom, who is being represented by Thaddeus. She's the real plaintiff, not Thaddeus."

"What's the allegation?" A school administrator asked. He was in town to visit with the Superintendent of Schools for Hickam County, something about a pregnant class president.

"Thaddeus claims Victor carved his name in the girl's chest!"

"What?"

"*Come again?*"

The lesser clerk dabbed a paper napkin at the corners of her mouth. "The complaint alleges that Victor carved his name in Ermeline's breast and then inked it in."

"Is it permanent?" Rich Tatinger asked. It had been a slow morning in the shoe industry. At last, something—some bit of gossip —had piqued his interest. This was sizing up to be good.

"Jeez, wonder what Betty Anne Harrow's thinking?"

"Never mind what his wife's thinking, what in the hell was *he* thinking?"

Attorney Bud Leinager banged inside—late from court—and motioned a visitor to slide around in Bud's booth. Bud waited while the man moved his plate and iced tea, then lowered his hulk in beside him. "I just read the entire complaint, front to back. It's outrageous!" he announced in his inherited voice, booming and piercing. "Thaddeus Murfee better hope to hell his own legal malpractice insurance is paid up."

"You Vic's lawyer?" Someone asked Bud.

"Not yet. Probably won't be. I have a conflict of interest." Bud would never admit it would be Bill Johansson III who would catch this gold ring. In order to keep face, Bud would beg off with a claimed conflict of interest, just to make people think that, while he had been asked to intervene, the ethics of law prevented him. He made a long face and scowled at the inquisitive looks around him. Victor Harrow clearly needed his keen help and steel-trap legal mind, but legal ethics held him at bay. He wasn't happy about it one damn bit, either; he let everyone within earshot know.

"What's the lawsuit after, Bud?"

"Ten million dollars," Bud answered after he quickly let Cece know he would have the roast hen, with new potatoes and creamed spinach. Coffee, bring the pot, but hold the cream, Doctor's orders. "Weight," he explained to his audience, and patted his sizeable girth.

"Ten million dollars and attorney's fees of one million."

"Damnation!" George Bingham cried. George was the owner of H&M Furniture, home of "No Tricky Financing." He remembered, for one, how it felt to be sued. It had happened to him after he had buried his Ping putter in another golfer's head. The *Hickam Press* had even sarcastically ranted that George had failed to count the cranium stroke on his scorecard. Bud had defended that case. It had been settled for an undisclosed amount, the court records sealed, but Quentin Erwin, who once again refused to prosecute because it had occurred on private land—the Red Apple Country Club—he knew the amount and let everyone know. George had had to mortgage both his house and the H&M Furniture Store to pay for the pleasure of creasing another golfer's skull.

"You should know, George," someone muttered quite loudly, then ducked his head.

Al Petty, owner of the *Hickam Press*, gravely asked Bud, "What's the legal theory of the case?"

"Well, there's several legal theories, Albert," said Bud, who was slowly stirring two sugars into his steaming coffee. "Count 1 claims there was a breach of a legal duty to provide a social invitee with a safe place to visit."

"That would mean Ermeline was on Victor's property?" someone asked.

"It does. Ermeline was alleged to be visiting Victor at the office. The bus."

Catcalls rang out and some whistling. Someone shouted, "What time of night was *that*?"

"Actually, it was at night," Bud continued, "if you believe the complaint. Which I don't. Victor wouldn't have Ermeline to his office at night. Not in a million years. Happily married, deacon at First Christian, Silver Star— "

"Yeah, we know all that Bud," the school administrator interrupted. "But what is the allegation?"

"Simple. That she was there at the trailer after ten at night and... Victor drugged her." This last portion was said almost under his breath as Bud shoved a partial chicken breast in his mouth. He licked his fingers and nodded approvingly. "Just fine, Cece!" he called toward the lunch counter, where Cece was busily pouring water for new customers. "Highly recommend the hen, everyone."

Al Petty stuffed a good pinch of Prince Albert into his pipe. Neither Hickham County nor the City of Orbit had seen fit to outlaw smoking in local restaurants. He who would object to another's smoke was always soundly booed. It was a free country and even if someone else's smoke was blinding you and ruining your meal, by damn, they had the right to smoke. This was Lincoln country, one man-one vote, and all that. He flipped a silver Zippo with a Marine Corps emblem on its case. "So you've told us failure to provide safe premises. What other legal theories are alleged?"

"Hell, Al," Bud said through a mouthful of new potatoes, "why don't you stop by the Clerk's Office and run off a copy? You're going to make front page news out of this anyway." Bud stuck up for his friend and sometime-client Victor Harrow, but he was also sounding slightly miffed, knowing that in the Thursday edition of the *Press* his own name wouldn't be mentioned because Victor would never hire him for such desirable work. Bud got many of Victor's contracts and employment disputes to handle, but the big stuff was always just out of reach, much to his utter dejection.

"I already have a copy, Bud," Al retorted. "I'm just gauging audience reaction here. It will be a novel case for a jury made up of these and other local people."

Bud didn't respond but appeared furiously engaged with slicing up the chicken's opposite breast into bite-size chunks.

"Any pictures attached?"

"To the complaint?" the minor clerk said. "No pictures. Those will probably only be seen by the jury. And then they'll be sealed."

"What the hell does her chest look like? Was it her boobs? Or just her chest?"

"Boobs," Bud suddenly erupted. "Someone is alleged to have engraved her breasts!"

There was a serious moment of reflection at this. Who in their right mind could do such a thing to Ermeline Ransom? This called for some serious debate and much more investigation and answers than what they had so far. Perhaps Thaddeus was right, then. Perhaps the case was worth ten million dollars.

"Does Victor have ten million?" Junior Grant wondered out loud. "Could he even pay a huge judgment?"

"Thad was smart," Bud said, using the shortened version of Thaddeus' name to indicate there existed an intimacy between him and the young and almost surprisingly aggressive lawyer. "Thad alleged negligence in Count 1, which gets Vic's insurance company in the game. Now it's got skin, so there's insurance money to be tagged, so Vic isn't hanging out all alone. Thad will want policy limits, not a dime less."

"Who will Vic hire? Bill Johansson in Polk County?"

Bud chewed thoughtfully. "It's the insurance company's call, which lawyer gets hired to defend Vic. But, yeah, probably Johansson."

"He wins every case he touches."

"Never has lost here in Hickam county, has he?"

The minor clerk agreed. "Never lost here. So far, anyway."

"Maybe this is a first."

"But what about Thaddeus? Is he experienced enough for this? Isn't he still learning how to patty-cake?"

"Pretty much," Bud opined. "But it doesn't take a legal genius to win this case: if, and that's a huge 'if', the facts as alleged are true."

"Damnation."

"Amen."

"Can they get the writing removed?"

"Dermabrasion," the school administrator suggested.

"Well, sure," some woman said whose own face had been recently peeled. "But that only gets the derma, the outer layer of skin. If the ink is actually *inside* the skin, they won't be able to get it out. Poor thing. Give her twenty million!"

"At least," Cece said as she rushed by with coffee in one hand and three waters in the other. "At least twenty million for that kind of assault. She works here, and she's a great girl. And she's got a kid."

"Is her ex still coming around? Is that why she was out at Vic's? Romancing?"

"It was purely business," Bud said.

"Oh sure, like she was hiring Vic to build a new freeway for her. Bullcrap."

At that moment Sheriff Charlie Altiman and two deputies entered. All eyes followed him and his crew as they waited for a table to be cleared. Once they were seated, pandemonium erupted. Everyone wanted to know, would Victor Harrow be prosecuted? Had he been arrested? Would Quentin Erwin, Jr. file criminal charges? Was there any truth to all this? Had the Sheriff gone to the premises and retrieved any evidence? Was there anyone else there when this allegedly occurred? Had Victor given a statement? Where *was* Victor right now? He usually joined the crowd for lunch. But not today.

When the entire clamor died down, Sheriff Altiman held up a hand. "There will be a press conference at noon tomorrow, courthouse steps. Until then, there's nothing more I can say."

Groans from the crowd. Publisher Al Petty pulled out his iPhone and entered a reminder on his calendar. He was relieved; the Sheriff had wisely called the press conference in time for the results of his investigation to make it into the Thursday paper. Smart move. But that's why he had been elected to five four-year terms. Smart, indeed.

9

Erwin Farms controlled the Quarter Horse competition in the Midwest. Twenty-five years before, Ed Erwin—District Attorney Quentin Erwin, Jr.'s father—had purchased a perfectly proportioned colt, the offspring of the Kingston Ranch's foundation sire Old Musket. The Colt, Captain Jones, had continued Old Musket's grand line of Quarter Horses—many of whom had been champions in the annals of the American Quarter Horse Association over the years since. While Quarter Horses were not only well-suited for western riding and cattle work, many race tracks offered Quarter Horses a wide assortment of pari-mutuel horse racing with purses in the millions. A few—not many—of Erwin Farm's Quarter Horses had also been trained to compete in dressage, where horse and rider are expected to perform from memory a series of predetermined movements. Erwin Farms boasted a dressage arena under roof, a standard size, which by rule measures 20 m by 40 m (66x131 feet).

Saturday, after Thaddeus filed the complaint, a certain late-20's rider was working a horse named Sister Andromeda in the dressage arena. She was taking Sister Andromeda through the complex series of maneuvers they might face should they ever compete. For Ilene

Crayton, the rider, competition was far from her mind, as she was deeply involved with the raising of her daughter Eleanor. For now, riding was a hobby, although a hobby much-loved and, in a way, a carrying-on of a Crayton family tradition. Ilene was a single parent; Doctor Bill Crayton had been instantly killed when kicked in the head by one of their own Quarter Horses three years earlier. Ilene, who was a philosophy graduate from Bennington, suddenly found herself head of household and without any marketable skills, as the Help Wanted ads weren't exactly falling all over themselves looking for philosophers. So, she enrolled in several online training schools and became trained as a computer programmer—the last thing anyone who knew her might have expected. "Simple," she said, "They pay eighty thousand a year and you can work from home." Thanks to Doctor Crayton's substantial life insurance policy, Ilene and Eleanor had been able to remain in the family home, a small horse farm five miles east of Orbit. The horses, however, had been sold off following the tragedy. There were just too many painful memories there. Lately, though, Ilene had been showing up at Quentin Erwin, Jr.'s spread, helping him clean stalls and drive the tractor and manure spreader, in exchange for dressage time with some of the smarter, competitive horses. While Ilene thus spent some Saturday mornings, Eleanor hung out with her grandmother and grandfather on Bill's side, both of them physicians as well.

Thaddeus had never met Ilene Crayton, though he had heard the story of Bill's premature death. So, when he parked and walked in through the barn he had no idea who was working Sister Andromeda in the dressage arena as he passed the door. Moreover, the woman— girl? —was wearing the standard headgear, so he wouldn't have been able to make her out, anyway.

Thaddeus quickly passed by and stopped at stall three, where his own Quarter Horse, Uncle Do-gooder, was waiting for him. It was almost as if Uncle Do-gooder knew it was Saturday and knew Thaddeus would turn up any minute loaded down with carrots and apples for the mounts. He held out a carrot and the roan horse nuzzled it from his hand. As the horse munched and blinked at a fly, Thaddeus looked back toward the dressage arena. The girl—woman? —sat a horse very nicely. And she seemed to have a damn fine figure too, he imagined, although he'd only had a glance at the pretty, trim legs and the loose denim work shirt, which was amply filled out. He thought he would like to know her name. He wondered if she wrote stories. That...was too much to ask for.

Thaddeus found Quentin at the north end of the barn, cleaning hay clotted with horse manure out of stall seven. "So who's the gal?" he absently asked, just generally making conversation.

Quentin, wearing Osh-Kosh coveralls and Wellington boots, stopped and removed his Cardinals baseball cap. He wiped his forehead with the cap. "That? Ilene Crayton. Bill's widow."

"Never met her."

"Well, you should. Very classy."

"I'm sure. If she's horsey, she's probably just your type."

"Yeah," Quentin laughed, "just don't tell Donna. I like having my genitals intact."

"Don't worry, I won't breathe a word. Is she pretty?"

Quentin ignored the question. "She's just coming over now and then. Likes to work Sister Andromeda and some of the others. Pure dressage. I never did much get that stuff."

"Is she pretty?"

"She's very pretty."

"Maybe I should meet her. Showmanship—ringmanship, it's all good." Thaddeus said. He had done some reading at the AQHA website and others. Maybe, at some point, he would have horses too, like Quentin. They were a great way to spend the day. And maybe, he would get a chance to say hello to this Ilene Crayton.

"I'm dressed for anything. Where do you want me to start?"

Quentin looked Thaddeus up and down. The rookie lawyer was wearing Redwing boots, khakis, and a flannel shirt. "Next time, lose the slacks," Quentin said. "This is horse crap we're forking around with here," Quentin laughed. "Tell you what. You take over the pitchfork, and I'll go fire up the Ford and back the manure spreader in. Then, we can clean the stalls and load the spreader, all in one move."

"Fine."

Quentin handed the pitchfork to Thaddeus, who bent at the waist and went right to work. He was glad to have purely physical labor to do for a while. The past week and the tension of the Victor Harrow case, the news media seeking comments from him for 100 miles around, and the questions from everyone he came in contact with, had worn him out mentally. It was good to clean stalls, good to be around Quentin. Who knew, maybe they would even talk some law, though law was off-limits in the barn. There might be time for that later, when they adjourned to the Red Bird Inn for lunch, like they did most Saturdays when stall cleaning was done.

Two DAYS AGO, Thaddeus had watched Sheriff Charlie Altiman hold his news conference on the north steps of the courthouse. The news conference was held just across the street from Thaddeus' office, and Thaddeus had to admit he had cracked his window and listened in to some of what was said.

Charlie had tapped the mic and said, "Testing?" before he launched into what he had to say. "Can you hear me back there?"

"Do you have a statement from Victor Harrow?" the NBC affiliate reporter out of Quincy piped up.

Charlie had lifted a hand. "Let me start with some opening comments. Maybe what I have to say will answer many of your questions. And first, in answer to that question from Marilee Sonigee, no, we don't have Victor Harrow's statement. Victor Harrow at this time is represented by Bill Johansson III out of Polk County, and Mister Johansson has instructed Mister Harrow not to discuss the case with anyone, as you might expect. Now, here's what we do know."

Charlie launched into the narrative: Ermeline Ransom coming to him in tears at 7:30 that morning; how they had brought her some black coffee and helped her to settle down; the story of the previous night and meeting Victor at the bus; awakening from a drugged sleep at 4:30 the next morning, disoriented and terrified; not knowing where Victor was; having absolutely no recall of the night before or what she had had to drink; the serious nature of her injuries and the fact that it clearly was an aggravated assault, a Class 2 felony in Illinois which could get the guilty party up to twenty years in prison; that pictures had been taken and that the District Attorney had been consulted no less than five times now.

"I already know the answer, Sheriff," said Al Petty of the Hickam Press, "but I have to ask for my readers. Will any of the photographs be made public to us?"

"You're absolutely right, Al, you do already know the answer. Next?" Charlie looked out over the small crowd of TV and news reporters, town merchants, a couple of city council members, and those holding TV lights and ensuring battery power for the filming.

"What exactly happened here, Sheriff?" someone up front asked.

"I'm getting to that."

"Will the grand jury consider the evidence?"

"Sorry, you'll have to ask the DA for that answer."

"What's your opinion? Should the DA seek an indictment against Victor Harrow?"

"Yeah," someone else chimed in before Charlie could answer. "*Should* Vic Harrow be charged with a crime?"

"Again, that's not my call to make. You'll have to ask District Attorney Quentin Erwin, Jr. that question."

"Sheriff Altiman, can you describe the injuries?" asked Marilee Sonigee.

"Letters carved in her breasts and then inked."

Great clamor, many shouted questions. Then Sheriff Altiman raised a hand and waited for quiet. Finally, he answered.

"What do the letters spell? They spell V-I-C-T-O-R. All right, I think that's all for now. Thanks for coming."

ERWIN FARMS' horse barn had been built in 1985 without regard to cost. Patriarch Ed Erwin had wanted the best for his animals, and he paid for what he wanted. Outside, the barn was a long, vertically planked, structure, whitewashed. The roof peaked to a flat plane, out of which arose a second peak, where rows of clearstory windows shed light on the stalls below.

But the interior was magnificent. It was built of dark-stained redwood front to back, eight stalls per side, with stall doors hung from rollers so the doors would roll to the side and allow the horses to come and go. Overhead, there were sixteen circular fans, one per stall, individually controlled. Same for lights, as each stall allowed bright incandescent and fluorescent light controlled from a panel embedded just outside. The center walkway of the barn was turquoise brick, laid in a herringbone pattern that allowed spray washing with sand underneath and gravel with drainage tile under that, to allow runoff. The whole idea of the brick was to have a walking surface that would give beneath the inhabitants' shod feet. Better than cement, Erwin thought, though others would have said the expense of building such a floor was excessive. The barn gleamed inside, thanks to a full-time stable staff that did everything from bathe the horses every day to lunge them, to ride them, to test their speeds on the regulation size track at the rear of the farm, to groom and curry. A veterinarian visited regularly and kept the animals in perfect condition, including ninety day checkups and individualized diets. A farrier cared for the horses' hooves, trimming the giant nails and creating fitted horseshoes. The idea of Thaddeus helping Quentin clean stalls was something they did for entertainment, to be outside, to perform physical labor, to be around the animals and the smell of the barn, the hay, the oats, the medications, and even, yes, the excrement, which was all a part of keeping living, breathing, 1500-pound horses. Thaddeus forked caked hay, and imagined himself with such just a spread someday. There was nothing about it he didn't already like and enjoy. He was clearing out stall eleven when he heard a voice call to him. "Hey in there! What's your name?"

Thaddeus looked up. She was tall, he guessed five-nine, slender as if stepping off a *Vogue* page, black hair, black eyebrows, pale blue eyes, with a playful smile at the corners of her mouth.

"Oh, hey," he said. "I'm Thaddeus. Is that you practicing the dressage?"

She laughed and tossed her head. "Just working Sister Andromeda. She needs it. Otherwise, she gets lazy. I'm Ilene Crayton."

"So you're horsey?"

"Was. In a past life. Actually, my husband and I kept horses, Quarter Horses."

Thaddeus knew the story of Doctor Crayton and his untimely death. He skipped over that, saying, "That's a breed I'm getting familiar with. I have one boarded here. Uncle Do-gooder." He removed his baseball cap and wiped his forehead with his wrist. "Hot work."

She smiled. "But the pay's good, right?"

"Top dollar. He'll buy my lunch for my efforts, which means I'm making about eighty cents an hour."

"That'll take you far. Well, anyway, I'd best get this little lady groomed and put away. She's already moving toward her stall."

"She likes her room?"

"Hmm. She likes her oats, you mean."

"Got it. Well, thanks for saying hello."

She started to move away then stopped and looked back across the English saddle at him. "Hey, we're having a little get-together Christmas Eve. You busy?"

Thaddeus' heart bumped in his chest. "I am now, thanks!"

"You know where I live?"

"Who doesn't? What should I bring?"

"Just your own sweet self. And wine, if you have a preference. Otherwise, I'll have Coors and all the rest of what you cowboys drink."

"Not much of a drinker, but I'll help tend bar. I bartended my first year in law school. I make a great White Russian."

"See you then. Bring an apron, barkeep."

"Will do."

10

Governor Cleman L. Walker was furious when Ricardo Moltinari dropped off the $25,000. They were huddled in the mansion's library, where the feds had hidden a bug every ten feet. The bugs were hot: downtown in a nondescript building the hard drives were whirring and recording every word that was said. The governor sputtered and his face turned red. His fists clenched and unclenched. Then he managed to get out a few words, hisses, really.

"Sumbitch stole my money!"

"Johnny tried everything with the guy. Put the fear in him."

"Oh?"

"Carved up Mister Harrow's girlfriend. Nothing structural."

"What's that mean?" The governor's face paled. "How seriously did he injure her?"

"He carved Victor's name in her tits."

"Damn! He what, cut her up and turned her loose to call the cops on him—on us?"

"Naw. She was sound asleep when it happened. Wouldn't wake up even if you engraved her tits."

"Oh hell."

"Hey, Your Honor, you said we should put the fear in Victor Harrow. Consider it done."

"Yes, and I also said nothing broken and nothing that shows."

"Relax. This don't show."

"Damn. Well, what's done is done. Now what about the seventy-five K he owes me? That's my money he's holding out!"

"Swears he ain't got it."

"Well, I've got the AG looking into that. He's got assets, we'll find them. Which reminds me, let me call Bob Amistaggio and see where we are with that."

Governor Walker hit 9 on his iPhone. Speed dial had the Attorney General on the line in seconds. This time a cell phone monitor sparked to life and recorded the conversation on the same hard drive downtown.

"Hey, Cleman, what's up?" Robert F. Amistaggio answered.

"We got anything yet on that Victor Harrow down in Orbit?"

"What do you mean, have we found assets?"

"That's exactly what I mean."

"There's a lawyer down there, name of Fletcher Franey. Fletcher is the chairman of the Hickam County Democrat Party. He's been through every public record in the county. Plus, he swiped a copy of our Mister Harrow's tax returns last five years. Franey tells me there's nothing that doesn't have a huge lien. The guy's judgment-proof. We get *nada*."

"Thanks," the Governor said, and clicked End Call. He turned back to Bang Bang Moltinari. "Nothing. We can't touch the guy."

"But we can make an example of him. That's our play, so word don't get out that he beat us."

"I hate that."

"Hey, you got another idea?"

"Does the guy have kids?"

"One daughter. Grown. Her husband owns a restaurant and package place. Small change."

"Any equity there we can get to?"

"Guy's only had it five years. He's still paying interest on the notes. No equity."

"Damn it all! So what do we do?"

Bang Bang Moltinari spread his hands and looked firmly at the Governor. "You got but one play. We take him out. Make an example."

"Damn."

"Just gimme the word. We can make it look like the girl did it."

"What girl?"

"The chick Johnny engraved. She has a motive to hurt Victor back."

"I like that."

"I knew you would."

"All right. Get it done. Just don't report it back to me, yes?"

"Done."

~

VICTOR HARROW FROWNED at his lawyer and shook his head. "No, we don't turn over the name of the guy that did this. That gets me killed."

Bill Johansson III nodded, "Because the guy's connected." Johansson was a bear of a man, Michigan Law, first in class, and had once worked at Brown and Doerr in Chicago, an 800 lawyer firm, where he became a senior partner in the unheard-of record-time of 34 months. Following that coup, he had cashed in his equity, taken his several million in cash and bonuses, and headed south to start his own firm, back in his home town. A life-long dream. But, he still had the same insurance companies in his pocket that had loved him in Chicago. He did the defense work, civil and workers' comp, for no less than 22 carriers all over downstate Illinois. Against his better judgment, Johansson-Hathaway had been allowed to grow to eight lawyers when Bill had put down his foot. "No more," he said. "If I can't review its files personally, then it can get me in trouble. I need more control. No bigger." Clint Hathaway, his partner, could only agree. Bill held all the cards, and Clint was in the game only because he had been in the right office setup at the right time when Bill had come back to town looking for space and a partner. Eight lawyers, no more, no less, and Bill controlled them all with an iron fist.

"So you're afraid to turn over this Johnny Bladanni's name," said Johansson. "I appreciate that."

Victor closed his eyes. "More than that. The guy's not only connected, he's the nephew of Ricardo Bang Bang Moltinari."

"How do you know this?"

"I've been dealing with the guys since forever. I know all of them."

Bill Johansson III made a note on the legal pad that said "HAR-ROW" in all caps across the top. "Subject related to Chicago. Uncle-Nephew." Johansson didn't use names in case his files were ever subpoenaed or seized—the feds had a new habit of seizing the legal files of certain lawyers who defended bad guys. Among other things, Johansson was one who defended just the kind of bad guys the government was very interested in. He knew Bang Bang Moltinari's name and knew what he did, but he didn't think he'd ever defended any of his middlemen or the lower echelon. Button men and some drug mules, that was about the extent of his involvement with the Chicago mob. He smiled to himself: it could never be said he had a conflict of interest, representing Vic Harrow in a case involving the Chicago mob. Would that be an ethical violation, he mused while he made his notes. Bill Johansson III was fifty-five, played racquetball competitively on weekends (seniors, but still) and had been married to Gretchen Johansson for thirty-five years. He was loyal to his wife, he was loyal to his clients, and he was especially loyal to the insurance companies that were forever hiring him to defend their policy-holders and even, once or twice a year, the insurance company itself when it was sued for Bad Faith. It was said he had never lost a trial for an insurance client. It was also said he had never lost a criminal trial. Thirty years ago, there had been a traffic violation and prosecution that he had lost, but that was chalked up to the fact his client hadn't bothered to show up for trial and the State Trooper wouldn't give him the foundation he needed to admit certain photographs into the case. That one had come back "Guilty" and, even now, thirty years later, he sometimes couldn't sleep, thinking about that case. He prepared his cases with all the attention a surgeon gives a new procedure he must learn. He knew where to cut, where to dissect, where to sew, and when to close. Never once in his professional life had he gone to court with anything less than his own statements in detailed outline form and cross-examinations and direct-examinations written out—complete with expected witness responses—beforehand. In short, nothing was going to happen in that courtroom that he hadn't anticipated and made full preparation to resist or encourage.

"Here's something I bet you *didn't* know," Bill Johansson said. "My little bird at the courthouse in Orbit tells me that Fletcher Franey had been going over your public records."

Victor's heart thumped. "Looking for what? Did they know?"

"Grantor-grantee indices, looking at all your real estate transactions. UCC Financing Statements to see what trucks and equipment and tools you own. Tax records to determine values of your assets based on their tax appraisal—everything on you there, Franey went through and made copies."

"Who the hell would he be working for?"

Johansson shook his head. "Unknown. That's what I wanted to ask you."

"No clue."

"Is he connected to Thaddeus Murfee?"

"Not that I know of. I've never seen them together."

"Would Franey be on the clock for Murfee?"

"Doubtful. Thaddeus Murfee doesn't have that kind of money he could afford to pay anyone. From what I hear, he's destitute, lives like a monk, doesn't drink or smoke, doesn't hang out with questionable women—nothing we can use against him."

"Sounds like me at that age," Johansson laughed. "No exposure means no pressure points. Smart man."

"Suppose so. What if you were to call Franey, ask him what the hey?"

"Might work," Johansson said, a thoughtful look creasing his forehead. "We know some of the same people, might use that. Course, if he's working with Thaddeus, then it gets back we're onto him."

"True. Damn! I don't like assholes prying into my private stuff."

Johansson laughed. "Did I just hear you say 'private'? In a small town? Dream on, Dreamer."

"True again. But, I'll tell you one thing, and I mean this from the bottom of my heart."

"Which is what?"

"I didn't cut that girl. I'm crazy about Ermeline Ransom. I would never do that to her."

"Well, your insurance company has a reserve on this case of $300,000, just in case a jury disagrees."

"Could that happen? I wasn't even conscious. I was drugged, too!"

"Anything can happen. It's an American courtroom with a jury of your so-called peers. Anything can happen. Except, we're going to micromanage things, so we lessen the odds of some of the negative things happening."

"What are we going to do?"

"We're going to turn over the name of Johnny Bladanni to Thaddeus. We've got a discovery document call a Request to Admit Facts. One of the things it asks us to admit or deny is that you, in fact, caused the injury to Ermeline. My strong suggestion to you, Victor, is that you allow me not only to deny that request, but also to name the actual cutter. Johnny Bladanni."

"I'm screwed."

"I doubt that. You're high profile, Victor. Nobody is going to make an attempt on you. Hell, from what you tell me you're judgment-proof, everything's mortgaged. That being the case, it's my guess the mob has already forgotten about you. They've already moved on to their next victim." Johansson knew he might be totally wrong about this, but he was being paid to talk with certitude, as if he had all the answers. That's how you earned $500/hour.

"Then you and I see it differently. I think they're coming after me."

"They wouldn't dare. You're too high profile. Everyone would know."

THE MOB LOCATED Hector Ransom living on Burgundy Street in a flophouse in New Orleans. He had been working offshore for BP, helping that obnoxious institution continue to hide the billions of dollars of damage it had done to the Gulf of Mexico during the Great Oil Spill of 2006. Three years after the spill, tar balls could still be found on the Mississippi coast. In July 2013, the discovery of a 40,000 pound tar mat near East Grand Terre, Louisiana prompted the closure of waters to commercial fishing. Hector Ransom had been busy at $125/hour working on a dredge around and through that horror story. While it was true BP paid extremely well for his services, Hector rarely saw any reason to send any part of that back home to his ex, Ermeline Ransom, for his son Jaime's child support.

You're needed back home in Orbit, the thugs told him. When he resisted and he told them Hickam County had a warrant out for him, the men hurt him. As usual, the injuries were invisible to other citizens. But, in reality, he pissed blood for weeks after, and he was missing the second toe of his right foot. Three days later, Hector was sitting in the lounge of the Sangamon Grill in Springfield, nursing a draft beer, waiting to meet someone he knew only as "Johnny." He had been told the man would introduce himself, that he had Hector's picture on his cell phone. He should follow Johnny's orders exactly to the "T" or they would be back. Next time, they told him, if they had to come back for him again, it would be the whole foot.

11

It was Christmas Eve and Ermeline was working straight through to midnight. Bronco Groski had joined her at ten, but tonight she was pulling a double shift. She always did on Christmas Eve, and really didn't mind, since Jaime was being watched by her mother, who would sleep over and be there to help the youngster open his presents on Christmas morning. They did every year and Ermeline was glad for it. She was also glad for the huge tips she took in between ten and midnight on Christmas Eve. Everybody loved her during those hours. Everybody wished her Merry Christmas. Several propositioned her; one offered her $100 to see her tattoo and was brusquely hustled out the front door by Bronco and told to go home and sober up.

Nobody heard the single gunshot at 9 a.m., certainly not anyone inside the noisy, boisterous lounge at the Silver Dome. Besides, the shot had been muffled by three inches of paneling and insulation and steel body.

At 10 p.m. who should show up, out of the blue, but Hector Ransom. He slid onto a stool at the bar, ordered a draft beer from Bronco, and received a curious look in return. Bronco knew the face from somewhere, but couldn't quite place it. Besides, the face was half-hidden behind a black and gray beard and bleary eyes that seemed to see everything and nothing. The draft was plunked down before him and Hector two-handed the mug to his mouth. He had the shakes as he hadn't yet had a drink that day: Johnny's orders. He was to remain sober for this one, no matter what. Hector was wearing his J.C. Penny fleece parka, which weighed twice its normal weight, thanks to the silver plated .38 snub nose in one inside pocket and the ten-inch switchblade in the other. He had been the most unwilling recipient of the two items, but he had known better than to argue. He remembered what they had told him about cold turkey amputation of his right foot. Damn! He thought, as he swilled down the beer, without a right foot you can't even drive! How scary was that? He tapped a quarter sharply on the bar and motioned for a refill. It was going to be a long night.

ERMELINE FELT his presence before she actually saw him. Something about Hector Ransom had given her the creeps ever since the first time she was alone with him when they were fourteen. She scolded herself for the millionth time: if only she had listened to her feelings back then. Sure, if only. But tonight wasn't a night for "if onlys," tonight was a night to make an apron full of cash in tips. She fastened the smile back on her mouth, ignored the creepy feeling, and went back to waiting on the rear booth.

An hour later, she brushed by Bronco, who was going the opposite direction, four Buds in each hand. "Guy at the bar. I think you know him." Ermeline looked. She certainly didn't recognize the guy from the back. All she could see was a rumpled blue parka and the heels of two cowboy boots hooked on the bar stool. The hair was shaggy and long but unwashed. Gross, she thought. But there was something about the guy's size—and *smell*—could she actually smell him? She decided to take a closer look. She went around the bar, flipped up the entry guard, and worked her way along to the other end, filling mugs, mixing drinks, keeping her head down while sneaking looks in the man's direction. The closer she got the worse she felt. "I think you know him," Bronco had said. Bronco knew his faces, and he rarely forgot one, especially those that had given him trouble in the past.

Finally, she was right in front of the man, and he raised his face to look at her. "Hello, Erm," he smiled.

She lost it. "Damn!" It was him, Hector. She felt faint and awash in the old creepy feeling. Still, she pulled herself together and managed to spit out, "What do you want, Hector?"

"'What do you want, Hector?' Is that any way to treat our son's father?"

"What do you want, Hector?"

"I want to spend Christmas day with my son. Divorce papers say I get him Christmas Eve one year, Christmas Day the next year. I want my Christmas Day with him."

Ermeline thought about this. The son of a bitch was right; he had been granted holiday visitation. Legally, he could probably have the boy all day, if he really pushed it. Her heart sank. Of all times for Hector to show his ugly face. Now what?

"I have no problem with you coming by for an hour on Christmas Day. That would be fine."

"Uh-uh," he said, and pulled a battered sheaf of papers from his pocket. "Read the divorce decree. All day. Not a minute less."

"But you haven't been around in months."

"That's because I've been off earning child support. So I could catch up."

"Catch up?"

"I've got it all right here," he smiled, and produced his wallet. "Fifty-five hundred bucks."

"It's sixty-five hundred now. Three more months to add on."

"I've got that, too. I'm ready to get current and exercise my visitation." He smiled ear to ear. He was saying exactly what Johnny Bladanni had told him to say. He had Johnny's money in his wallet, and Johnny had made him go by the court and get copies of the divorce paperwork. He had come prepared and—it was working.

"Come by in the morning around ten. It'll just be Jaime, me, and my mom."

Hector vigorously shook his head. "No, no. I wanna be there when he wakes up. I want him to see what Santa brought him."

"Meaning?"

"I've got my pickup full of toys and presents for my son."

"Sure. Like what, for instance?" She figured she had him. He wouldn't have a clue what five-year-old boys would want for Christmas.

Then he floored her. "We've got a boys' superhero costume set. A compound archery set—with rubber-tipped arrows but a real metal target. We've got the oldest standby of all, the Lionel Electric Train. The Polar Express, which cost me over $250. An electric excavation truck, sort of like what his old man operates in Louisiana. And there's more."

"I got my break in fifteen. We can go out and talk."

"Sure. I'm not going nowhere."

She leaned across the bar and whispered, "Go on out. I don't want to be seen leaving with you. What you driving?"

"Ford F-150, Louisiana plates. East parking lot."

"Meet you there. Have it warmed up."

"Will do."

"And no more drinking. Or I don't even sit down to talk."

He finished his beer and left, while she was down at the other end of the bar, pouring drinks with both hands.

Ilene Crayton's' house occupied five acres and was set back behind a circular drive that swept in from the highway east of Orbit. It was a large, sprawling Victorian, white with a green porch surrounding three sides. Thaddeus parked the Buick near the entrance to the drive and set off walking. The place was packed. As he got closer, he could see the Christmas tree boughs encircling the front door, the giant wreath, and the stained glass windows on either side of the front door. Two fireplaces were pouring smoke into the sky, one at either end, and the air smelled of wood smoke, a great smell, and he was happy to be there, happy to be alive, and happy that his law practice was finally getting off the ground. Thanks to the case of *Ransom v. Harrow*, filed by his firm. He liked thinking of his practice as a "firm." Many lawyers who wrote to him—even from mere partnerships—signed their letters "For the Firm." He thought it had a nice, substantial ring to it, and he wondered whether sole practitioners might seem overboard if they signed "For the Firm." That was a Quentin Erwin topic, TBD. He climbed the three steps to the porch and stood before the front door, where he gathered himself and drew a deep breath before knocking. He was a little nervous, and he hadn't stopped to ask himself why. But deep down he knew: there was something about her skin tone and her black hair, the aristocratic nose and bearing, and the great, warm smile. There was something about her that, frankly, was a huge turn on. He hated to admit it because he wasn't looking for anyone at the moment, because dating took money, and he was always low on funds. He still had in mind his ideal—the English major-sometime-author who enjoyed discussing Faulkner and Raymond Carver and Michael Chabon. Those were the people Thaddeus loved to read, and they were where his ideal woman dwelled in thought and in writing. As he rang the bell, he found himself wondering who Ilene Crayton read.

He didn't have time for much wondering. Ilene herself answered the door and greeted him with a huge smile. When she saw he was wearing an apron under his blue blazer she folded her hands down on her knees and laughed with full force. "You *are* a bartender," she cried. "You remembered!" Thaddeus spread his blazer so she could read the writing on the apron. "Don't Fiddle, Heat the Griddle?" she read. "Not exactly bartender-ish," she declared.

"It's all I could find at the last minute. But sentiment's there. I really will help tend bar if you need."

She took him by the arm and walked him to the coat closet. "Not at all. We're catered tonight, including the bar. We'll just get you something to drink and introduce you around. My roommate from college is here. Let's start with her. C'mon!"

AT BREAK TIME, Ermeline joined Hector outside the Silver Dome. It was just beginning to snow, but it wasn't all that cold. The cloud cover had kept the air warm, and Ermeline took a deep breath when the Dome's side door closed behind her and locked.

He rolled down the window of the F-150 and waved. "Here's my truck. It's warm in here."

"Okay," she said.

She settled into Victor's truck which, to Ermeline's surprise, was a somewhat recent vintage, maybe a 2010 or even later. Within minutes, she was warming up, and she removed her hands from her coat pockets. She next removed her mittens from her hands and lit a Salem.

"When did you start smoking?" Hector asked, a surprised look in his eyes.

"I don't smoke. Just sometimes."

"You nervous?"

"Seriously? I'm very nervous. I don't much trust people anymore."

"Yeah, I heard someone cut you."

"Really, who told you that?"

"My sister. I stopped by her house and paid her $1000 I owed her."

"From last time you left town. I *thought* that's where you got the money to disappear."

"That's what family's for."

"To help you disappear when the sheriff's after you?"

"Sure, why not? But not to worry." He pulled the wallet from his coat pocket and counted out sixty-five one hundred dollar bills. He placed them in her hand and closed her fingers around them. She was stunned. Never in her most outrageous dream would she have ever imagined Hector Ransom actually catching up his child support. Never. It made her feel much happier than she had been in a long time. She swiftly went through the mental inventory she kept of the items Jaime needed: New winter coat, new Nikes, new bicycle—the list went on and on, all the things five-year-old boys need to keep up with their buddies. She was at once surprised and very grateful for the money. "Thank you, Hector," she managed to say, her voice faltering. "I'm shocked; I guess you know."

"Figured you would be. But Erm, I'm not a bad guy. I just don't have any education and finding work in this economy has been tough. Really tough."

"So where are you working?"

"Louisiana, for BP. We're still collecting oil balls."

"What's that?" She took a drag on her cigarette and wished she had something to eat. Her stomach was rumbling. This was the time of day she usually had her dinner—a late, ten o'clock dinner after work. Except tonight she was on until midnight. Food would just have to wait.

"Oil mavericks, they call them. Oil that's broke loose and still clogging up the Gulf."

"Good money—obviously."

"Good enough. At least it lets me get caught up with what I owe in support," he lied. Johnny Bladanni had provided the money to catch up. It was all part of Johnny's instructions to him. "So here's what I need. You let me stay over tonight—I'm not talking about making love, nothing like that—and I'll watch Jaime open presents in the morning. You'll make the usual Christmas morning breakfast. We'll eat. Then I'll split. Gone from your life until next time I come back to see him. Maybe another three months, if that's all right."

She thought about this. Actually, there was no room for him to stay over. Her mom had the couch, and Jaime had a single bed in his room. The only other bed was her own, and there was no way he was getting in bed with her.

He seemed to read her mind. "Tell you want. We go to your place; you get in bed. I come in fully dressed and get on top of the covers. We turn our backs to each other and sleep for six hours, then we get up, and I unload Jaime's toys from the truck and put them under the tree. You make coffee, we talk to your mom until Jaime jumps up and comes running. What do you say?"

She was tired. She just wanted to get it over with, the whole visitation thing. And she was still in shock: she had $6500 in her pocket and would knock down another $200 in tips tonight. That was almost seven thousand dollars. That was almost enough for a down payment on an FHA loan—in Florida! She knew this; she had wanted for three years to get into something, to give Jaime a permanent home to grow up in. Another three grand and they would have their dream. Maybe her mom could loan the difference. They could even get a three bedroom, so her mom could stay with them—at least until Jaime started school. Plus, she could stay over on nights when Ermeline had to work late. More and more that was happening lately. The Silver Dome drinking crowd was expanding as the economy got worse.

She sighed. "But no touching. Not even holding hands."

He made the Scouts' sign. "I promise."

"It won't ever happen again. We're divorced."

"Next time, we'll plan it out better. I get him the night before; you get him Christmas Day. Like it says in the papers, we trade off."

"All right. Follow me home when I get off. Midnight."

"This will be great for Jaime."

"Maybe so."

Hector Ransom smiled to himself. It looked like he would be keeping his foot after all.

12

Thaddeus had been introduced to Marvis Michelmann, Ilene's roomie at Bennington; to Justin and Eustice Loveland, her older sister and brother-in-law from Iowa City; to Ilene's mom and aunt; to Rex Howe, a dashing commercial pilot out of Saint Louis who, Thaddeus feared, probably already had something going with Ilene; to Father Emil Pritchard, the priest who would be conducting the Midnight Mass at Ilene's church; and many others, too many to remember all at once. The house was bright and noisy and small children were scampering and retrieving presents from under the seven-foot tree and holding them up and shaking them and listening for clues. Two white English sheep dogs wound their way back and forth through the crowd, seeking handouts and begging when ignored. They were both plump and looked well-fed to Thaddeus, as did most of the guests.

At eleven o'clock, they all became aware of a huge commotion and much stamping on the front porch. Thaddeus watched as Ilene went to answer the bell. She swung open the door and was greeted with the curious head of a horse, poked just inside and peering around, while outside could be heard Quentin Erwin's laughter. "C'mon Illie," he cried, "I've got your Christmas present with me."

"Sister Andromeda!" Ilene shouted at the horse. "On my front porch!"

Quentin had parked the horse trailer right outside the front door, and his brother Johnny had helped him back Sister Andromeda out of the trailer and up onto the porch. The Quarter Horse was wearing a warming blanket and being led around by a white halter. She was calm and unruffled, as if she went visiting on Christmas Eve every year.

Quentin explained to Ilene that Sister Andromeda was, indeed, her Christmas present. "Let me grab my coat." Thaddeus grabbed his too, and tagged along. If it was about horses, he was definitely in. They steered Sister Andromeda out back. They turned on the exterior and interior lights to the horse barn, and opened the corral to make their way back. Thaddeus, along with several others, followed the procession. Johnny Erwin led Sister Andromeda back through the corral and inside the barn. Ilene chose the horse stall closest to the house and turned on its overhead. The stall was empty.

"Not to worry," said Johnny Erwin. "We've got thirty bales of hay in the trailer. You all go back inside and I'll get Miss Andromeda bedded down. We'll leave the blanket on her until the barn warms up in the morning."

Thaddeus could see the tears in Ilene's eyes as Sister Andromeda was tethered to the bar outside the stall. "I haven't kept horses since— "

Whereupon Quentin Erwin, Jr. hugged her to him and patted the back of her head. "We know, we know."

At that moment, Quentin's wife, Donna, pulled up in the Range Rover and began carrying riding tack inside the barn. "English saddle," she said, "the one you like. And all the rest. You can come out and get what else you might need." Ilene hugged Donna and thanked her. Next, she hugged Johnny and thanked him. Thaddeus was stunned when she next approached him and threw her arms around his shoulders and gave him a huge bear hug. "Thanks for coming," she whispered. "This is really nice."

ERMELINE AND HECTOR RANSOM arrived at Ermeline's home at 12:22 a.m., early Christmas Day. She had had to stay a few minutes and help Bronco and Bruce close up. The tills had been counted and the night deposit made by Bruce. The Orbit square was now buttoned up and ready for a holiday. The only light on the entire square was on the northeast corner outside the sheriff's office. Interior lights were on as well, but it was impossible to tell how many deputies were on duty. Hector had guessed not that many, since it was Christmas Eve and everyone wanted to be home with the family. Ermeline led Hector around to the back door; Ermeline's mother was asleep in the front room. They wanted to avoid waking her if possible. She owned the couch for the night, and that was fine with Hector, he didn't plan on staying all that long anyway. Without turning on any lights Ermeline led him into the bedroom. "Now, turn your back. I'm getting into my jammies." He watched as she set her purse on the dresser and glided up to the head of the bed where she retrieved her pajamas from under the pillow. He turned his back to her and waited for her whisper. His eyes quickly became adjusted to the dark. There was the closet, there the door into the bathroom, there the dresser with the purse, there the door back into the hallway. It was a moonless night as it was still snowing outside, but the light reflected up from the snow bathed the room in soft blue light. Good enough to find my way around, he thought. Finally, she whispered. It was okay to turn around. She quietly pulled back the covers on her side of the double and slid under. He waited until she was settled, and then laid down on his back beside her. He was at her side but fully clothed, complete with cowboy boots. "Lose the boots," she hissed. "I don't want those clod-hoppers on my bedspread." He did as he was told and lay back down. It was all right; the boots would slip back on quietly with no effort at all. It was all part of the plan Johnny Bladanni had laid out for him.

She was asleep, lightly snoring as she always had, within fifteen minutes. Hector didn't move. Johnny had told him to wait a full hour and he would. He watched her out of the corner of his eye. Her chest rose and fell under the covers about fifteen times each minute. He was counting and keeping track of the minutes on his fingers. Plus, he had his watch. They weren't to meet until 1:30, so it was all good. He closed his eyes, certain that he would not fall asleep. There was too much to do, and he had switched over to coffee anyway, after leaving the Silver Dome. The Phillips 66 on the west end of town had had fresh coffee in huge canisters, and Hector had helped himself to a thirty-two ouncer, while filling with gas. He paid with cash; no paper trail. His only other option was a prepaid MasterCard, which he kept for those rare occasions where he might have to rent a car. The plastic remained in his wallet the entire trip.

At 1:12, he lifted his arm slowly, slowly, and checked the time. Perfect. She had been sleeping without moving, and no other sounds had reached him from inside the house. In slow motion, he sat upright, and then moved his feet over the side and back down inside the cowboy boots. They immediately slipped on and he stood up, keeping pressure on the mattress until he was upright and only then slowly releasing the inner spring. If she suddenly awoke, he would say he was looking for the bathroom. Simple enough. He made his way over to his parka and felt inside the inner pocket. It was all there: gun, knife, gloves. He soundlessly shrugged into the coat. Then, he removed the latex gloves and gradually slipped them on both hands. He removed the gun, followed by the knife. With these items exposed, he crept around the foot of the bed and gently stepped up beside Ermeline's hands. With the greatest of care, he slipped the gun barrel under the fingers of her right hand and, ever so gently, placed her fingers on the barrel. Just enough, just so, just capturing finger-prints along the smooth portion of the gun. Then, he did the same thing with the closed switchblade. With his gloved hands on both weapons, he slowly crept back around the bed and went to the bath-room door. He waited while his eyes adjusted to the inner darkness, to lessen the chance of stumbling over something there and giving himself away. Satisfied after several minutes that he knew where things were located inside, he entered the bathroom and opened the top cabinet above the towels. He felt around and felt nothing metallic or hard plastic that might rattle against the weapons. He then placed them on the top shelf of the cabinet and slowly closed the door.

Back in the bedroom, he paused to listen to her breathing. He satisfied himself that she was still asleep—very asleep. She had worked a long, hard shift, and her body was tired and resting deeply. So he crossed to the dresser, found her purse, and stuck his hand inside. Instantly, he located the clip of 65 $100 bills with his fingers, and eased them out. Still wearing his gloves, he inserted the money back inside his own coat pocket. Then, he stopped and smiled. Why not? He thought, and put his hand back inside her purse. Just as he thought: her wallet. It felt like it was stuffed with bills, although he had no idea how much. It was from her tips for the night and would come in handy once he was back on the road. He pulled the wallet out and put that in his other outside pocket. He had been told to take nothing but the $6500, but no one had to know about the wallet. Then, he did his inventory: he had left fingerprints only on the bedspread where he had placed his hands and there was no way they would ever lift prints there. He had touched nothing else since entering the small house. With the greatest of care and caution, he eased himself back down the short hallway and into the kitchen where they had come in through the back door. He slowly twisted the knob and let himself out, closing the storm door all the way as gently as possible behind him.

EARLIER THAT DAY, Hector had met with Johnny Bladanni at Moe's Aces, a Springfield watering hole on the south side of town. Moe's featured a huge sign out front comprised of four aces peeking from a deck of cards. Inside the joint, there was sawdust on the floor and peanuts in baskets along the bar and on all the tables. They were salted, of course; studies showed that by simply offering free salted peanuts a pub owner could expect to sell 35% more drinks and beer. For Moe (there was no Moe, there was only Arnold C. Goldsmith, Jr.)

the peanuts were a no-brainer. So were the very dim lights and the feeling of anonymity enjoyed by the denizens of the dive.

They met just after four, while an NBA game was blaring over the flat screen. Johnny entered and limped by several regulars at the bar; he didn't know they were regulars, but it was a strong guess, for they had that settled-in, comfortable look that regulars always have. The limp was a hoax, but if anyone remembered anything about him, it would be the limp. He passed by them and beyond the bar, averting his eyes and face, wishing to enter, meet, and leave without being remembered. He found an empty booth along the back wall, just off the bathrooms, where a strong odor of urinal cake and vomit held on. Johnny slid into the booth and partway unzipped his black leather coat. He was wearing a nondescript black baseball cap pulled low over his eyebrows and when a sturdy little man wearing a white apron approached and took his order, Johnny kept his eyes fastened on the table top, as if preoccupied with his cellphone to where he couldn't be bothered to look up. He ordered a Scotch and water and kept poking cell keys. The little man disappeared and Johnny put the cell away. Five minutes later, he was joined by Hector.

"Know anyone here?" were the first words out of Johnny's mouth.

Hector turned around and eyed the other patrons. "Naw. First time here anyway."

"Okay. Now listen up. You been drinking today?"

"No, sober like you said."

"Any drugs, crack, speed?"

"No, Dude, you said sober and here I am."

Johnny studied Hector's face. He looked into his eyes and studied the pupils. Satisfied at last that he had a sober co-conspirator, he launched into the plan. Johnny went on for a good five minutes, explaining to Hector how Hector would drop in at the Silver Dome no earlier than nine p.m., talk with Ermeline and get her on board with the Christmas Eve plan. Hector would leave there by 9:25. He would then leave his truck unlocked while he went inside the Phillips 66 on the west end of Orbit around 9:30 p.m. Johnny would be filling the Escalade also at the Phillips 66, and Johnny would walk from his

Escalade over to Johnny's truck and leave the gun and the knife on the passenger seat. By then, Victor Harrow, of course, would be lying face up in a pool of his own blood inside his mobile office, shot once between the eyes by the same nickel plated snub nose .38 caliber. Hector would handle the weapons only with the napkins he would bring with his coffee. He would wipe them down totally and drop them in his inside coat pockets. Hector would give Ermeline the $5500—which Johnny slipped to Hector under the booth—in order to enlist her participation. They wanted to prove to her that Hector's intentions were only good. Hector would accompany her home just after midnight, place her fingerprints on the gun and knife, and plant the weapons in an obvious place of hiding where, "even the stupid butthole cops could find them," as Johnny put it. Hector would then retrieve the money out of Ermeline's purse and quietly leave. "Take nothing else," he was warned. After that, Hector was free to keep the $5500 and go wherever he wanted, just not back to the Gulf Coast. Johnny preferred L.A. or New York where Hector could get lost for at least a year, working at some menial job for cash. Then they would be even. "Even?" Hector asked him. "How does that make us even?" Simple, Johnny told him, you get the cash and you get to keep the foot—in return for helping us dispose of Victor Harrow. That makes us even. Hector could only shrug. $5500 was better than nothing. He was glad he had packed his things in the suitcase under the F-150 bed cap. He had enough jeans and flannels to make it through the winter. He would be okay.

CHARLIE ALTIMAN RECEIVED the call from deputy Dale Harshman at 4:30 a.m. Christmas morning. Deputy Harshman was so excited he was stuttering.

"Victor Harrow's dead, Charlie. You-y-y-you'd best come to the bus."

"Calm down, Dale. Secure the scene. Touch nothing."

Sheriff Altiman's next act was to call the Illinois State Police and talk to the desk sergeant. "There's been a shooting," he calmly told them. "I need the crime lab in the next thirty minutes. Victor Harrow's office-bus. Two miles east of Orbit, Washington Street. Purple monstrosity."

The State Police beat him to the crime scene. By the time Charlie arrived, Dale Harshman had encircled the bus with yellow crime scene tape, and one of the crime scene techs was scouring the parking lot for any evidence that might even resemble a tire track. Evidently, there was nothing obvious, as she soon disappeared inside the bus. Charlie Altiman put the squad car in park and went inside. He found Sergeant Mel Himmelmann inside with a photographer and two crime scene technicians. Photographs were being taken and measurements made. Plastic bags had been taped over the victim's hands. Evidently, Vic Harrow hadn't been moved. They all acknowledged each other and Sergeant Himmelmann said, "Notice anything about Vic?"

"I notice he's deader than hell."

"Look closer. Use your light."

Charlie shone his flashlight along Mel's body, toes to head. At the forehead he paused. "What is that? Somebody scratched him?"

"Look closer," said the sergeant. "Step over here by me and bend down so you can see."

"Okay. I'm looking. What the *hell*? E-R-M?"

"I guess she ran out of space."

"She carved her name in his forehead?"

"Like I said, she started to. But she ran out of room."

Charlie looked again. Dried blood outlined the deep cuts across Victor's forehead. There was no doubt; someone had carefully engraved E-R-M in large, blocky letters. His mind reeled. It couldn't be. Nobody would be that stupid. "Ermeline didn't do this," Sheriff Altiman finally said. "This isn't something she would even think of doing."

"You're the Sheriff," said the female tech. "Your job is to do the sheriffing now, right?" she laughed a dry laugh and Sergeant

Himmelmann scowled at her. "Well—" she exclaimed, "*some*one did it."

"You'd best go straight over and talk to her," the state policeman said. "You know how this looks. And if anyone asked me, I would have to say that would be my first item on my list. Talk to Ermeline."

"Of course I'll talk to her," Sheriff Altiman said. "Take plenty of pictures."

He went to the door and jumped to the ground. "Dale, have you notified Betty Anne Harrow?"

"Thought I'd wait for you, Sheriff."

"Right. Thanks."

Sheriff Altiman returned to his squad car and placed a call. However, the call wasn't to the new widow; he was calling District Attorney Quentin Erwin, Jr.

"Quentin, Charlie. We've got a situation here."

"Damn, Charlie, it's not even five. Couldn't wait?"

"Victor Harrow's been murdered. We need your direction."

"Go ahead."

"You ain't gonna believe this. Somebody carved E-R-M in his forehead."

"Ermeline? No way! Ermeline wouldn't shoot Vic Harrow in a million years."

"Totally agree."

"But we'd better make a record. I'll call Judge Prelate and get a search warrant for her place. You swing by and pick it up then pay a visit to Ermeline. Then report back to me."

"You've got it."

Sheriff Altiman hung up and called the new widow. It went about like they always went. Shock, disbelief, anger, depression—all within about three minutes.

13

W hile judges usually didn't prepare search warrants, the Honorable Nathan R. Prelate was the exception. After serving four terms as Hickam County District Attorney, and having served for ten years on the bench, he knew the recitations of the common residential search warrant front to back. When Charlie Altiman called him early Christmas morning, he promised Charlie that he would have the warrant ready and signed, waiting for him, by the time Charlie arrived at Nathan's house. Judge Prelate lived in a white saltbox with a sea blue roof, right on Washington Street four blocks west of the square. He was the father of two college age girls who threw outrageous parties and caroused with young men —and women—no end, all to the Judge's ongoing embarrassment and mortification time after time. While Judge Prelate himself was no goody-goody—he did like a beer or two every now and then—his daughters were beyond the pale. When he got up out of bed that morning to go downstairs to his office and print out a search warrant, he peeked inside the girls' rooms as he went by. One girl was asleep with the bare arm of some unidentified individual—man or woman? —across the daughter's T-shirted chest; the other daughter was missing from her room, evidently, deciding to spend Christmas Eve "away." She was MIA, Judge Prelate thought to himself. All in all, he had given up trying to control them while they were yet in high school. Now, he only hoped and prayed that they didn't commit some horrendous crime or kill someone while they were driving under the influence. So far—he crossed his fingers for the umpteenth time— the girls had avoided those plagues and poxes. In pajamas and bathrobe, he stole into his office and turned on the computer. He hit the printer switch. Both machines kicked into their startup routines and Judge Prelate went to fix two Keurig coffees while he waited for Charlie to show. They had done this often enough that he knew Charlie liked his coffee black, two Sweet N' Lows, in a to-go cup. He was always in a hurry at these moments, and this morning would be no different.

Just before dawn, Charlie swung into the Judge's driveway and pulled even with the back door. He leapt up the concrete steps and knocked on the porch. A white plume of air escaped his mouth as he waited, shifting anxiously from foot to foot. This wasn't going to be fun. They all liked Ermeline. They all felt sorry for what had happened to her at Victor's bus.

"This is going to be a sad Christmas morning," Judge Prelate said as soon as he opened the door for Charlie. It was almost as if he had been reading Charlie's mind.

"Not for a second do I think she was involved, Nathan," Charlie replied. "Got the coffee ready?"

"C'mon in the office. We're all set."

In the office—a small, mahogany paneled room with a trestle table desk and a computer desk—they took a seat on either side of the table. Judge Prelate raised his right hand and Charlie copied him. "Do you solemnly swear that the testimony you're about to give is the truth, the whole truth, and nothing but the truth?"

"I do so swear," Charlie replied, and reached for his steaming Styrofoam coffee.

"Please proceed. There will be no record."

"My name is Charles M. Altiman, and I am the duly elected sheriff of Hickam County," Charlie began. He then went into a long recitation of what he had heard that morning and what he had seen. He believed there was probable cause to believe a crime had been committed—a murder—and he believed there was a reasonable suspicion to search the premises inhabited and controlled by, one, Ermeline Ransom, in an attempt to locate evidence of said crime. He described the single gunshot wound between Victor Harrow's eyes, and the strange carving embedded in his forehead E-R-M. He described how Ermeline had been earlier attacked by Victor Harrow, who had made a similar carving—it was alleged—in her breasts, when he carved his name in her breasts one night while she was drugged inside the same bus where Victor Harrow's body was found just this morning. Based on all the foregoing, he believed there was reasonable suspicion to search her home located at 323 Sycamore Drive, Orbit, Illinois.

Judge Prelate listened attentively. When Charlie finished, he nodded and removed the cap from one of his many Mont Blanc pens. With a great flourish he signed his name boldly at the bottom of the search warrant, stamped it with the Clerk of the Court's seal—he kept one at home just for such occasions—and signed and stamped a second copy, which he handed to the sheriff, along with the pink return. The return was the sheet on which Sheriff Altiman would enumerate the items seized, if any, from Ermeline's residence. The sheet would then be returned to the Clerk of the Court for filing, which would close the loop on the search warrant process.

"If you see Leona," Judge Prelate said, "lying dead alongside the road somewhere, please tell her that her Dad's looking for her."

Charlie winced. He was glad he had no daughters.

Back inside the squad, Charlie radioed Dispatch and asked for two city cops and two deputies to meet him at 323 Sycamore Drive, 6 a.m. Dispatch acknowledged, and Charlie sat in Judge Burrow's driveway, sipping his coffee and killing ten minutes while the troops assembled for the search. At 6 a.m. they converged on Ermeline Ransom's home and Charlie Altiman rapped his gloved hand sharply against the front door. "Ermeline!" he called out, "Sheriff Altiman. We need to talk to you."

AT NINE O'CLOCK Thaddeus arrived at the Hickam County Jail. It was the earliest he could get in to see Ermeline, who had been instructed not to say one word to the police. This was hours earlier. Charlie Altiman had honored that—went beyond honoring that, in fact, making sure that none of the peace officers spoke with her—in order to keep her from saying anything she might later regret. Upon his arrival at the Sheriff's Office, he was immediately ushered into Sheriff Altiman's office, where he found Charlie waiting to meet with him, a very grim look on his face. He scowled at Thaddeus, shook his hand, and said, "Helluva way to spend Christmas morning, Thad."

Thaddeus nodded. "Poor girl. Please tell me what we know so far."

They had converged on Ermeline's house at six that morning. The warrant team consisted of Sheriff Altiman, Deputy Michael Smith, and patrolmen Stafford and Arnot of the Orbit PD. They had met no resistance to entry. The door had been answered by Georgiana Armentrout, Jr., the mother of Ermeline Ransom. Evidently, she had been asleep on the davenport. Mrs. Armentrout had asked them to wait while she summonsed Ermeline. Ermeline was still getting into her robe when she came into the living room. Ermeline's heart thumped in her chest when she saw them. This couldn't be good—four police? In her house? At six a.m. Christmas morning. Which was when Jaime leapt from bed to see what Santa had brought with his reindeer. The Sheriff asked Mrs. Armentrout, Ermeline, and Jaime if they would please wait on the couch. He explained to Ermeline that he had a search warrant to search the premises. It had been signed by Judge Nathan R. Prelate just an hour before and was all "legal and adequate." Ermeline took the search warrant and started reading. Her hands were shaking, and the paper rattled as she read. Tears came to her eyes. "Fruits of the crime?" She asked Sheriff Altiman. "You're looking for fruits of the crime? What crime was that?" she wanted to know.

"Ermeline, this isn't easy to say. Victor Harrow was murdered last night. Shot to death."

"Oh my stars!" cried Mrs. Armentrout. She reached and took her daughter's hand.

"But why me?" Ermeline exclaimed, her voice anguished and frightened.

"Someone carved E-R-M in his forehead."

"Oh, no!" she cried. "Charlie, on my honor, I swear that wasn't me!"

"Ermeline," Charlie said softly. "Let's have an agreement. Let's have you not say anymore for right now. Is that okay?"

She sniffled and wiped her eyes with the back of her hand. "Get Mommy a tissue," she told Jaime, who climbed off the couch.

"No, son," said Sheriff Altiman. "You wait right there. Please don't anyone leave the couch until we've finished."

"Okay," the Sheriff told his deputy and the two cops. "Search the premises. Remember, we're looking for a gun. And maybe a knife, which is doubtful."

The men spread through the small house and began opening drawers, looking behind pictures, kicking aside rugs, and moving furniture, books, potted plants, lamps, knick-knacks, jamming their hands inside the pockets of clothing, turning boots and shoes upside down, and feeling across the top shelves of closets, spreading linens and sweaters on the lower. For the next thirty minutes, Ermeline and her mother exchanged whispers and shed tears while the police went about their business. They made her open her closet safe. They counted the money inside and made notes. Then it was locked again.

Then one of the cops called to Sheriff Altiman.

"I think we've got something," he said, excitement creeping in his voice. "But I'm afraid to move things around. Bring a stool."

Sheriff Altiman picked up the kitchen stool and met the patrolman in Ermeline's bathroom.

"Top shelf," he directed. "On top the towels there."

Sheriff Altiman climbed to the second rung and peered inside.

He recognized it immediately. A .38 caliber snub nose, affectionately known as a "Detective's Special." It was silver nickel plate, though most were gun metal in color.

"Somebody hand me an evidence bag," Sheriff Altiman muttered with his head partly inside the bathroom wall closet. Someone else handed him latex gloves, which he snapped on. The evidence bag followed, which was nothing more than a plastic bag about the size of a woman's purse, and across the top seal there was a writeable label. Sheriff Altiman withdrew a ballpoint from his shirt and wrote on the label, "Bathroom closet, top shelf. Sheriff Altiman." With his gloved hand, he then withdrew the pistol and carefully laid it inside the bag. He was careful only to touch it once, so that any fingerprints went undisturbed. Then he stuck his hand further inside the cubby and withdrew a ten-inch switchblade. There were streaks of blood along the bone handle. "Gimme another bag." A second bag was handed up and Charlie repeated the same process: into the bag, write the location of recovery, sign name of officer. He stuck his head all the way inside then, and shone his light around, going down shelf by shelf until he was once again standing on the bathroom floor. He switched off his flashlight. "Not good, boys," he said to the deputy and patrolman who had made the find. "Not at all good." He was speaking almost in a whisper, as if not to alarm the small family waiting in the living room. The search then continued inside the house.

Thirty minutes later, they were finished. The evidence bags were removed through the back door; Ermeline, son, and mother never saw them. "No need to upset them anymore than we already have," Sheriff Altiman told his assistants. "Mike, you take the seized items back out to Vic Harrow's bus. The ISP crime lab is there. Please turn it over to them and ask them for the usual workup."

"Will do," said Officer Smith, who took custody of the two bags with the greatest of care and tore off in his patrol unit, lights flashing, siren silent. It was just after seven a.m., and the search was concluded.

Sheriff Altiman returned to the living room. "Mrs. Armentrout," he said, "would you keep your eye on the little guy today? For a while, at least."

"Why?" said Mrs. Armentrout, her hand at her throat protectively. "What is Ermeline going to be doing?"

Sheriff Altiman turned to Ermeline. "I wonder if you would put on your clothes and ride uptown with me? I've got a few house-keeping chores I need to do with you."

"Am I under arrest?" Ermeline managed to say. Her mouth was dry; she had had nothing to drink since coming awake, and her breathing had been frantic all the last hour. A cold bead of sweat had broken across her forehead, and her pupils were constricted with fear.

Sheriff Altiman said nothing at first. Then, slowly, he nodded. "I'm afraid you are. I'm afraid I'm going to have to arrest you on suspicion of homicide."

"Dear me!" said Mrs. Armentrout.

"Call Thaddeus," was all Ermeline had to say. Her mother nodded she had heard and would do so. "Let me get dressed."

Sheriff Altiman sat down on the couch to wait for Ermeline. He was certain she had no access to a weapon of any kind in the bedroom where she was dressing. They had searched every inch of it that morning—not once, but twice.

Ermeline reappeared, purse over her arm, and she told Sheriff Altiman she was ready. She hugged Jaime, kept the tears from flowing, and told him she would be back before he knew it. The little boy cried. This wasn't how Christmas was supposed to go; he knew that for a fact. Sheriff Altiman looked away.

THADDEUS HAD BEEN SITTING in the Sheriff's office while the account of the search and seizure was repeated, by the Sheriff himself. He was holding a Starbucks in one hand and writing furiously on a legal pad as the story was told. Finally, he looked up. "That's it? Nothing else seized?"

Sheriff Altiman shook his head. "There was nothing else to seize."

"And the gun and knife. They're with the Illinois State Police crime lab as we speak."

"They are. Officer Smith reported in on the radio. I'll file the return on the search warrant tomorrow when the Clerk's office opens."

"Please, let me see her now."

"Thad, one more thing."

"Yes?"

"She rode up to the office with me. In the front seat, no cuffs. We fingerprinted her, took her picture, and got her some coffee. She sat in my office while I filed out the arrest report. Then we put her in the women's cell. No one else with her in there. She asked to be let out once, to use the restroom. Most important: we haven't tried to state-mentize her. Nobody's asked her a thing."

"I appreciate that, Charlie. I'll tell her what you've done. Thank you."

"You're welcome."

They led Thad to the cells along a narrow dark hallway, and opened a second door. Two cells were in a shorter hallway. It too was dark. Ermeline was in the cell on the right, half in and half out of a shaft of Christmas morning light pouring through the window. Her face was tear-stained, and she was clutching an empty Styrofoam cup. The coffee was long gone. The cup shook in her hand. She gave out a small cry when the jailer opened the cell and Thaddeus entered. She leapt to her feet and threw both arms around his shoulders. "What is going to happen to Jaime?" was all she said. Then she was weeping uncontrollably. She soon stopped crying and sniffed hard, once, and half-smiled. "Help me."

"I'll make sure he's okay," Thaddeus responded. "If this goes on beyond today, we'll make sure your mom has temporary custody."

"Who gets to decide that?"

"Judge Prelate makes the final decision. Actually, he just rubber-stamps whatever recommendation is made by Naomi Killen over at DCFS. Department of Children and Family—"

"I know who they are. They helped me when Hector flew the

coop and left me without a penny even for groceries. We ate that first week because of DCFS. I know June, too."

"She's a good lady. She'll do the right thing for Jaime."

Thaddeus took a seat on the bunk opposite Ermeline's bunk. They were actually concrete slabs embedded in the concrete walls, on which lay mattress pads, the kind that unroll, probably two inches thick. A folded army blanket covered the foot of each bed. On the far wall was a stainless steel toilet, no lid, with several sheets of toilet paper loose on the floor. He opened his iPad, fired up his litigation software, and started in.

"First off, do you know why you're here?"

"They think I had something to do with Vic's death."

"Did you?"

"Did I kill Vic? Absolutely not. I swear it, Thad. On my mother's name."

"I'm sure, but I have to ask anyway." He made a note on the iPad then again lifted his eyes. "Do you know anything about it at all? Anyone tell you anything? Any rumors at the Dome?"

"Nothing. I just heard of it this morning."

"Have you seen or heard anything unusual in the last day or two?"

"Only Hector."

"Tell me about that."

"Hector came in the Silver Dome last night. He came over to my place after work. He was gone when I woke up this morning."

"You're not getting back together with him, are you?"

"Damn, no. He wanted to be there for Christmas. He paid me over six thousand dollars in past support."

"Where's that money?"

"In my purse, I guess. I didn't look. They took my purse." She indicated the front of the jail.

"Where would Hector have gotten six grand to pay you?"

"Working, I guess."

"And you let him come over to your house? Did he sleep with you?"

"He slept on my bed. On top the covers while I was under. He never touched me the entire time. He didn't see me naked, nothing."

"What happened once you were in bed?"

"I went straight to sleep. I had just pulled a ten hour shift and was dead."

"What did he do? If you know."

"Went to sleep too, I guess. Like I say, he was gone by the time Charlie Altiman came."

"Do you know where he went?"

"Unknown."

"Do you have a number for him? Cell phone?"

"No. He was just gonna be there a couple hours this morning then leave. We didn't trade numbers or anything."

"What did you find out about him, anything?"

"He told me he was living in the Gulf of Mexico somewhere. Working for some company. Something about cleaning up oil spills."

Thaddeus typed "BP?" in the margin of his notes, followed by, "Get BP records on Hector."

"Let me change the subject just a little. Did you see Victor Harrow last night?"

"He hasn't been back to the Dome since I got cut up. No, he wasn't there last night, either."

"You didn't go out to his bus? Or even to his house, for that matter?"

"No and no. Like I said, I went straight home after work."

"What time did you get off?"

She thought a minute. "Off at midnight. Left about 12:10, after the tills were counted. Everything balanced, and so we left right away."

"We?"

"Me, Bronco, and Bruce. But Bruce was in the package store, mostly. It was just me and Bronco."

"When did you first see Hector?"

"He came in the Dome. About nine or ten."

"Did he talk to anyone?"

"I didn't see him talking to anyone."

"Did anyone else know he was there?"

"Well...Bronco told me he was there; he had seen him. No, that's not quite right. Bronco told me someone was there who I might know. That was it."

"Where was he when you first saw him last night?"

"At the end of the bar. Closest end to the front door. Drinking a tap Bud."

"Was he talking to anyone?"

"Not that I saw."

Thaddeus raised a hand. "Let's get some coffee." He called to the jailer, a frail-looking older gentleman wearing khaki jeans, boots, and a brown deputy shirt without any of the insignia, chevrons, badges, or other emblems that police wear. "So you're the stripped down model," Thaddeus said to the man as he unlocked the cell. Do you think we could get a couple of coffees in here?"

"What do you think this is, the Ritz?" the old gentleman said with a laugh. "I guess so. How do you take 'em?"

Thaddeus and Ermeline gave their orders and the man shuffled off. "Nice thing about being in jail in a small town. Room service," Thaddeus said jokingly, but Ermeline's eyes filled with tears and she sobbed again. It was all too much and the reality hit her again.

"But you get to leave!" she cried. "How long do they plan on keeping me today? And what about Jaime and his Christmas? Am I just going to miss that?"

Thaddeus reached across and gave her shoulder a squeeze. "Listen, Ermeline. There's something else. The police found a gun and a knife in your house."

"What?" she said incredulously. Her fists pounded the thin mattress. "Hector left those. He—he—planted them! I don't have a gun!"

"That's what I think, too. That's why I'm asking you all the questions about Hector. We need to prove he was inside your house."

"My mom was asleep when we got there. I doubt if she ever saw him."

"I doubt that too. But I think I see what's going on."

"Which is?"

Thaddeus and Ermeline stopped talking when the jailer returned with two steaming Styrofoam cups. "Charlie says with his compliments," he said.

"Please, tell Charlie we said thank you. And thanks to you, too."

"Just whistle when you're ready to leave."

Ermeline gave a harsh laugh. "Does that include me, too?"

The old man stopped on his way out. "I think you might be our guest for a while, Ermeline. They booked you in when you got here."

"Meaning?" She blew across the coffee cup. "What's booked me in?"

"You're being held now for something."

"Will I get to go home today?"

"Better ask your lawyer about that." The man disappeared out the door.

"What about that?" she asked Thaddeus.

"You're being held on suspicion of murder one. Pending the result of fingerprint evidence on the gun and knife. The State crime lab has the gun and knife, and they're dusting them for prints. Probably also looking for DNA. At least on the knife."

"That's a relief. They won't find my prints there."

"Yes, that's a relief. We need to keep that hope alive. That they'll see you haven't touched the weapons and decide there's no reason to hold you."

She shuddered. "How long will it take?"

"Crime lab evidence usually takes two weeks." He looked down. He took a small sip of coffee.

"Two weeks!"

"Yes. Afraid so."

"I'll be locked up for two *weeks*?"

"We'll have an initial appearance tomorrow before Judge Prelate. I'll ask him to release you on your own recognizance. Meaning, you would sign a bond and get out."

"Will he allow that?" She sipped her coffee and made a face. "Instant."

"He'll probably want some security. Real estate or a cash bond. Something to ensure you show up for trial. Something to guarantee you don't flee."

"I'm not fleeing. This is where I live."

"I know. But the system looks at it differently. It's a statutory requirement that bail of some sort be posted in certain cases. Yours is one of those."

They talked on for another thirty minutes about bail and the possibilities for release. Ermeline asked, at the end of it, "What about Jaime? Does he just stay with my mom?"

"I don't see any reason why not. That would probably be the court's first choice."

"What's the court got to do with it?"

"Ermeline, sometimes when a parent gets jailed and there's no other parent around, the court has to place the child."

"Meaning?"

"They look for someone to keep the child while the single parent is being held. Locked up."

"Well, my mom gets him. That's a no-brainer." She began weeping freely now. "Oh my stars," she repeated over and over. "Oh, my stars."

"We'll know once I talk to the District Attorney. He's the one who would bring a dependency petition for placement of Jaime. I'm sure he won't want to file. He'll just let your mom step in."

"Thank goodness."

"And there's one more thing I have to ask."

"What's that?"

"Officially, do you want me to represent you in this case?"

"Absolutely. I wouldn't have it any other way."

"I'm just asking because you could probably get the public defender."

"Why, in heaven's name, would I do that? You're my lawyer, Thaddeus. I chose you."

"Well, when—and if—charges get filed tomorrow, I'll enter my appearance and a plea of not guilty. I'll also file a motion for conditions of release and try to get you sprung from here."

"That would be appreciated."

"Okay, so we've got a lot of work to do. Now, I'll see if I can get you a TV or radio or something in here."

"Not necessary. I don't plan to be here that long."

"I'll ask anyway. Just in case."

THADDEUS' next stop Christmas morning was Quentin's home. The house itself was a ranch style of salmon colored brick and a red slate roof. It sat on a small hill, set back off Washington 300 yards, with no trees and no landscaping. The horses were fenced off by a white fence that encircled the entire ranch, and then made geometric shapes, rectangles and squares, on the interior of the property. The closest they got to District Attorney Erwin's house was twenty-five yards. The horses often were found close by, grazing along the nearest fences, in hope the Erwin kids would bring carrots and apples as they often did. Thaddeus pulled up on the east side of the house and parked just outside the three car garage. He entered through the garage and rang the doorbell.

Quentin Erwin, Jr. answered the door. He was wearing jeans, a T-shirt that said "Go Cardinals!" with a stylized picture of a quarterback about to pass the ball, slippers, and he was holding a glass of eggnog. He lifted the glass to Thaddeus. "You can come in and drill me with your questions. But only if you'll have an eggnog."

"Done," said Thaddeus. "Because I've got a million questions."

"Sure you do. Come on in. I don't have an office here, but we can sit at the dining room table and talk."

Quentin led Thaddeus to the dining room, and they both sat. Donna Erwin appeared in minutes, two fresh eggnogs in hand. "Hey, Thad," she said. "Hear there's trouble up town."

"Thanks," Thad said, accepting the drink. "Yeah, your husband is after my client."

"Whoa," said Quentin. "Let's get one thing straight. It won't be me prosecuting Ermeline. I've got a conflict of interest. I've already called the Attorney General. They'll be handling any prosecution. If there even is one."

Thaddeus' ears perked up. "You mean there might not be a prosecution after all?"

"Depends on the crime lab, I'd say. The AG may see it differently, but without positive results from the crime lab, I don't see a case."

Thaddeus frowned and lowered his voice. "Quentin, someone's after my client. Someone's trying to frame her. She would never shoot Vic Harrow."

"Agreed. But right now it *looks* like she did. It's your job to prove otherwise."

"I thought it was the State's job to prove her guilty beyond a reasonable doubt."

"Sure, that's what the books all say. Truth is, you're gonna have to prove her innocent. That's how it works in the real world."

Thaddeus sat back and took a large mouthful of the drink. His mind was churning. How was he ever going to prove her innocent?

GEORGIANA ARMENTROUT WAS in her mid-fifties, lived in a single wide in Shady Oak Acres north of Orbit, kept two parrots and a Pekingese and had one daughter, Ermeline Ransom, and one grandson, Jaime. She was a widow. She had killed her husband in a hunting accident ten years earlier, when they were hunting in LaGrange Township. They had been hunting deer, using shotguns and shotgun slugs as authorized by Illinois law, when Dan Armentrout handed his gun to Georgiana and ducked through a barbed wire fence. He made it to the other side and was holding down the bottom wire with his foot, when Georgiana went to hand him the two guns, to pass them through the wire. Unfortunately, they were passed muzzle first, the trigger of Dan's gun caught on her hunting jacked button, and the gun fired, blowing a hole the size of a Mason jar in his chest where his heart used to be. Quentin Erwin, Jr.'s predecessor in the District Attorney's office, a mean spirited little man named Blaine Mattock, now deceased in a boating accident of his own, sought to bring charges against Georgiana for the shooting death, and through some legal wizardry, Blind Man's Bluff, and Hide the Ball, managed to convince a Hickam County Grand Jury to indict Georgiana Armentrout for Third Degree Murder. Things went from bad to worse for her from there, because she had no money, had to accept the court-appointed attorney, and the luck of the draw wound her up with Attorney Fletcher T. Franey. Since receiving his law license in 1970, it had been Attorney Franey's practice, with criminal defendants, to plead them guilty first and find out the facts later—if at all. Which is exactly what he did in Georgianna's case. Against her better judgment, she let Franey talk her into a plea agreement, where she would plead guilty to manslaughter, serve six months in the Hickam County jail, and two years of probation. She did her time, talked to enough jail house lawyers while incarcerated to understand that she had been hornswoggled by Franey, and came out a new woman with one goal in life: to avoid lawyers, judges, police, and prosecutors for the rest of her life. She wouldn't even let them pass her by on the street, always preferring to cross over, literally, than have any chance of eye contact or contamination by their ilk. She never voted in general or special elections and didn't care who held what office. She had seen enough government in her forty years to swear off forever. "I've been cured of that," she would say about officialdom. It was Georgiana who awoke to Charlie Altiman's knock at Ermeline Ransom's door that Christmas morning, and it was Georgiana who was told in no uncertain terms that the cops outside had a search warrant, and they were coming in.

Georgiana pulled open the door and stood aside, clutching her robe at the neck. "What the hell do you devils want?" She spat at Sheriff Altiman as he came through the door.

"Mornin' to you to, Georgie," said Altiman with a smile. "Sorry to bother you good people on Christmas morning, but there's a little problem uptown we need to tend to. Hope you folks can help us out."

"I want nothing to do with you and your problem. Neither does Ermeline. So, state your business and leave!"

"Afraid it won't be that easy. You see, we have to search the house. Ermeline home?"

"She's getting decent. She'll be right out."

And at that moment, Ermeline emerged, looking drowsy and flustered, and wearing a sweatshirt that said "BS" and a pair of blue jeans rolled at the ankles. "What's up, Charlie?" she asked the Sheriff. "What in the world all you peace officers after?"

"We've got a search warrant, Ermeline."

"For what? What did I do?"

"Probably didn't do anything. But we need to take a look around."

Which was the moment Jaime Ransom, all of five and full of pep and Christmas morning angst, chose to come bounding in the room, expecting to find a slurry of presents dropped off by Santa, and finding, instead, four complete strangers standing in his living room. He noticed the guns and the badges, and his face clouded over. Tears came to his eyes. "My daddy got hurt?" he asked.

Sheriff Altiman reached across the small room and tousled the youngster's brown hair. "Your dad is just fine, son. We're just here to look for something we lost."

"Lost it in my room?" the little boy asked. "C'mon I'll show you my room."

"Jaime, come up with grandma," Georgiana said, and patted the couch beside her. "The men need to find something someplace else. Probably not in your room. Probably not here at all," she ended, her tone menacing toward the cops. "So's the quicker we all get set down the sooner they can leave. Ain't that right, Sheriff Altiman?"

"That's exactly right, Georgiana. Ermeline, you too, on the couch, if you would please."

"Whoa, can't I brew up a pot first?"

"Go ahead, but hurry it along, please."

Ermeline, not particularly nervous about the interruption, went into the kitchen. She figured they had found out about Hector and had come looking for him, which would explain his total absence this morning when she woke up. At first, she had thought he was in the bathroom getting ready for Christmas morning. But then she heard the police voices and her mother's voice in the living room and she guessed that Hector—as usual—was in some kind of trouble, maybe even for the warrant Hickam County had out for non-support. She wondered if the $6500 could be used to bargain his way out of any arrest. After all, she thought, he had made good and he shouldn't have to be arrested for non-support now. She filled the coffee pot with tap water, scooped three scoops of Folgers' into the basket, and hit the switch. Within seconds, Mr. Coffee was happily underway with its daily routine. She returned to the living room and took a seat on the couch, as the Sheriff had requested. By now, the police had spread through her house, and she could hear them trading information through the thin walls, although she couldn't make out what was being said.

Fifteen minutes into the search warrant's execution, Sheriff Altiman returned to the living room. He was scratching his head. "Ermeline, do you own a gun?"

Ermeline was taken aback. A gun? "Never! I've got a five year old living here! Whose grandfather was killed in a gun accident—" emphasis on *accident*. "No gun, no way, not ever, not here, Sheriff."

"That's what I figured. Okay, thanks."

The Sheriff disappeared, and Ermeline dashed into the kitchen and poured two cups of coffee and a small glass of milk. Using her cocktail waitressing skills she balanced all three, with saucers and two Christmas cookies apiece, and returned to the couch. Jaime inhaled his cookies and immediately asked for more. Before Ermeline could placate the little boy, one of the police officers, Michael Smith, appeared out of the bedroom. Smith was known as the Great Spirit of the Red Bird Inn because he spent so much time at the restaurant chewing donuts and chatting up the farmers and truckers. He came through the living room, exited out to his car—Ermeline supposed—and returned with what looked like a black gym bag. She never did see the opposite side of the bag that read EVIDENCE TECHNICIAN in red letters. The cop disappeared back inside Ermeline's bedroom, and what sounded like a conference was held in the bathroom. Five minutes later, the same cop returned, snugging the evidence bag tight under his arm. He managed a stiff smile, and disappeared back outside. Ermeline heard a car trunk slam, and he didn't return again. Evidently, the search was then continued, as the threesome on the couch didn't see any sign of the remaining three officers for another fifteen minutes. Finally, they all three returned to the living room, and the two uniformed city cops began looking under furniture and inside drawers and behind the entertainment center, looking for heaven only knew what, as far as Ermeline could tell. Sheriff Altiman again reached to tousle Jaime's hair, but this time the boy ducked. He stuck out his tongue. Clearly, he had inherited his grandma's distaste of law enforcement officers. Ermeline told him that that was enough, that these men were guests and should be treated nicely.

"Tell the truth, Ermeline," Sheriff Altiman all but stammered, "I'm gonna have to ask you to ride up to the office with me."

The little boy's ears perked up. "Mama ain't leavin'. We gotta do Christmas, Mister."

"I'm sorry, son, but I need to borrow mama for a while. She'll come back soon," he lied, and the whites of his eyes showed as he said it, knowing he had just lied to a five year old. There were some things about this job a man could really come to hate, and Ermeline picked up on his thoughts and feelings. This wasn't good; she could read that between the lines. Something was definitely up, and it involved her, too, maybe not just Hector.

"This about Hector?" Ermeline asked. "What's he done now?"

"We can talk on the way uptown. I'd just as soon wait for privacy," Sheriff Altiman said and nodded at the boy.

"Let me get a coat and slip into some boots. Be right back."

Sheriff Altiman waited, and Georgiana totally ignored him, hating him from a distance, until she could finally stand no more and went to the kitchen for a refill.

"Mama," Ermeline called to her, "you watch Jaime while I'm out?"

"Of course. No need to ask," she shouted back. "Just take the cops with you when you leave, and we'll be fine here."

Sheriff Altiman could only smile. He knew all about Georgiana and her hatred of all things official, especially cops. In a way, he didn't even blame her, he thought, kicking himself for telling a whopper just minutes before: they had found a gun and a bloody knife; Ermeline wouldn't be returning any time soon. He was getting too old for this crapola, he told himself. Three more years and he'd have his twenty, then adios. He was off to Florida like every other sane mortal.

Ermeline reappeared dressed for the weather. Jaime leapt into her arms and she bear hugged him, whispered in his ear, and carried him into his grandma. Sheriff Altiman held the door for Ermeline as she went outside before him. Neither said a word on the way to the Sheriff's Office and, finally, to jail. She was booked in at 7:45 a.m. Christmas morning, and the jailer escorted her back to the jail cell she would now call home. At least for now.

THAT AFTERNOON, the Governor and Mrs. Walker welcomed the Governor's cabinet to the Christmas Day Dinner that was always held in Springfield at the Governor's Mansion each year. This red brick Italianate mansion in downtown Springfield had been the home of Illinois governors since 1855, when Joel A. Matteson and his family moved in. On February 13, 1857, the Lincolns attended a party, which a writer from the *Illinois State Journal* called, "a delightful and magnificent entertainment. Carefully restored in 1971, the building houses many treasures. When you walk inside, you immediately see the exquisite elliptical stairway which leads to spacious rooms decorated in British Regency style."

Once upstairs, you could see portraits of the Lincolns and their friend Edward D. Baker, a bust of Lincoln modeled from life by Thomas D. Jones, bedroom furniture given to the Lincolns, and a spectacular table presented to President Lincoln, which contained more than 20,000 pieces of inlaid wood.

After greeting his guests and their husbands and wives, Governor Walker managed to sneak away with Attorney General Robert K. Amistaggio. They crept upstairs to the Lincoln bedroom where they sat at the great man's inlaid writing desk and put their heads together. The Governor had downed two quick gin and tonics in anticipation of the day's guests, most of whom he hated and most of whom were trying to replace him with themselves, and he wasted no time getting down to the real reason for the get-together.

"That girl in Orbit. I want her prosecuted with every last atom of power in the Attorney General's office," the Governor spat at his AG. "Without her held responsible, people are going to start digging deeper. Bury her now, and do it fast."

The Attorney General took a long pull at his Bud in a bottle, his drink of choice. "We're already working on that. I've assigned the case to my chief prosecutor, Rulanda Barre, now that Quentin Erwin, Jr.'s declared a conflict. She's a magnificent trial attorney. Her record is 62-0 and counting. All homicide cases, all conflicted out by local DA's."

"There was a stroke of luck."

"Mister Erwin claimed he had counseled the girl in his office. The alleged assault on her by Vic Harrow. You know—the name carved in her boobs."

"Yes. What about that?"

The AG shrugged. "You said to put the fear of death in Vic Harrow. Johnny Bladanni did that with his knife. It worked."

"It worked only to the tune of twenty-five thousand."

"Cleman, that's all the guy had. We've been over all his records. Everything was mortgaged to the hilt. Liens everywhere like Democrats in South Chicago."

"Funny man. Okay, so strike fast and get me a conviction. Other contributors to the Governors retirement campaign will get the message. Pay up or leave in a cheap coffin."

"So when you retire—it will be my turn to take on the responsibilities of the Governorship. Let's not forget where we're headed here."

"Never forgotten. You will have my endorsement and the party's leaders in your corner. It's a shoo-in in 2016."

"Excellent."

"Now get me a conviction. I just hope this Rulanda Barre is everything you say she is."

"Not to worry. She could convict John the Baptist at the Mount Israel First Baptist Church."

"Music to my ears."

"Music to our ears."

"Now let's go rub shoulders with the criminals I call my cabinet."

14

Thaddeus arrived at the office just after 7:30 the day after Christmas. He had stopped by the Silver Dome and listened to the gossip. Oddly enough, no one seemed to have heard about Ermeline's arrest yesterday. Instead, the tables were overflowing with talk of Victor Harrow's murder, which some were calling a suicide, which some were calling an act of terrorism, and which some were calling the result of one-too-many dalliances with some married woman whose husband found out. Only Cece knew the truth: she had personally delivered an early morning breakfast of scrambled eggs and sausage to the Hickam County Jail, a courtesy to Sheriff Altiman. Cece had seen the truth with her own eyes: Ermeline was housed in the one of the two women's cells. When the two friends saw each other, they both cried out. Cece had been briefed before going in that Ermeline was being held on a "very serious matter," but, other than that, nothing more was said. Now, when she saw Ermeline, she whispered "Why are you here?" To which Ermeline replied, "Victor Harrow was murdered. They say I did it!" Cece returned to the Silver Dome determined not to breathe a word of what she had found out. Let the gossips and their fools find out for themselves. She and Ermeline worked together at the Silver Dome, and Cece had nothing but profound respect for that girl. She had been through it all and had come out the other side all the stronger for it. Her till always balanced when her shift was over, and she never gave away Bruce's alcohol to free drinkers. She made every dime for him she could, and the only time she lazed was when she was on break, often coming next door to Cece's side and having a bite to eat before returning to the din and clamor of the tavern side. They had always traded hellos and the war stories typical among those who serve the American public their food and drink. No, she was protecting Ermeline from the masses that would try to devour her, any way she could.

THADDEUS FOUND two bombshells waiting for him at the office. When he arrived, he made his coffee, took a seat at his desk, and dialed up his voice mail. Three messages awaited. Bombshell Number One was a call from a woman who identified herself as Rulanda Barre, an Assistant Attorney General at the AG's Office in Springfield. Thaddeus played her message and then replayed it. The second time, he made notes

"Mister Murfee," the message said, "My name is Ruland Barre, and I'm an assistant AG with Robert K. Amistaggio's office in Springfield. I've been asked by the Sheriff of Hickam County to review the circumstances surrounding the shooting death of one Victor Moreland Harrow, of Orbit, and I have made some preliminary inquiries. As you are probably aware, Mr. Harrow died as the result of a gunshot wound to the head, or so it appears at least, pending the coroner's final report, of course. It also appears that your client, Ermeline Ransom, was savagely attacked by Victor Harrow sometime within the last little while. That being the case, we believe she had sufficient motive to retaliate against Victor Harrow. Along with that, Sheriff Altiman and police officers from the City of Orbit PD executed a search warrant yesterday morning at your client's residence. A .38 caliber pistol was seized, as well as a ten inch switchblade knife. The knife exhibited what appear to be blood stains. The shooting wound to the forehead of Victor Harrow appears to be a .38 caliber wound, according to the State Police Crime Lab Incident Report which I've been provided."

At this point Thaddeus paused the message and took a long drink of coffee. His mind was spinning. These people had wasted no time, no time at all, in coming after Ermeline. How much worse was this going to get before the end of today, he wondered. He punched PLAY, and the message continued from Ms. Barre.

"As a result of these preliminary—and I emphasize preliminary—reports, I have prepared, and today, will be filing a criminal complaint against Ermeline Ransom, charging First Degree Murder in the shooting death of Victor Harrow. Initial Appearance will be this morning, according to rule, and I can only assume that you will be representing your client at the appearance. I will be available to discuss the case with you after the Initial Appearance, but only briefly, as we are moving a temporary office into the law library of the Hickam County Courthouse to serve as our official presence in your county as this prosecution proceeds. Oh, yes, one last thing. I will oppose all bail motions. Here the evidence is strong and compelling against your client, and I believe Judge Prelate would be hard-pressed to find legal ground on which he could impose a condition of release that would allow your client her freedom while the prosecution goes onward. So bring a checkbook that's got a whole bunch of zeros in it, she's gonna need them."

The last was clearly intended as a joke, but Thaddeus was in no joking mood. He would send Christine across the street for a copy of the criminal complaint as soon as she arrived. Then, he would take the complaint across Madison Street to the jail and meet with Ermeline. In the meantime, he would need to make arrangements with her mother for some clothes suitable for courtroom dress. He didn't want her looking like some frazzled truck stop babe in an orange jumpsuit. She would be dolled up, but demure, and would look every bit the mother of a healthy five-year old who needed her at home.

Thaddeus then skipped to the second message on voice mail.

Bombshell Number Two was a call from District Attorney Quentin Erwin, Jr. himself. In small counties such as Hickam, it is customary for the District Attorney in Illinois to represent not only the State in criminal matters, but also to represent various departments in their administrative matters in the county. One of his common clients was the Department of Children and Family Services, DCF, which held 100% final say-so on any juvenile dependency matter in Hickam County. Thaddeus hit PLAY.

"Thad, Quentin. This isn't the best news you're going to get today. It appears that now that Ermeline has been arrested the DCF folks are going to be filing a dependency petition for her little boy. I believe his name is Jaime Ransom. Naomi Killen is representing DCF in the matter. As you know, child dependency cases have priority in Illinois courts. This morning, at 10 a.m. sharp, I will be appearing before Judge Prelate and attempting to have Jaime made a ward of the state. I know that Ermeline felt right about leaving the boy with her mother yesterday, but it turns out the mother has a criminal record, as we all know. Because of that, she's not a person qualified to have custody of this five-year-old while the mother is out of the home. I know this sounds like bullcrap to you, and it probably is, but I wanted to give you a heads up. Please spend some time on the horn this morning talking to Ermeline's family and try to find another candidate to take custody. I hate this as much as anyone, but it's my job, and sometimes my job sucks. Tell Ermeline I'm sorry and that I promise a placement will be made that's suitable for Jaime while she's going through her own criminal case. I guess you know by now that I did follow up Charlie's call to the AG and claimed a conflict of interest there, so I don't have to prosecute Ermeline myself. It's bad enough I have to take her kid away from here. Later."

Thaddeus hung up on voice mail. There was a third call waiting, but right now he just couldn't take anymore. He stood up and took a deep breath. He could feel his pulse racing, feel his heart beating a fast rhythm in his chest. This was all just happening too fast. He was going to have to go talk to Ermeline about Jaime without waiting for Christine. Jaime would be the most important thing on her mind,

and he didn't want to let her down. He wanted her to know he had
come to her aid as soon as he heard.

THE F-150 with Louisiana plates pulled into the rest stop just south of
Normal, Illinois. Hector rolled into a parking slot outside the men's
restrooms. He shut it down, removed the key, and climbed out. Then
he had a second notion and reached back inside the truck, to the
driver's side, beneath his crumpled parka. He removed a pink wallet,
about as long as a checkbook, snapped along the side. It was well
worn and smelled of a perfume Hector knew from his years with
Ermeline. He undid the snap. There was her Illinois Driver's License,
color picture, Social Security card, several folds of Jaime pictures at
different ages, and a First National Bank check cashing card and two
credit cards. He removed the two credit cards, an Amex and a MasterCard. Both cards were slipped into his shirt pocket. Why not? he
thought. Might be good for laughs, one last jab at the old lady. Run
up a few grand on her cards, and then watch her squirm. He remembered Johnny Bladanni's admonition to him to take nothing else from
her purse but the cash, but he could only shrug. Son of a bitch
thought he ran Hector's life, too? Guess not, damn greaseball! On the
way back to the men's room Hector passed an orange garbage can
hanging from a pole. He tossed the wallet into the trash and walked
on. He really needed to take a leak. Man, he needed to piss. Chicago
was another three hours, he calculated. But it was going to be fun. He
had almost seven grand in cash, two stolen credit cards, and that old
deep-down ache for some lady fun. He would find the nearest
Pussycat club, get a lap dance, drink a pitcher, and get laid. Prospects
were looking good. Very good, indeed.

15

News of the criminal complaint charging First Degree Murder against Ermeline Ransom spread like wildfire through the courthouse that morning. Immediately upon hearing the news, Hickam County Clerk Herman McKenna wasn't buying it. Something just didn't add up about the arrest of Ermeline Ransom for the shooting death of Victor Harrow.

As County Clerk it was McKenna's job to care for the official county records of Hickam County. This included real estate records and property records. Real estate records in Illinois were known as grantor-grantee indices, meaning that you could search by the last name of the person who made a deed of real estate (grantor) to someone else (grantee), or you could search by the last name of the person (grantee) who received a deed of real estate from someone else (grantor). The records also included what are known as UCC-1 financing statements. Whenever tangible personal property such as furniture, machines, cars, trucks, construction equipment—anything that wasn't attached to real estate—was purchased with a lien, then the seller filed a UCC-1 financing statement. The purpose of the UCC-1 was to give a subsequent purchaser of the property official

notice that there was already a lien on the property, and that if he or
she purchased it, they would be taking title subject to the lien of the
original seller. At least until the original lien was paid in full by the
first purchaser. When that happened, the lien was marked as paid,
and a subsequent purchaser then took 100% title to the asset upon
payment of the second selling price. It was a complicated office that
Clerk McKenna oversaw, but he thought it the most important office
in the Hickam County Courthouse, because of the assets involved.
After all, the assets registered in his office proved that people owned
things. The records proved their wealth. And wealth, in Hickam
County, as in most counties in America, meant everything. So when
Clerk McKenna's assistant clerk, Clarice Jones, came to him and told
him that Attorney Fletcher T. Franey was spending the second of two
full days in the Clerk's office looking through the records for assets
owned by Victor Harrow, McKenna's antennae had gone on alert.
First, it was rare that the attorneys themselves pored over the records
McKenna kept. Most often, the records were viewed by clerical
people from the banks and S&L's. When the attorneys needed a
record they 99% of the time sent a secretary over to make a copy. But
it wasn't until Vic Harrow had been murdered did the recollection of
Franey's visits to the County Clerk's office really come into focus for
McKenna. Now it had him wondering.

Clerk McKenna's own daughter, Angel McKenna, had grown up
best friends with Ermeline Ransom (nee Armentrout). They had
played paper dolls and dress-up together, had raised hamsters and
turtles together, had performed in ballet and piano recitals together,
had served on the high school spirit squad together, and had
married, to everyone's wonder, two second cousins upon graduation
from high school. That Ermeline was now charged with first degree
murder just didn't click for McKenna. That Franey had personally
spent two days in McKenna's office with Vic Harrow's records did
raise a red flag for McKenna, as those visits were only a day or two
before Vic Harrow's death. Something was skewed and McKenna
planned to get to the bottom of it.

So, he made a call to the feds in Chicago. "It's probably nothing," he told Special Agent Pauline Pepper of the Chicago Office of the FBI. "It's probably just coincidence. But it's something I think the feds need to look into."

Special Agent Pauline Pepper wasn't so sure. "It could just as well have been coincidence," she told McKenna. "Lawyers visit Clerk's offices every day and review records. That doesn't mean there's been a crime committed."

"You would be doing me a favor just to nose around down here some afternoon," McKenna said. "Let's say I'm requesting that as an official act."

Special Agent Pepper paused. A hunch or a "feeling" was one thing; an official request from a county official was something entirely different. She would now have to make a record of the call and, at least, do some cursory footwork. "How about this," she said, "how about my partner and I come and check it out with Mister Franey. No big deal, just some standard questions, that sort of thing."

McKenna smiled. "That would be a great idea. Like you say, it's probably nothing. On the other hand it could be something. I know Ermeline Ransom, and I don't believe for a second she murdered Vic Harrow. It's just not in her to do that, I don't care what he did to her."

"He carved her up pretty bad, then?"

"Horrible. I hear he cut up her entire chest area."

"Damnation," said Agent Pepper. "Okay. We'll do our due diligence, and I'll file a report. I'll copy you on the report, even though I'm not supposed to. But seeing as how you're a county official and all, I see no harm."

"Stop by when you're down. I'm buying the coffee."

"Will do."

AFTER THE SECOND voice mail message, the one from DA Erwin, Thaddeus slipped his suit jacket back on, pulled on his London Fog,

and crossed Madison Street in a snowstorm to the Hickam County
Jail. Sheriff Altiman was up front, reviewing the booking record when
Thaddeus came clomping inside, kicking the snow onto the rubber
mat. The doorbell chimed beside him, as there wasn't always a recep-
tionist up front, especially at night when the staffing was cut down
due to budgetary constraints.

The Sheriff looked up from the booking clipboard. He was
dressed in his standard outfit: gray slacks, blue button down, brown
tie, and badge and gun on his belt. When he would go out, in this
weather, he would add the standard nylon cop's jacket with the fur
collar. "Thaddeus," he said, "it couldn't get much worse for her."

"I know. I better break the news, Charlie."

"Let's go back. She's already had breakfast. Cece brought it over."

"Chris is coming with an outfit for court. She's going by Ermeline's house. As of right now, she still doesn't know anything, right?"

"None of us have said a word. That's your job."

"Thanks."

Charlie led Thaddeus back to the door at the end of the first bank
of cells. He slipped a key in the door, and they entered the women's
holding area. When Ermeline saw Thaddeus she closed the Gideon's
she was reading and turned away. "This isn't gonna be good, is it?"
she said. "Oh, damn."

Charlie left them alone. Thaddeus entered the cell and took a seat
on the second bunk, across from Ermeline's. "No, it's not good."

He went over the two phone calls in detail, describing the criminal complaint that would be filed. He then explained the dependency petition that would be filed concerning Jaime's temporary
custody. Ermeline's eyes filled and tears streamed down her face. She
jumped up and down on the cement floor and hit the cement wall
with her fist. Then she threw herself down on her mattress. She was
pale, and he could tell there had been little, if any, sleep. Her eyes
were bloodshot, and her fingers tightly clutched the Gideon's as if it
was all she had to support her. He started in again. When he was
done she became very quiet and non-communicative. It suddenly
occurred to him that he would have to request a suicide watch on

Ermeline. She was too quiet. "Well?" he asked her. "Are you ready to get to work with me?"

"I suppose," she said dreamily. "I'm going to lose, aren't I?"

"As long as there are no fingerprints on the gun or the knife we're home free. I can walk you out in front of jury on those facts. You're sure you didn't handle either one?"

"Positive. My mom won't allow a gun within a football field of the house. Not after what happened to my dad."

They launched into a long discussion about Jaime's temporary placement. It turned out that Ermeline had an aunt in Louisiana, Missouri, who would almost certainly take on the responsibility. Thaddeus called the aunt on his cell. There was no answer, so he left a message. The clock was creeping around to 9:30, which was when Nancy Kelly, Quentin Erwin, Jr.'s secretary, knocked once and entered the women's area. She shoved a handful of papers through the bars. "This is from Quentin," she said, avoiding Ermeline's eyes. "He says he's sorry, but he has to do it." She immediately turned and left. Thaddeus slowly studied the paperwork. "This is your standard dependency petition, signed by Naomi Killen of DCFS, and set for hearing one-half hour from now before the Honorable Nathan R. Prelate, Circuit Court Judge. They're going to try to make Jaime a ward of the state while you're locked up. It says here your mom doesn't qualify for temporary custody. Let me call Christine."

Ermeline sobbed once and cried, "Help me, Thaddeus!"

Thaddeus called Christine Susmann. He asked her to meet him in court just before ten o'clock. He had an idea that just might work.

He stood up and drew a deep breath, tossing his shoulders back. A chill ran down his spine as he realized that he was all that was standing between Ermeline Ransom and the ruination of her life. His law practice had suddenly become very real and loomed very large before him. He was certain most new lawyers in just their second year never found themselves facing anything quite this serious. "It just ain't gonna happen," he said. "We'll figure out something, but you're not losing Jaime, not if I can stop it."

Thaddeus was waiting in the courthouse hallway when Christine came up the stairs two at a time. "We've got a problem, he told her. Naomi Killen is trying to make Jaime a ward of the court and place him in a foster home while Ermeline's locked up."

Christine winced. "What can we do?"

They discussed the possibilities, and finally Thaddeus had to go inside the courtroom. He told Christine to stay put. He would send the bailiff when he was ready for her.

JUDGE NATHAN R. PRELATE was in a good mood. It was the day after Christmas, every gift he had bought for the wife and two girls fit, so returns wouldn't be necessary. All three had seemed pleased with his selections. The girls had made it home by 1:00 a.m. almost every night since Christmas break, and there had been few strange sleep-overs going on inside their bedrooms. Finally, he was beginning to hope, Leona may have outgrown that open and notorious sexual stage she had been going through since her sophomore year in high school. This past week there had been no bed sharing with members of the opposite sex—or even with members of the same sex. Wynell was a different story and probably always would be. So when he took his seat in the courtroom on the morning of December 26 he was in a good mood and ready to see justice done. He told those in attendance to be seated, which included Ermeline Ransom, who had been brought from jail to the court by Deputy Dale Harshman. Ermeline was wearing dark slacks and a herringbone sport coat, white shirt buttoned to the throat. Deputy Harman had removed the handcuffs and had placed Ermeline so she was sitting at counsel table on the left side of the courtroom, Deputy Harshman sitting just behind her in the first spectator row.

Judge Prelate looked out over his domain. First up was the peti-tion entitled "In Re Jaime Ransom, a Juvenile." He had the clerk call the case and watched as Quentin Erwin, Jr. and Thaddeus Murfee took their seats at counsel table. Quentin had the burden of proof, so he sat at the table closest to the jury box, although, of course, there was never a jury in juvenile dependency cases. At Quentin's right, Naomi Killen took a seat. She was there representing the Illinois Department of Children and Family Services, and it was her signature that appeared on the dependency petition itself. At the table on the judge's right sat Thaddeus Murfee, who took a chair beside Ermeline. She had been sitting alone and looked nervous and very frightened, Judge Prelate noted. He couldn't blame her.

"Gentlemen," he said to the two attorneys, "are we ready to proceed?"

"Yes, Your Honor," said Quentin Erwin, Jr. and Thaddeus Murfee almost in unison.

"Very well, if the clerk will call the case."

Clerk of the Court, Wilma Smith, scrolled to the top of her computer screen and called the case of "In Re Jaime Ransom, a Juvenile." Quentin announced that he was present and representing the State of Illinois. Thaddeus announced that he was present and representing Ermeline Ransom, the mother of the juvenile. At that moment, the courtroom door behind them banged open and attorney D.B. Leinager strode noisily up to the bar and entered through the swinging gate.

"Mister Leinager," said the judge, "we've just called the juvenile case the clerk called you about this morning. Are you able to serve as guardian ad litem for the minor?"

The 89 year old attorney pulled out the chair next to Ermeline. "I am, Your Honor. As an officer of the court I take that responsibility very seriously and will do my very best to properly represent the child's interests."

"Good enough," said the judge. "Counsel," indicating Quentin Erwin, Jr., "it's your petition. Please call your first witness."

"The State calls Naomi Killen."

Naomi Killen stood before the clerk of the court and raised her right hand. She took her oath and climbed the step up to the witness chair.

"State your name for the record."

"Naomi Killen."

"And Miss Killen, what is your business, occupation or profession?"

"I am the lead case worker for the Department of Children and Family Services of the State of Illinois for Hickam County, Illinois."

"And, in that capacity, have you come into information concerning the minor named Jaime Ransom?"

"I have."

"And where did that information come from?"

"Sheriff Altiman called me yesterday."

"Christmas day?"

"Yes, my job is 365/24. I'm on call for dependent juveniles around the clock all year."

"And what did you learn in that call?"

"Objection!" said D.B. Leinager, rising to his feet. "Calls for hearsay."

"Sustained. Miss Cooper, please just tell us what you did as a result of that call."

"Well, like I said, Sheriff Altiman called me and gave me some information. As a result of that information I paid an afternoon visit at the home of Ermeline Ransom of Orbit." She nodded at Ermeline, who only returned a blank stare. Ermeline almost couldn't believe this was actually happening and felt like pinching herself. But she didn't; it was real, and it was a horror story, and she had nothing to hang onto except Thaddeus Murfee. She said a silent prayer for him and for Jaime.

"What happened there?"

"I spoke with Mrs. Georgiana Armentrout at Ermeline's house. She was babysitting the minor. Evidently, the child's mother had been arrested for First Degree Murder and removed from the home by the Sheriff. The child was therefore dependent as there is no father living in the home, and the father cannot be located, from what I learned."

"As a result, what did you do?"

"I determined that it would be in the child's best interests to leave him with the grandmother, Georgiana Armentrout, pending today's hearing. He is still with her this morning, as I didn't feel he was threatened in any way by being with her Christmas day. However, it is my belief he should be removed from that home."

"Removed," said Quentin Erwin, Jr., "why is it your opinion that he should be removed from the home?"

"Georgiana Armentrout is not a fit and proper party to have temporary custody of the minor. She has a criminal record involving violence."

Judge Prelate spoke up. "The court takes judicial notice of Ms. Armentrout's record. This court took the plea in that case and accepted the plea bargain. It is noted that Ms. Armentrout did indeed plead guilty to one count of involuntary manslaughter, which is, under our laws, a crime of violence. Thus, Ms. Armentrout is unqualified as a person with whom placement of the minor might be made. Please continue."

Thaddeus shuffled his feet. He could see Ermeline in his peripheral vision. The color drained from her face as the court took judicial notice of the grandmother's plight. She pulled a tissue from the box and clutched it hard. Damned if they were going to see her tears, she decided. "Unbelievable," she whispered, though Thaddeus responded by holding up his hand. "No talking, please," he whispered back.

Erwin continued. "Do you have an opinion regarding proper placement at this time?"

Naomi Quentin nodded. "The child's legal custody should be vested in the DCFS, and I will locate an appropriate foster home for him. This should happen immediately so we can remove him from the home."

Ermeline gasped. "No, please," she said weakly.

Judge Prelate smiled down. "You'll get your chance, Ermeline. All right, Mister Erwin, anything further?"

"No, Your Honor."

"Gentlemen?"

D.B. Leinager shook his head and Thaddeus said, "Not right now, subject to recall, please."

"Then you may call your next witness, Mister Erwin."

"Your Honor, the State rests."

"Gentlemen?" said Judge Prelate, indicating the men on either side of Ermeline. "Witnesses—either of you?"

"I have one," Thaddeus said. "Respondent Ermeline Ransom calls Christine Susmann as her first witness."

The bailiff went into the hallway asked Christine to join them. Up until then, she hadn't been allowed in the courtroom as all juvenile hearings and records are sealed.

Christine stood before Clerk Smith and was sworn. She stepped up to the witness stand and took a seat.

Thaddeus started in. "State your name."

"Christine Susmann."

"What is your occupation, for the record?" Everyone in the courtroom knew she worked for Thaddeus as his paralegal. Still, a record had to be made in case of an appeal by either side.

"I am a paralegal. I work for Thaddeus Murfee in Orbit, Hickam County, Illinois."

"Are you a mother?"

"I have two children, a boy and a girl."

"Names and ages, please."

She related their ages, that they were in perfect health, and that they were normal, happy children.

"You're married to Buddy Susmann?"

"I am. Ten years now."

"What does Buddy do?"

"He works—worked—for Victor Harrow of Harrow and Sons. Since Victor's death, we're not sure. So far, so good."

"Meaning, he still has his job."

"Yes."

"Are you and your husband able to provide proper support and care for your children?"

"We like to think so. We work hard and play with the kids every chance we get. Everyone gets along."

"And prior to working as a paralegal for me, what other jobs have you held?"

"I left high school, turned eighteen, and enlisted in the Army. They sent me to Basic Training, then to Military Police School. Following that, I was sent to Iraq where I served two tours."

"Doing what?"

"Working as an MP."

"Where?"

"Baghdad."

"I see. What happened after those two tours?"

"The Army wanted me to re-up for another four years, so they offered me a school."

"Did you re-up and go to school?"

"I did. I went to Military Justice School. They trained me as a paralegal."

"Then what?"

"Then I was stationed in Germany with a JAG unit. I was one of three paralegals for seven very busy prosecutors."

"What were your duties?"

"The usual—witness statement review, deposition summaries, research and briefs, correspondence, filing, plus I ran the calendar for all seven, which was huge by itself."

"Everybody got to where they needed to be on time?" Thaddeus smiled.

"They did while I was there."

"And why are you here today? Do you have any relationship to the minor child known as Jaime Ransom?"

"I do. My husband and Jaime's father Hector are second cousins. So that makes me a relative."

"Objection," said District Attorney Erwin. "She's offering a legal conclusion."

"Oh, I think she can say she's a relative, in a general way," said Judge Prelate. "Overruled. You may continue."

"As a relative, do you have an opinion regarding the appropriate temporary custody of Jaime Ransom?"

"I do," Christine said. "He should be placed with me and Buddy."

Ermeline gasped and Quentin Erwin, Jr. rose up out of his chair. "Your Honor, while that's a nice offer and certainly good of Chris and Buddy, I don't think that legally she is of the correct degree of family to qualify her and Buddy for foster placement."

Judge Prelate nodded and sat back in his Judge's chair. He looked up at the ceiling. He pressed his fingertips together and finally leaned forward. "Tell you what, Mister Erwin. I'm going to ask you to brief the law on that issue. Get me a written brief by oh—let's see, today's December 26. Can you have something to me by February 1?"

Erwin said, "Really? You really want a brief?"

"Really. I do. Right now, the court is leaning in favor of the place of the child with Chris and Buddy Susmann. While the Court isn't one hundred percent positive on the degree of relationship required to create a priority for placement by family relationship, it is an issue worthy of no small amount of research. I think you're just the man for that job, Mister Erwin."

Quentin Erwin, Jr. took his seat. He couldn't help but smile.

Judge Prelate pointed at the lawyers. "Anything further?"

D.B. Leinager raised his hand. He had questions. "Miss Susmann, you say you worked in Baghdad as an MP?"

"I did."

"Isn't it true you were actually working with the CIA doing black ops?"

Thaddeus was quickly on his feet. "Objection. Relevance, materiality."

"Oh, it's relevant," said D.B., "it goes to whether she has ever been engaged in violence of any nature herself. My suspicion is that she has been, knowing what went on in Baghdad at those prisons."

"She may answer," said Judge Prelate, "as long as the service isn't classified."

Christine looked up at the Judge. "It is classified. I am under lifetime orders not to disclose my role in Iraq."

"Your Honor," said D.B., "she's claiming to be a fit and proper person. Her history is very relevant."

"But it is classified, Mister Leinager," responded Thaddeus. "You are swatting at gnats."

"CIA agents and torture prisons aren't gnats, Sir, I can assure you," D.B. spat at Thaddeus. "I represent this little boy, and I just want to know what kind of people are going to be watching over him. That's my job to find out."

"You're correct, Mister Leinager," said Judge Prelate. "But at this point, I'm afraid I'm going to have to draw the line and make a ruling. The court specifically finds that Miss Susmann's duty details while on active duty in Iraq are neither relevant nor material. Mister Murfee's objection is sustained."

"Very well," said D.B. Leinager. "I have nothing further."

"Anyone else?" asked the judge.

They all shook their heads. "Very well," the judge began, "I have known Christine and Buddy Susmann since they were children themselves. When she got older, Christine babysat one summer with my own girls while Ginny was playing Golda in *Fiddler on the Roof* at the Hickam Players Theater. Christine did a great job, my girls loved her, and we thought the world of her. We were very happy with her work, and I have nothing but the greatest respect for her ability to care for children. It is the order of the court that temporary placement of Jaime Ransom be with Christine and Buddy Susmann until further order of the Court. Mister Erwin, I will expect your brief by five p.m. on the first of February. Anything further?"

All three attorneys shook their heads. Christine came down off the stand and stopped. She leaned across counsel table and gave Ermeline a hug. Ermeline thanked her and patted her back. Thaddeus turned away and watched as Deputy Harshman watched the transaction between the two women, as he was required to do. Quentin Erwin, Jr. walked up to Thaddeus, leaned close, and whispered, "Don't that beat all? You're writing this bullcrap brief, Thaddeus. You owe me one."

Thaddeus smiled. "Done." He breathed a huge sigh of relief.

Catastrophe had been averted. At least for a while. But, at any time, the State could renew the motion for the most minor reason and throw mother and son into uproar again. Thaddeus was determined not to let that happen.

"Later. Good luck with her initial appearance."

"Thanks."

16

As Hector Ransom was headed north on I-55 toward Chicago, he was passed by a black Ford Interceptor headed southbound. Of course, there were four lanes and a median separating the two vehicles; not that any of the drivers would have known each other or even been looking for each other anyway. At this point, there was no reason. Behind the wheel of the Interceptor was Special Agent Pauline Pepper, who worked out of the Dirksen Building in Chicago. Riding shotgun was Special Agent Giovanni Henrici—"Gio"—who shared the same windowless office with her.

"More than anything else," Pepper was saying to Gio, "I wanna move out further west. Maybe out near Schaumburg or Arlington Heights. But it takes money."

"You can get a nice four bedroom in Schaumburg for around four hundred grand," replied Gio. "We're talking four bedrooms, den, family room, granite in the kitchen, hot tub in the master. I know 'cause I've looked, too."

"I thought you liked the loft gig downtown. Don't tell me you want out of the city?"

Gio frowned. "Not while I'm single. But I won't always be single. Then I'll want the 'burbs."

"That's me," Pepper said. "I've got Maria and Adam. I want them in Catholic school—none of that public school crap."

"All it takes is money," Gio sighed.

"*That's* what I'm telling you. That's why I gotta make my next GS grade like yesterday. Then I can finance."

"Well, you're never gonna make it by working some nothing case out of—where was it again?"

"Orbit. If you can believe it. Orbit." She said it as if the word left a bad taste on her tongue. She said it again and scowled. "Orbit."

"What's the connection to Spandex?" He was referring to Operation Spandex, so named because it was rumored the governor wore Spandex athletic wear under his suits to hide his bulging waistline. Pepper and Gio were assigned exclusively to Spandex. The operation itself was a net that had been cast over the governor's dealings with known mobsters, henchmen, bagmen, and crooks, both petty and white collar. He used those people, and the FBI knew it. They knew the governor kept close company with them, and was constantly chatting them up. The FBI knew this because every phone the governor had ever used, or ever would use, was tapped, along with his office in Chicago, his office in Springfield, and every room in his house, including his sauna in Chicago, all tapped, thanks to a FISA court order which was general enough that the Governor's grade school report card would have come within its purview. The FISA court had agreed to jurisdiction (FISA was a court designed to sniff out foreign terrorist threats) because several of the men the Governor kept company with were Sicilian by birth and by citizenship. Weren't even U.S. citizens and he was doing business with them like they were Mr. Smith, the manager down at the Safeway store. The Attorney General's phones and calls were likewise tapped and analyzed and parsed and saved to the Chicago DELL servers. The AG had made the happy list because, based on the Governor's talks with him, the same keywords-of-interest were being traded in those conversations. First order of business every day when Pepper and Gio arrived for work was to read over the previous night's phone calls and private conversations. Same thing at the end of each day. They were all summarized, of course, and critical components highlighted in yellow. They were also entered into the FBI computers in whole, because they could be broken apart word by word and sliced and diced and jammed into databases that would have made the NSA blush. Pepper and Gio had complete and exclusive access to the databases thus created and maintained by the FBI out of Chicago, and could even call them up on their iPads. Just login and bam! Search everything the governor or AG ever had to say about this or that topic. In this case, they had searched on "Victor" and "Vic" and "Harrow" and "Orbit" after Pepper's talk with the County Clerk, McKenna. They had come away with a ton of hits—bits and quarks of conversations where the governor or his AG had mentioned the keywords. Which was why they were headed to Orbit. Evidently, the Attorney General, himself, had spoken by phone to some nobody lawyer in Orbit—Franey—and had mentioned Victor Harrow no less than four times. It was just a hunch, but it was Pepper's hunch, and Pepper's hunches always got followed up. That's why she was once again up for promotion, and that's why she was on her way to Orbit. Franey was about to get Peppered, as they said around the halls in the Dirksen Building.

They entered Franey's office just after ten a.m., at the same time Judge Prelate was presiding over Ermeline Ransom's initial appearance across the street in the Silver Domed Hickam County Courthouse. They entered Franey's office with badges out and flipped open. Franey was found alone in the office, feet up on desk, drinking cold coffee from his favorite mug and wondering when, if ever, he was going to master the art of pipe smoking. He nearly choked on the pipe stem when he saw the embossed gold badges glistening across his desk.

"Good morning!" he cried, determined to keep the upper hand with the more boisterous voice. "How can I help you?"

Pepper spoke. "Special Agents Pepper and Henrici, Chicago FBI. You're Fletcher T. Franey?"

"I am. Please, have a seat."

"We'll stand. This should only take a few minutes."

"How can I help you?" Franey stood to his feet too, though he couldn't have explained why.

"Let me cut to the chase, Attorney Franey," Pepper said in her most commanding voice. "Two weeks ago you had a conversation with the Attorney General. He asked you to review some records for him. Recall that?"

"Let me see," Franey was immediately treading water, attempting to discern from their faces and their body language and their words just how much he could play hide-the-ball with them. Was he under investigation here? The sudden thought frightened him. He felt his bowels loosen and immediately wished he were near a restroom. "I do recall that. We talked, yes."

"And you reviewed records for him, yes?"

"Let me see," Franey tried again. Then he gave it up. These people were the real thing. Martha Stewart had done 21 months for lying to them, not for the insider trading they were investigating her for. He decided to cash in his chips. "He asked me to review Victor Harrow's records in the courthouse. Yes, that was it."

"And did you do that?"

"I spent two days going through courthouse records."

"What did you learn?"

"Everything Vic Harrow owned was mortgaged to the hilt. He owned nothing free and clear of liens."

"How did you know what all he owned?"

"I obtained his—the AG instructed me to obtain his...tax return."

"The AG instructed you to obtain Vic Harrow's tax return?" Pepper's tone was incredulous, although it was mostly a damn good drama job. She was leading Franey right down the merry path where she knew she could lead him. She had known two weeks ago where she could lead him, and she had rehearsed this conversation several times.

"Yes, he instructed me."

"Were you aware that it would be illegal for you to obtain

someone else's tax returns without their permission? I assume you never had Victor Harrow's permission to obtain his tax returns?"

"I never did. No—Yes, I was aware it was illegal. But I thought since it was the AG telling me to do it that I had a legal duty to comply."

"Wait," said Gio. "You're telling us you believed the Attorney General of the State of Illinois had the legal authority to direct you to violate federal law?"

"Yes," he managed through a voice husky with fear. "I did think that."

"Seriously. Where did you go to law school, Mister Franey?"

"Creighton."

"Is that an ABA law school?"

"Far as I know."

"Was it an ABA law school when you attended?"

"Far as I know."

"At Creighton, did they teach you that state officials had the right to violate federal law and to encourage citizens to violate federal law?"

"Not really. Not exactly."

"Not exactly? Tell us which course came close to authorizing state officials to violate federal tax laws."

"None."

"So you are telling us the AG directed you to violate federal law. And that you followed his instructions?"

"I guess I did."

"You guess you did, or you did?"

"I did. I obtained Victor Harrow's federal tax returns. We wanted to see what he was depreciating so we would know what all he owned."

"Who is 'we'?"

"Me and the Attorney General."

"So you and the Attorney General conspired to violate federal law?"

Franey suddenly sat down in his high back lawyer's chair. He slumped forward on his elbows. "Shouldn't I have a lawyer representing me now?"

"Mister Franey," said Pepper. "You have the right to have a lawyer present during any further interrogation. You are being questioned for your role in a possible violation of federal law. Everything you say can and will be used against you in court. If you can't afford a lawyer one will be provided for you. Knowing these things, do you wish to continue answering our questions?"

"I do. I don't. I don't know. Can I cooperate and make a deal?"

"You can cooperate if that's what you choose. We're not here to make any deals today. We're here to get the truth and move along. No arrests will be made today."

"Bleah," said Franey weakly. He realized that he sounded like a cartoon character, that he didn't have any strength left to resist. They had him dead to rights. He wondered if lawyers were still in demand in federal penitentiaries. He wondered if he could write appellate briefs for inmates and avoid getting raped. Then the tears came to his eyes. His cheeks were suddenly wet, and he reached for his pipe but only succeeded in knocking it to the floor as his teared-up eyes made everything double. He saw the pipe fall, hit the floor with the bowl down, and a live ember spark up and begin smoldering on the gray industrial carpet. Finally. He had managed to keep it going. He pulled a handful of tissues from his divorce client tissue box. He removed his thick glasses and wiped his eyes, dabbed his cheeks. "What do you want me to do?"

"Okay," said Pepper. "Here's how it works." She went on to explain how she would dial a secret Chicago number and be connected to the FBI's computers and servers, how she would conference Franey in on his phone and merge the calls, how she would then take him through a series of questions and he would give his answers. The questions would be exactly the same—well, almost exactly the same, she said—as the questions he had already answered. His job was to be forthcoming and truthful in his answers. He was to leave nothing out and to volunteer information he considered pertinent if it were left out or unasked by her. Anything less and he would be looking at obstruction of justice charges, not to mention perjury, falsifying federal documents, conspiracy, and the rest of the laundry list of federal crimes one can commit without even being aware. Especially a small town lawyer like Franey, who knew about wills, divorces, and deeds, and Marlin City Laws, but knew zip about federal criminal laws, racketeering, RICO, FISA courts and all the rest, of which Pepper and Gio were confident masters. In the end, he agreed, and the questioning began all over again. Except, this time, he was plugged in directly to the FBI computers, which recorded every word, extracted keywords, massaged his statements into database artifacts, cross-referenced it all, and made it instantaneously available to all other FBI and NSA and CIA agents worldwide. The entire process took only one hour, then the agents left, and Franey went home, defeated, intending to read about extradition laws in Columbia, S.A. He had heard Columbia was friendly to American fugitives. It was the next best thing to cutting a deal, at this point.

17

While the FBI agents were taking Franey's statement, Ermeline Ransom was across the street having her first day in court, such as it was. Although Chris Susmann had brought her the decent clothes to wear to court, leaving the orange jailhouse jumpsuit in her cell where she had changed, the court appearance turned out to be much ado about nothing, as far as Ermeline was concerned. First, she waited around for half an hour after the custody hearing for Jaime. Thank goodness Chris had come through on that. Outside of her own mother, Ermeline couldn't think of a better place for Jaime to bide his time while mom waited in jail than with Chris Susmann and Buddy Susmann and their two kids. The Susmanns went to the same church as Ermeline; their daughter and Jaime did Sunday School together; they had the same teacher in half-day kindergarten; and the mothers were similar disciplinarians and love dispensers. Her son would never go without, and Ermeline was grateful and thankful to Chris and Thaddeus for making that happen at the last minute. Plus, Chris had an inner strength—probably from serving in the army—that Ermeline had always wished for herself. The last two days had been frantic for Ermeline, and she had alternated between crying and glumly sitting alone and silent in her cell, watching the spiders and dust mites pass through her vision. Three times a day she was fed; all three times were Silver Dome food, so she had no complaints. Charlie Altiman and the jailer even allowed her to choose from the daily specials. Now, the courtroom was about half full of people she didn't know, so they weren't from Orbit, she was quite certain of that. No, these were press people, from the local TV stations and radio stations, and there was even an AP representative there, though Ermeline wouldn't have known that. Something was definitely in the air, though, and she assumed it was only about her and the Victor Harrow charge of First Degree Murder. She couldn't have known that the AP was following the FBI agents who had come to town that day. She couldn't have known that while the agents stopped in at the Silver Dome for early lunch the AP reporter had diverged and come to the courthouse, as much to stay out of the way of the agents as to snoop around. But now the AP reporter found herself watching an appearance by a young woman actually accused of murdering the man the FBI agents were known to be inquiring about. The AP had its sources, even inside the FBI, and when the AP reporter found herself in that courtroom at that exact time she said a silent prayer. Serendipity was alive and well, at least in Orbit.

At long last, Judge Prelate told the clerk to call the next case, and the clerk announced the case of *People of the State of Illinois v. Ermeline Ransom, Defendant*. Ermeline stood up when she saw Thaddeus stand up, and he motioned her to join him at counsel table. She took her place beside him and looked directly at Judge Prelate. Judge Prelate had his glasses up on his forehead and was squinting while he read from the case file before him. Finally, he looked up and the glasses slid down to their proper perch on his nose. "Counsel," he said, "have you been given a copy of the complaint in this case?"

Thaddeus spoke up, strong and firm. "I have, Your Honor, and I have discussed it with my client. We waive its reading in open court."

"Very well. And you do represent Ermeline Ransom in this matter?"

"I do, and I'll be filing a written entry of appearance later today."

The Judge smiled. It had been a busy morning for Thaddeus Murfee, and he knew that. "Very well."

At which point, Rulanda Barre, the Special Assistant Attorney General who had been directed by the Attorney General to prosecute Ermeline Ransom, spoke up. "Your Honor," she said in an equally strong voice, "the State requests that the conditions of release continue. That no bail be set."

Thaddeus pondered this for several moments. "Your Honor, I will also be filing a motion today to set conditions of release. I'm wondering—could we have that heard first thing in the morning?"

"I don't know about first thing, Mister Murfee, but we can certainly come back in the morning for a hearing on Ermeline's conditions of release if that's your preference. Counsel?" he added, looking over at AG Barre.

"Tomorrow morning would be too soon for the State, Judge," she said. "I was hoping to have at least a week so that I could become more familiar with the defendant and her connection with the community, so that I could participate in an informed discussion of her conditions of release."

"Nonsense," said Judge Prelate with a broad smile at the Special Assistant Attorney General. "You've had plenty of time to find out everything there is to know about Ermeline by talking with our sheriff and DA. We'll hear the bail motion in the morning. We'll start at eight sharp. Madam Clerk, please issue the order."

"Yes, Your Honor," both attorneys said in unison.

"And preliminary hearing will be set one week from today. Assuming there's no indictment between now and then. Same time next week."

Thaddeus felt himself warming to the coming fight. This was going to be a knockdown-dragout and he knew it. Already, SAAG Rulanda Barre, had tried to draw blood, and the judge had quickly dispossessed her of that notion. Now, they would go toe-to-toe in the morning. Thaddeus was determined to get reasonable bail set for Ermeline, something she could afford and, if she couldn't afford anything, he would ask for release on her own recognizance—

unheard of in Murder One cases, but hey, this was Orbit and everyone knew everyone, and Judge Prelate, himself, wasn't out to get Ermeline, he had already proved that. Thaddeus was already drafting the bail motion in his mind.

The court continued the case to the following morning, ten a.m., and Ermeline left the courtroom in the custody of deputy sheriff Dale Harshman. There were no handcuffs, nothing to indicate she was even in custody, except an official hand on her elbow, guiding her along the aisle and out the doors.

"Counsel," said Rulanda to Thaddeus. "Would you like to meet and discuss this afternoon? I owe you discovery anyway."

"What time?"

"Two good?"

"I'll be there. Thanks."

After the Franey statement, the two agents dropped in at the Silver Dome for an early lunch. They both ordered salads and iced tea. They asked if Bruce Blongeir were available. They knew Bruce to be Victor Harrow's son-in-law, the ex-basketball coach who had been given Bruce's Juices (the package store) as his prize for marrying Marleen Harrow. Bruce had then parlayed the package store into ownership of the Silver Dome Inn. The agents were simply asking to see the owner. It raised no eyebrows, not even Cece's quivering antennae. "No," she told them. Where might we find him, they asked. "He'll be out at his father-in-law's bus, on the east end. Can't miss it. Purple monster. Says 'Harrow and Sons' on the side. Can I get you anything else?"

BANG BANG'S office was actually a converted three-stall automobile paint shop in Skokie. The undercoat pits had been filled in and a new floor poured. Four steel desks ringed the walls, and Bang Bang, himself, occupied the furthest from the anonymous steel front door. There was no sign on the place, and there was no phone number to call. Nothing to identify it from any of the other fifty-some structures in the office park. But it was here that most of Chicago's mob business got decided, planned and staffed. There was a small galley kitchen off to the east side where a gofer made coffee and refreshments.

Bang Bang was wearing his blue navy pinstripes, two-toned Allen Edmonds, and a fat diamond on his pinkie. His goatee was freshly trimmed, every graying hair was in place on his head, and, for once, he wasn't hungry. It was barely 9:30; too early to even think about lunch. Eating was his main addiction anymore, since he had learned he was impotent. It was the diabetes that had really taken hold and done its damage down below. Anymore, his one solace was the food, and the food he preferred was killing him. It was a bitch, and he wasn't happy about his life. Now, he had some jerkwater lawyer down in Bumtown Illinois interfering with the scheme he had master-minded on Victor Harrow. Another bug to be squashed. Johnny Bladanni sat beside Bang Bang's desk, just waiting. Bang Bang liked Johnny, always anxious to do the big guy's bidding, ready to kill or be killed on a moment's notice—just be sure it paid enough and he would literally do anything asked. "Just squash this lawyer, Thaddeus Murfee," he was told that morning. "Don't bring me his head. Just make sure it don't work no more when you're done. Got me?"

"How much?"

"Ten large. Five now, five when you bring me the news clipping."

"Done. Could you make it fifteen?"

"Johnny, whattayou take me for? Have I ever screwed you? Are you calling me a homosexual?"

"I ain't callin' nobody nothin'. I'm just negotiatin' on price. Fifteen I'm askin'."

"Ten and be damn glad you got it. This economy everybody's gotta pull their weight."

"Just askin'. I'll report back."

"In person. No phones."

"No phones."

"Now get outta here. I got real work to do."

18

The law library was an archaic, under-served mess. Under-served because there was no real law librarian; the Northeast Reporters were actually the books of Judge Prelate; he merely lent them to the Hickam County Law Library, kept them there. All Illinois judges received the reporters by law as part of their budgets, for the legislature wanted judges immediately updated on all cases coming out of the courts of appeal and the Illinois Supreme Court. Judge Prelate was, in that respect, different from most other Circuit Court judges: he actually read the books, actually took them home with him and read the cases front to back, before shelving them in the law library.

Special Assistant Attorney General Rulanda Barre looked around her makeshift office in the Hickam County Law Library. What a dump, she thought. Compared to the vast law library she had enjoyed at the University of Illinois Law School, this was a sad joke. Compared to the computerized legal research on her laptop that gave her instant access to every law in the civilized world, every case decided in every Western country, this dump was totally unnecessary. They should bust up the bookcases for kindling and pass it out to the poor. Unnecessary? For that matter, so was Orbit. Farthest thing from her mind was coming to Podunk and prosecuting some floozy for killing her John. At least that's how she viewed the case at this point. All it represented to her was a minor irritant while she made ready her bid for the AG's job when her boss, Attorney General Robert Amistaggio, ran for Governor in 2016. She would be running for AG and she was counting on her long history of wins of criminal prosecutions to so impress the electorate that it would be as if she were running unopposed. And, come to think of it, another murder conviction under her belt could only help her Won-Loss record, on which voters put tons of weight. 63-0? Maybe this case could generate some publicity in this part of the state, and her name would be remembered for sending Victor Harrow's killer to the death chamber. Lethal injection of a local woman would make great headlines for surrounding counties too, and her name would be right up there at the top of the story.

JOHNNY BLADANNI WAS on his way to Orbit when he stopped off in South Chicago. Big Jim's Wholesale said the hand-painted sign on the rundown storefront where he roared the black Caddy up to the curb. He checked his hair in the mirror, slicked his eyebrows down with saliva, and jumped out. He looked up and down the sidewalk and was satisfied he was alone and no one was following. If they were following they were damn good. But he would lose them anyway, on the freeway. Who they were or why they might be following, he had no idea. He was born paranoid and had learned that paranoid was the best mental state for staying out of prison—or worse. It was the street warrior's best psychology, screw what the pop psych books said about these or those feelings or emotions.

He made his way inside Big Jim's, was immediately waved through the steel-grated door at the rear, and found Frankie "Good Man" Goodnichi waiting for him by the work table. Frankie gave him a high-five and waved his hand over the gun. "She's beauty, no?"

Laid out before him, still tightened down in the gun vise where a final patina of Hoppe's gun oil was being lovingly worked into its action, was an AR-15, complete with scope and flash suppressor. The gun would be loud, so there would only be time for one shot, and Frankie warned him about that. "You lay rubber as soon as you pull the trigger because this baby's gonna send the doves scattering and the cops running Code 3. Wear these gloves. They don't leave fingerprints inside. Toss 'em from the window and leave 'em there. If you're within a hundred yards there's no need to adjust for windage. She fires a .223 caliber projectile and she'll knock a man's hand off if you hit him in the finger. Every round hits, explodes, cuts, and slices and dices. Don't point it at nobody you don't mean to kill. That's three grand."

Johnny withdrew Bang Bang's expenses roll and counted off thirty hundreds. He placed them on the table and Frankie tenderly removed the weapon from its mount. He carefully slid it muzzle-first inside the gun bag. Next came a thirty round clip, "All dum-dums and armor-piercing ammo, though you don't give a rats ass about that. What's this guy do? He ain't a cop with a vest or nothin'?"

"Nobody lawyer."

"Oh, then shoot him for me, too. Just kidding. One round and you're gone."

"Thanks, Frankie. What do I do with the gun?"

"Drop it. Use the gloves, drop it outside the car. You don't wanna be pulled over with this baby in the backseat. She can't be traced, you've used the gloves, so no worry. Just drop her and tear ass."

"Will do."

Johnny headed back to the sidewalk where he again checked both directions. Satisfied, he laid the gun in the back seat and carefully edged away from the curb. No fancy driving now until the deed was done. The hit was worth $10K. He was going to get his new wheels after all. He looked again at his palm, where he had carefully lettered the target's name: Thaddeus Murfree.

SHE STUDIED the fax on her desk. The SAAG was secretly happy and
ready to flex some serious muscle around this sorry dump of a town.
State workers would arrive at 7 a.m. and begin tearing out walls
around the law library and installing new ones, installing paralegal
cubicles, and a new phone system hooked directly into the AG's main
offices in Springfield and Chicago. They were going to ramp up for
this. She had no doubt: she would soon have at her disposal more
square feet and more manpower than any other entity in the Hickam
County Courthouse. They really wanted this one nailed, and they
were going to spend taxpayer dollars to get the job done. She would
have two paralegals, a junior associate, which meant one of the newer
University of Chicago grads they loved to hustle onboard, and at least
two undercover AG investigators to run down all the leads in the case.
There would be a stack of witness statements a foot high by the time
those two finished their tenure in Orbit. It was going to get hot and
heavy. She only wondered if her opponent had any idea the drubbing
he was in for.

THADDEUS ARRIVED at the law library/office at exactly two p.m. SAAG
Barre was sitting at the lone table in the law library. She looked tired
and disgusted. Her hair was up, bun in back, but she was wearing an
expensive silk suit with a small diamond necklace that fit perfectly to
the hollow of her throat. There was no wedding band; there was no
engagement rock. She was, and her deportment said, a woman of the
world, alone, and in the hunt.

For the afternoon, the maintenance staff had scrounged up a
lawyer chair and she had positioned it on the far side of the table, so
that the table now served as her desk. Makeshift, but effective, Thaddeus thought, as he took a standard law library chair across from her.
He noticed how close they were—he could have reached out and
coldcocked her. They were very close, compared to how a regular
desk keeps a safe distance between two people. For a moment, he felt
empowered; he was the male, she was the female. By any law of any

jungle, he should win here. He decided against the crazy inspiration to just hit her; that would only wind him up in the cell down from Ermeline. He chased the thought from his mind like some magic rabbit that wanted to lead him down the crazy hole. No, he had to play this just right, make his position known, and start convincing the SAAG that his client was innocent and that somehow things had come to look horribly bad for her.

"I want to begin by saying—"he announced in his strongest voice, but she abruptly cut him off.

"Here," she said, and tossed an inch of documents at him. "Here's your discovery. The dead guy photos are there, but they're all copies. I can get you glossies if you've got the stomach for it. Some lawyers don't want the real close-ups. You're probably one of those." She smiled as she made the comment about his stomach for all this. "That said," she held up a hand to counter his reply, "—let me finish, please. I am only going to say this one time, Mister Murfee."

"Thaddeus or Thad is fine."

"I prefer Mister Murfee. Keeps it official. I'm only going to say this one time, and I'm only going to make this offer one time. I will allow your client to plead guilty in return for her serving a full life sentence, no possibility of parole or early release. I put an AG's rush on the gun and knife, and your client's booking prints are a 100% certain match to what they found on the barrel and the knife handle. She held the weapons, pulled the trigger, cut the letters of her name. This offer must be accepted by nine in the morning or it is forever withdrawn. If it is withdrawn, I will personally be in the witness room when your client receives the lethal injection. So far, in my practice, I have watched eight dirt bags get the needle. I put every last one of them on that table, and I'm about to do the same to Ermeline Ransom. Any questions?"

"I—I—"

"I agree. You need to discuss this plea offer with your client. You should do that now. The deal is only good until nine a.m. At nine a.m. in the morning we both go to the Judge's chambers and tell him we have a plea. He accepts the plea in open court on the spot. If that isn't underway by 9:01 in the morning, there will be no deal. You will have put the needle in your client's arm yourself. You may leave now."

The next thing he knew—when he fully regained his sense of conscious thought—he had climbed downstairs, out the courthouse doors, and down the stairs again, and was now headed toward the jail. He was on autopilot, and he had no choice but to go directly to the jail and tell Ermeline what had just happened. There would be no sugar-coating, no holding out false hope. She would then be left with a decision: Go to trial and risk making her son an orphan, or plead guilty and try to see him once a month until he got old enough and embarrassed enough that he no longer cared. Thaddeus felt as if he might throw up, and would have, if he hadn't known she was even now standing at the law library window, watching him struggle to the jail, a huge smile on her face. She had put the fear in him, turned him into a believer, and he didn't have the slightest idea what came next.

Within minutes he was in the jail, said hello to no one, and found himself in Ermeline's cell as the jailer shut the door on his way out. He was in shock, and he knew it. He thumbed the stack of discovery documents the SAAG had just thrown across the desk at him. Ermeline gave him a puzzled look. She had had lunch and was dozing lightly when he came in. He looked at her and shook his head. "It's not good." He went on to tell her all about what had just happened. And he dissected it for her, what the elements of First Degree Murder were—willfulness, premeditation, and intent. The State could prove, he explained to her, that she had willfully confronted Victor at his bus. That she had planned out the confrontation because she had obtained a gun and knife and taken them with her. The State could prove that there was intent to commit murder because it could be inferred from the fact of Victor's death. There was willfulness all over the place, he said, and there was intent not only from the fact of the death but also because she had the motive: she had sued Victor for cutting her up. What about manslaughter, she wanted to know. The jailer had said she might get a plea to manslaughter—was that possible? He explained how manslaughter applied to heat-of-the-moment killings, a sudden flare-up, a mental state that no one could have seen coming due to the immediate nature of the act which prompted the violence. She had taken a gun with her; there was no sudden flare-up, no heat-of-the-moment. He explained the fingerprints and how they were lifted from the gun and compared to her booking prints, how the computers analyzed, matched, and analyzed some more and how the computers were never wrong.

Tears came to her eyes. "I don't feel like you're on my side anymore," she said, and wept.

He could stand it no longer. He stood up from the bunk and sat down beside her. He put his arm across her shoulders and gave a hug. "I'm sorry," he whispered. She leaned into him and put her head on his shoulder. For several minutes they sat this way, nobody moving, barely breathing. Finally, he relaxed his grip and stood. He took two steps and sat back down on his side of the cell. "Now," he said simply, and he suddenly knew what came next. "Now we have to figure out how to kick some ass."

Her head popped up. "Kick some ass? That's the best thing I've heard since I got here!"

He stood and began pacing. "Ermeline, I don't know how I'm gonna do it, but you're not going down. This is not going to happen to you. We're going to find a spot, a weakness, and we're going to attack. We're going to find some chink in their armor and we're going to—to —kick some ass!"

She stood up then, and threw her arms around him. "Save me, Thad," she pleaded. "Just let me go home to my little boy."

"You have my word. You're walking out of this a free woman."

19

He walked outside and paused on the brick porch. He looked up at the sky and inhaled the clear morning air. Mourning doves cooed and skateboarders could be heard clacking along a block away. The start of another day in the ongoing saga of Ermeline Ransom and her Magic Breasts, he thought, and then hated himself for the thought. Poor kid. She would have her day in court today and maybe—if the heavens smiled down—he could get her released somehow at the bail hearing. He doubted it, but maybe. He flipped the Oakley's down on his face and took one last look around before beginning his trek uptown.

Which was just long enough for Johnny Bladanni, parked directly across the street with just the muzzle of the black AR-15 pointed out the top of the window, to draw a bead. He put the crosshairs on Thaddeus Murfee's head and carefully squeezed the trigger. At the last second, the young lawyer took a step and the muzzle involuntarily followed and fired at the same instant.

Thaddeus heard the blast, and that was the last he knew. Everything went black. As he lost consciousness he thought he heard sirens. He thought, but couldn't be sure.

20

Hector Ransom was infatuated, and he loved the feeling. He was in love with love, he admitted, and after spending all those dreary, mosquito-crazed months working the Gulf in the wilting heat and the drizzling rain, he was ready for something light, something pleasant, even something romantic in his life. He had come to Chicago in search of the almighty dollar and, while he hadn't found the perfect scheme yet, he had found the PuzzyKat Klub, just off the Loop on Clark Street. It was a topless, five-dollar-a-dance joint, where the liquor was watered down and the girls were underage runaways. Hector had visited there four consecutive nights and had hit it off with seventeen year old Rosemary Yuerl from Waltham, Maryland. Rosemary was a bright girl who had outscored her classmates on their math SATS, but rather than accept one of the three Ivy League scholarships she had been offered, she chose to make her way to Hollywood and become an actress. It was a great time in America, fame was there for the taking, all you had to do, basically—she had imagined—was to suit up, show up, and reach and pluck the golden ring when it came around. Chicago was where she ran out of money, and she did what all runaway girls do, she sold her body. At seventeen, there were tons of men willing to pay $5.oo to have that body lap dance, table dance, and private dance for them, and she was knocking down over two grand a week. She had fifteen hundred dollars locked up in a CD at Fifth Third Bank, and she was working on a second.

The night she met Hector he was just another face, just another admirer. He followed her every move when she worked the pole, and when she finished and came out on the floor he raised his hand immediately. He paid for seven lap dances in a row and talked to her while she ground her hips inches above his lap. She turned her back to him, she rotated and turned her front to him, nude from the waist up, and he learned some of her story. He was touched, as she was half his age and innocent beyond anyone he'd met since he was in high school. On the fourth night, she accompanied him back to the flop-house where he was logged in and he gave her the card. He gave her the card because he had actually run out of cash—the $6500 was down to $2500, and Ermeline's tip money had all been tossed away on the dances. He had just enough in reserve to keep off the streets until he found Johnny Bladanni and talked him into a score of some kind. He knew that Johnny had told him to go either east or west, and he knew Johnny would be angry as hell that he'd come instead to Chicago. But he had his ace in the hole: he had the goods on Johnny, and the guy wouldn't be able to turn him down when he came snooping around for work. So Rosemary accompanied him home at 1:15 a.m. on a cloudless late December night, wind chill -10 degrees, blowing snow off the Lake, and they crawled into his bed and made fast, unsatisfying love. She asked for money. He told her he had something better than money and laid Ermeline's American Express between her bare breasts. "What's this?" she asked.

"Plastic money. All for you. I've been saving it for a surprise."

"This isn't your name. Who the hell is Ermeline Ransom?"

"My Ex. She knows all about it. I've got her okay, because she owed me."

"So how much is the limit?"

He smiled and took a pull of a Bud Lite. "That's the great part. Amex has no limit. You can probably buy up to three-four thousand."

"Damnation!"

"I told you I liked you. Stick with me and I'll take even better care of you."

"C'mere," she said, and pulled his head under the blankets. "We aren't done here yet."

He did as she said, and she carefully reached behind her, to the purse she had left hanging on the bedpost, and dropped the card inside. A great start to an otherwise boring night. Two days later, she had run up over $3200 in plastic purchases, all over Chicagoland and as far west as Barrington. Nothing was cheap, and her tastes became more expensive as she shopped and learned what treasures were available to a person with Amex green. She had avoided Hector by skipping two nights of work, in case he wanted her to tone down the spending. She planned another attack tomorrow, this time along Michigan Avenue. She needed exquisite tops for her Hollywood head shots, and now she had the card to access those items. Just before she had maxed-out the card she would charge a ticket to Hollywood and leave this Midwest hell-hole. Her luck ran out in Macy's; the store detective nabbed her, called the cops, and she was processed through on two criminal charges. They took her name, current address, phone, place of employment (she lied and told them she worked a night shift at Mickey D's), and notified her parents. She was a minor, so the result would be acceptable and wouldn't make even a dent in her plans. Her parents would ignore the entire matter as they had ignored her all her life. To top it off, she got to keep everything else except the Macy's stuff, which was fine.

21

I n one way, the City of Orbit was blessed. One of the best cutters in southern Illinois headed up the surgical staff at the Hickam County Hospital. The hospital stood set back on the west end of Orbit. It was a four story structure, red brick with white porticoes, and an emergency room entrance around back with an entry way off Madison Street and a large lot, carved from the yards of the two houses that had been razed to make room. This was where the EMT's brought Thaddeus.

They had applied a tourniquet and pressure at the scene, had inserted a trachea tube, and had him hooked up to a heart monitor while the ambulance raced to the hospital. It all happened so fast that the kid on the skateboard had barely made the 911 call and the ambulance could be heard in the distance. The two skateboarders had crept closer to the downed man, wondering if they could help and wondering what a dying guy really looked like. They had seen enough by the time the EMTs came racing up the short walk.

"Scram, guys!" they shouted, and unfolded a transporter and lifted Thaddeus' limp body onto the table. They quickly rolled it up the walk and back inside the flashing van. Two EMTs jumped in with the shooting victim; the third drove. It was the left leg. They tied it off and managed the loss of blood best they could. They were only blocks from the hospital, and that's probably what saved the young lawyer's life.

The general surgeon who repaired and sutured together the femoral artery was Skip Russet, a graduate of Johns Hopkins who had done four years of surgical residency at Chicago's busiest south side hospitals. Gunshots were a walk through for Dr. Russet; he had repaired literally thousands of them by the time he moved his small family out of the city, downstate, where they would have more of a chance at a decent life and small town habits and manners. The schools might not be as good as the parochial schools around the North Side of Chicago, but by the time they were in high school, too many of the kids were lost to drive-bys, drugs, and alcoholism and unwanted pregnancies anyway, so it was a good trade to come south.

He began life-saving procedures on Thaddeus by getting an anesthesiologist on-board in the operating room, staffed with his usual OR nurse and surgical techs. They switched on the music—the doc preferred REO Speedwagon—and began clamping, irrigating, suturing, testing, and closing. Then the orthopedic surgeon bellied up to the table for his turn. He was a massive ape of a man and had no difficulty wrestling arms and legs into the weird positions favored by orthopedists in the operating room. The high-velocity bullet had shattered the left thigh bone at the neck and a steel rod had to be inserted, plated, and screwed in place. The entire surgery took nearly four hours, but Thaddeus held up well, which the doctors later attributed, at least in part, to his youth and to his excellent aerobic conditioning. He would remain in the hospital a week, and then be released in a wheelchair, with orders for physical therapy and home health care.

He awoke that first night just after seven. The morphine kept closing his eyes. As the room swam into focus he had to blink several times, trying to understand what he was seeing. Ilene Crayton? In his room? He turned away, and the nurse explained what had happened. She explained the shooting incident. She explained the surgery. She explained how Doctor Crayton's wife had insisted on being there when he woke up. He turned his head back. She smiled that incredible smile. She touched his hand. "Welcome back."

"The city police are standing right outside your door," the nurse reassured him. "They will be there 24/7 until your release. Orders of the District Attorney."

He reached for Ilene's hand, found he couldn't move his own, and fell back into a deep sleep. He awoke at four a.m., leg throbbing, and they replenished the morphine drip. He then drifted away again. By the time he awoke, she was gone. He wondered if he had been dreaming, so he asked the nurse. "No," she stayed with you until midnight, then left."

"Oh."

"But she said she'd be back later today."

"Oh."

"It's nice to have visitors when we're not feeling well."

"Yes."

"Do you want to try to sit up?"

"Yes. Do you have a mirror?"

"Oh my, we're going to be fussy now?"

"Yes."

THERE HAD BEEN NO WITNESSES, and the police had no clues. There was a gun, plus two gloves found at the scene. They had been turned over to the crime lab, but so far no reports were available. The AG didn't put a hurry-up on this workup, so everyone was in the dark. DA Quentin Erwin was on the ten o'clock news swearing that the IBI was in on the hunt for the shooter, and he had no doubt that they would be found and charged and prosecuted for attempted murder. They would leave no stone unturned, he promised. Yes, the victim was a lawyer, and yes, Thaddeus was defending a young woman accused of homicide. No apparent connection between the two shootings. Not so far, anyway.

22

A gents Pepper and Gio paid a call to Victor Harrow's purple
bus. It was just an after-thought; they didn't expect to turn
up much of anything, but Pepper insisted. They parked
their Ford Interceptor out front, climbed the three steps, and banged
inside, badges drawn and showing. "FBI," they told the gum smacker
at the front desk. "We need a desk and access to all of Mister Harrow's
records. We won't be long." The gum smacker buzzed Bruce
Blongeir's desk, and he got the news.

Bruce Blongeir was 6'-7", lean as a whippet and started three
years at power forward on Eastern Illinois University's varsity squad.
The team went nowhere, but Bruce graduated in physical education
with a minor in secondary ed and took the jayvee coaching job at
Orbit High. A year later, he was varsity coach, where in five seasons
he proved himself less of a coach than he had been a player. All five
seasons the team was below .500, and he was released from his
contract. Thereafter, he married Marleen Harrow, just back from two
spins with the Army. Victor had made a wedding gift to his daughter
and new son-in-law of what became known as Bruce's Juices—a
package store—which was instantly successful. Bruce immediately
parlayed his new equity into the purchase of the Silver Dome Inn.

After Victor's murder, Bruce had stepped into Victor's shoes at Harrow and Sons Construction, upon the widow's request. He knew next to nothing about construction or running crews or construction cost accounting or making multi-job payroll or meeting deadlines, but he was inquisitive and had an unusually sensitive nose for effective business practices. So far, following Victor's death, the business was surviving. In fact, some days it was even thriving, though it had only been weeks, so no one really had a clue yet what the end result would be. In return for taking over the reins at the construction company, Marleen had assumed Bruce's management role at the restaurant and package store. Each night they went to bed and kissed each other before immediately falling into the deserved sleep of the over-extended. But each knew, and it was no secret to anyone in town, that if this distribution of duties in the family worked and the businesses survived, the couple stood a chance of becoming very wealthy very fast. When the FBI agents showed up and flashed around their embossed gold, Bruce was quick to respond to the page and met them at front before they could gain any more of a foothold inside the mobile office. He wanted no trouble; he had enough trouble already and meant to get rid of them as quickly as possible.

He extended his hand and walked boldly up to them. "Bruce Blongeir, acting manager. How can I help?"

"FBI. We are interested in learning more about Harrow and Sons."

"Do you have a search warrant?"

"No, and we need one. Unless you'll cooperate."

"Why would I cooperate? No one likes the FBI nosing around their office."

"We think you might. We think Victor Harrow might have been making payoffs to certain officials in the State of Illinois."

"I don't see how that benefits me," Bruce said good-naturedly. He wasn't trying to make a scene or create any certain outcome, he was just being cautious.

"It could benefit you like this. If payoffs were made, you might be in a position to get that money back. With our help."

"How much we talking about?" Bruce was suddenly curious. He had been totally unaware of any payoffs ever.

"Possibly millions."

"You mean you might help me get back millions of dollars? Cash?"

Pepper smiled, which she rarely did when dealing with the public. "Cash."

"C'mon back to my desk. Let's talk some more where we're comfortable."

They arranged themselves around Bruce's desk. Coffees and colas were ordered and received. Bruce had become an instant concerned host.

Pepper went first. "We need two desks and access to your accounting data online. That's for me. For your information, my master's is in forensic accounting and what I plan to do won't take more than one afternoon. Next, we need all bank records. Gio— Mister Henrici—gets those. He's going to perform a bank deposit analysis for openers. That will give us an idea of the income/outgo picture of the business according to what the banks say. As for me, I can tell you I will be looking at the general ledger primarily. What the IRS calls LUQs—large, unexplained, questionable transactions. As I turn these up, I might have to bother you for more info. I'm sorry if that happens; we're not here to disturb you or injure your work flow."

"We can make that happen right now. What's my part?"

Gio smiled. "Just turn over passwords and records. We'll do the rest."

"Can I ask something?"

"Shoot."

"You don't think these payoffs might be tied to why he was killed?"

Pepper looked at Gio who looked away. Bruce had his first whiff of something more going on than what had been said. "Possibilities are hard to estimate at this juncture," Pepper said as vaguely as she could make it without appearing deceptive. "What do you think?"

"Here's what I think. Ermeline Ransom has worked for me two

years. I never have thought she killed my father-in-law. It just doesn't fit who she is."

"Which is?"

"She's a good, moral person with a kid to raise. That's all she's trying to do. And I've seen Victor try to hustle her down at the Dome before. She wouldn't give him the time of day. For her to somehow come out to the trailer with him and then wind up getting engraved with a knife, that doesn't fit either. The whole thing stinks. And now, the Attorney General has stepped in. From what I hear, they're after the death penalty. I can't say it enough. The whole thing stinks."

"Have you told this to anyone else?"

"I've told Thaddeus Murfee. He knows where I stand. I mean, I told him I couldn't offer cash help or anything like that, but anything else, let me know. Anything more wouldn't look right. This is a small town. Things get around."

Two hours later, Pepper had her LUQs: One journal entry read "Walker 150K/Harrow 450K." Another read "Walker 90K/Harrow225K." There must have been ten of them. And that was just for the last year. There were many years before, years when Victor had obtained and worked State contracts. Pepper cleared her throat. She was sitting at the bookkeeper's desk, next to Bruce. Bruce looked up. "Bingo." she said. "He made no effort to hide anything. Come over here, please. Let me show you what I'm talking about."

Two hours later Bruce had his answer. He was more certain now than ever before that Ermeline Ransom hadn't murdered Victor Harrow. The way Bruce saw it, Victor had gone and gotten himself killed when he quit playing ball with the Governor and the mob. Pepper showed him how this worked. Over the last six months of his life, there were no payments from Harrow and Sons to the Governor out of the general ledger. Nothing, although there had been at least a dozen receipts of State funds, payments on construction jobs. Victor Harrow, after years of cooperating and paying off Chicago, had suddenly stopped. For six months he had let them cool their jets. For six months he had let them stew or led them on, Pepper wasn't sure exactly how he handled it. But one thing she was sure of:

the payments had been turned off. Cold. She had it now, and she was sure, which made Bruce sure: Victor Harrow met his end because he quit the payoff franchise Chicago had him playing. Pepper didn't know who or why or the whens of what happened, but she was certain she was on the right track. She made Bruce swear that what they discussed that afternoon was absolutely confidential and not to be repeated to anyone, not even to Marleen or Victor's widow. Bruce understood and agreed. He wasn't about to do anything to drive away his new friends. He could see a huge pot of money somewhere out at the end of this, and he had become a convert. He wanted that money, and he was willing to go after whoever had it. One thing sports had taught Bruce, was this. When you're losing, you have nothing to fear because it's already been taken from you. When you're losing, that's the time to get reckless, to go all in, because it can't get any worse. Losing is losing and winning is winning. He had lost enough on the hardwood. He was determined not to lose it out here, on construction sites and inside courtrooms, where he knew he had to win. This wasn't about pennants on the wall or trophies in a glass case. This was about one, final item: money in the bank. And he intended to drag back as much as he possibly could. He owed that much to Victor and his family. Hell, he owed that much to himself, now *he* was family, and an important part of it.

"The payments leave your local bank here and go to the Cayman Islands," Pepper told Bruce. "I'll have to order the Grand Cayman records and trace out where the funds surface in the U.S. again. This just means Victor was washing the money before he paid off. Unless I miss my guess, the funds went to the Grand Caymans then to a federal bank in Chicago, where a withdrawal slip allowed the Governor's people to make the pickup. It was all banking, and it was all above-board. Victor has even filed his FBARs, so his foreign accounts are all reported and legal. He was doing nothing wrong, except partnering with the wrong guys. Eventually, it got him killed. I'm 99% sure of it. He quit paying off, and they made an example out of him. Happens every day in America. Go on home now, get some rest, we'll call after we have the foreign bank account records. You'll be kept in the loop by me personally."

But Bruce had a question. One that had started rolling around in his mind after she first announced finding the LUQs, which was this, "What do I do about this? I mean, do I send the Governor a demand letter from my lawyer and ask for the money back? Is that even safe to do? Will you be protecting me?"

"We've discussed that. We have other operative facts I'm not at liberty to discuss with you. But once those facts become public knowledge you'll know exactly what you should do."

"Does it involve suing the State?"

Pepper and Gio both smiled. "That wouldn't be the worst thing you could do," she said. "Let us talk that over."

23

She had stayed with him until midnight that first time. The next day she came by in the morning, with a Starbuck's, and returned in the evening. They talked and watched CNN. Then she read to him. She read his favorite stories by Michael Chabon. By the third night, he was feeling better, and the staff had him up and around. He was blowing in the spirometer and avoiding pneumonia. He was still wearing the anti-clot pneumatic hosiery and avoiding blood clots. He was standing with the help of crutches; they were very insistent about this and ignored him when he said how much it hurt. It was all part of his recovery, they assured him.

She brought a Scrabble board, and they played until ten o'clock, when he drifted off to sleep. He thought she kissed him goodbye on the cheek, but later decided he must have been dreaming. Ilene Crayton was not his only visitor; but she was the visitor he most enjoyed. Christine dropped by on the third day with documents to sign. There were also one or two fires to put out, nothing big, and he handled those with his cell phone. The pain was starting to relent, but it still hurt immensely when they forced him to get up and move around and put weight on the leg. That part of the recovery came much sooner than he would have liked, but it was according to the doctor's orders, and so he complied.

Police were still stationed outside his door. Quentin Erwin dropped by twice that week, one time smuggling in a six pack, and Thaddeus had several swallows before Quentin took the can back and finished it off himself. "Doctor's orders," Quentin said, and wiped his mouth with the back of his hand. He belched. "Ain't it great you have friends like me to drop by and harass you?"

"Seriously, what about the cops outside? Do I really need those?"

"Probably only while you're in here. Then you're going to want to carry a concealed weapon after that. Until we locate the perps and put them away."

"Do you think there's more than one?"

"There's always more than one. That AR-15 was clean, it was a professional job, probably someone out of Chicago."

"But why? What's the interest in me?"

"Something to do with Vic Harrow, I'm almost positive. I've got some feelers out with the feds. I'll see what I can run down. We'll talk again in the next day or two."

"Thanks for the soldiers outside. It was pretty frightening but also reassuring. You're my buddy."

"You bet. I hear Ilene's been dropping by."

"She told you?"

"That's a class act, Thaddeus my boy."

"Wow, I guess."

"Well you take care. Later."

"Thanks again."

He went home on the fifth day. Ilene helped him from the exterior door of the hospital to the Range Rover she had pulled under the portico. With the nurse's help he got the injured leg up and in, though he had to move the passenger seat back and recline it, to fit. His length made it difficult and flexibility in the leg was still nearly impossible and very painful. They had thought he would need a wheelchair, but his recovery was so fast that they released him with crutches only. He would need a cane after four weeks and might need the use of a cane for long time. She slowly drove him the four blocks home and helped him inside. She made lunch and got him propped up in the recliner she had made him buy. Lunch was chicken noddle soup and grilled cheese with a sweet pickle. He drank down a Diet Coke and finished off with a handful of Cheetos. He was suddenly starving and realized how much he had missed regular food. She tidied up the kitchen and wiped her hands. "So," she said. "All good."

"I really can't thank you enough."

"Yes, you can."

"How?"

"By giving me a quick tender kiss before I have to run home. The kids are in school, but I want to check in with their sitter. I'll be back in time for supper. Anything you'd like me to pick up?"

"Hey, I'm still back on the quick tender kiss. C 'mere."

She knelt beside the monstrous recliner, and he leaned up and put his arms around her shoulders. He kissed her cheek, and she turned her mouth to his. They kissed, and he was almost shocked at how good it felt. He released her, but she stayed close by. She pecked him on the cheek and then was gone. "Back around five," she said. "Cheerio."

"Cheerio."

He slept the rest of the afternoon.

24

"Hold it up," Thaddeus said to Chris. "C'mon, humor me!"

Chris extended her upright hand across the lawyer's desk. He placed his right hand to hers. He was correct: her fingers extended beyond his at the tips. "I'm right!" he cried, "Your hands are bigger than mine!"

A tinge of red colored her cheeks. "I work out. You don't."

"Wanna bet on an arm wrestle?" he invited. "Just for giggles?"

She placed the elbow of that same arm in the center of the desk and stood. He followed suit—putting his weight on the good leg— and also stood. They interlocked hands, and it was on. He strained, he gripped, he pushed, and he tried bending her hand backwards and down— nothing worked. It was like wrestling a four foot wrench, steel and fixed. She yawned and looked at her watch. "What time do I get to end your misery?" she asked without breathing hard. Just as he was about to make a smart-ass reply, she suddenly leveraged her full bicep and slammed the back of his hand down on the desk. "Wanna go two out of three?" she calmly asked.

"Damn," he said. He rubbed his shoulder. "Damn."

"Hey, I lift. I do tricep dips. You read. I'm strong here," she indicated her body, "and you're strong here," she touched her head.

"What gets used gets stronger. You were never in the military were you?"

He flashed on his one feeble attempt at interviewing for the Navy JAG corps the day following law school graduation. They had told him he certainly *could* expect to be stationed in Hawaii, *after* he had done two years on either an aircraft carrier or the southernmost island in the Aleutian chain, he had his pick. He had backed fearfully away from the recruiting table and looked over what remained of a very poor job fair. That was the moment he had decided he would have to go it on his own. Nobody worth a damn was hiring, and he didn't want to freeze his balls off in Alaska for two years or spend it in the sick bay of some aircraft carrier when it became clear he never would adjust to the fall and rise of a ship at sea. "No," he told her. "I never served my country."

"Army strong. Be all you can be. I went for it. And it worked. I can out-arm-wrestle all the farmers in my family. I can kick most of the athletes' asses."

He looked at her broad shoulders beneath the gray sweater she had received for Christmas from Buddy. She was such an athlete— plus a great wife and mother.

"How's Jaime been getting along at your place?"

"He's fine. He already knows the kids. It's a holiday to him. Only thing sad is he cries when I kiss him goodnight. He misses his mommy."

"That is really hard. I know Ermeline must be dying away from him. We've got to make this bail hearing work. I've drafted a pleading entitled 'Motion to Set Conditions of Release.'"

It was his first full day back at work, nine days after the shooting. He had trouble driving himself uptown, and had a terrible time on the office stairs, but he had finally made it. The coffee klatch was skipped; just not enough time to meet with his group and still get to work at a decent start time. "So I'm going to go for bail. We're set for hearing in the morning."

He slowly read it to her.

When he was done, she asked, "So any person accused of

committing a crime is presumed innocent until proven guilty in a court of law—we've all seen that movie. So they should always be able to bail out?"

"Unless there's a good reason not to."

"And that would be?"

"Well, if it looks like the defendant might flee, no bail. Or commit other crimes, no bail. Or interfere with witnesses, no bail."

"Ermeline is none of those. So she gets bail?"

"This is the part that's killing us. She can't get bail where the proof is evident or the presumption strong."

"The presumption that she did it, you mean."

"Exactly. So let's look at our facts."

She began making notes. "One, we've got a dead guy."

"Two, we've got Ermeline with a motive to kill the guy. For the job he did on her breasts. Motive isn't an element of murder, but it's like icing on the State's case."

"Three, she's got the murder weapon and the knife in her house."

"Four, and worst of all, her prints are all over the weapons. That's enough to not only convict her but to send her to the death chamber."

"She gets the needle."

"Unless we come up with a defense."

"So she's not getting out on bail tomorrow morning?"

"Her fingerprints closed that door."

"Damn it, Thad! She didn't do it! You know it, she knows it, and I know it."

"Probably Judge Prelate, Quentin Erwin, Jr., and Sheriff Altiman know it, too. But the evidence says otherwise. The evidence sends her to the death chamber."

"Damn! I hate this. It makes me want to walk across the street and beat the crap out of that lady lawyer."

"The SAAG? You could take her, Christine. I have no doubt."

"I'm just waiting for her to look cross-eyed at me. Can't stand that bitch."

"Hey, let's try not to personalize, all right?" he said, but on the inside he felt the exact same way. For a nickel he would shove Rulanda Barre out of the law library second story window. She flaunted it, used her position of extreme power as the senior prosecuting Special Assistant Attorney General in all of Illinois. And she lorded it over him, but at the same time, she was so cagey. She spoke softly and played so demure. But lurking just under that ingénue exterior there was a raging lioness, ready to devour even her own young if they crossed her. She was a killer and Thaddeus knew it, and she knew he knew it. He found himself starting to shake with rage while at the same time growing increasingly queasy toward the hearing to set bail. He was going to get blown out of the water, and he knew it. The bitch had him. He felt powerless in the face of the full strength of the State piled up against him. The State had the money, had the cops, had the crime lab, had an unlimited budget—everything they needed to bury Ermeline. Now they had a huge office complex in *his* courthouse. It occupied an entire third of the floor.

What did he have? He had a cheesy walk-up office in Nowheresville, eighteen months of wholly unrelated experience, and a client who had no money to defend herself with. Plus, a bum leg. Luckily it was the left leg, and he could still drive just fine with his right. For that, he was infinitely grateful. For just an instant, it crossed his mind to withdraw from the case and allow Ermeline to get a court-appointed lawyer so there might be some county funds for a second opinion on the fingerprint analysis and other crime lab workup. But he quickly nixed the idea. Ermeline had chosen him, and he felt honored. Most of all, felt a professional obligation as big as the courthouse. It loomed inside of him, filled his dreams, and occupied his every waking thought. When he read, he thought about Ermeline's plight. When he drove, he played it all in front of his eyes, sometimes nearly swerving off the road in his preoccupation. It was eating him alive, and he knew it. Now he knew what it meant to be obsessed. He was that: totally, 100% obsessed with one case. Would he ever get over it if he lost? How could he ever face another client and assure them he could help if he lost Ermeline to the execution chamber? His career would be over, flat out, kaput. He would be done. He would go back to school and train as a...maybe a welder. Something that didn't require him to stand up for people because he would have failed that responsibility in the worst way, and deep down he knew the worst secret about himself of all: he would never have the courage to try it again. He would be finished.

Christine leaned back and took a long drink of the tea—Earl Gray —on her side of the desk. "How is it looking? Terrible."

"I've got to get to court and file this. Make two copies, please."

HE DIDN'T WANT to admit it, but finally it kept pressing against his brain so often and with such ferocity that he had no other choice. The shooting had changed him in a huge way. No more did he simply walk to work, carefree. Now he drove. And he watched the rearview mirror every inch of the way. No more did he ride the Lifecycle to start the day. Now he had ordered a bench from Amazon and Ilene had helped him put it together. He was doing bench presses, rows, sit-ups and a dozen other exercises, all to keep the aerobic conditioning going as best he could. No longer did he stop in the mornings for his coffee klatch. Between the crutches and all the doors to navigate, plus in and out of the Buick, it was all just too much. Besides, the Silver Dome was an area where many faces could congregate, and in his mind he couldn't control his surroundings there. Too many people to try to identify and keep track of. The wrong one could sneak in and walk up to him and press a gun against his chest and that would be the end of him. So public places were, for the most part, avoided. He didn't like who he was becoming, but he didn't know how else to act. The police were parked out front of his apartment when the sun went down; the police were out in front of his house when the sun came up. Quentin Erwin and Charlie Altiman were making sure of that. But he knew their help was limited and finite. The day would come when they would have to take their manpower assets and align them differently with different cases and different needs in the community. What then? He wondered. What kind of protection would he have then? It made him shiver to think of what might happen once the cops went away.

THE BAIL HEARING went about as well—or poorly—as he had guessed it would. Rulanda Barre was there, of course, wearing the same outfit as she had worn yesterday, Thaddeus noticed. And of course Erme-line was there; but this time she hadn't changed, and she was wearing the jail-issue orange jumpsuit that said Hickam County Jail in stencils across the back. The Hickam Press was represented by a city news reporter and two reporters had come over from Quincy. A much smaller crowd this time, and in a way Thaddeus was relieved. This wasn't going to go well.

"Your Honor," he began, once Judge Prelate had gotten them started, "Defendant moves to modify the conditions of release. I have prepared and filed a written motion, and I believe that about says it all. This is a case of a hometown girl with lots of family and profes-sional contacts to Orbit, she's well-known and has a son and mother here, and she poses no threat as a flight risk. She has no passport and no need for one. She has no money or assets with which to post a cash or property bond. We ask that bail be modified to allow her to execute a recognizance bond." A recognizance bond would release her just on her signature. Thaddeus abruptly ran out of things to say and thanked the court for its time and took his seat. Ermeline didn't seem to notice she was being represented by a lightweight today, at least as he saw it. But he just didn't have that much to go on, and he knew what was coming.

"Miss Barre," the judge said, "what's the State's position?"

The SAAG jumped to her feet. "Bail should remain as is, Your Honor. I would like to advise the court that I made an AG Special Request with the ISP crime lab and that we have the preliminary fingerprint analysis back from the two weapons seized from the defendant's home. I'm placing a copy before the court—for the record —and handing one to counsel. As you can see, Judge, the Defendant's fingerprints are all over both weapons. And preliminary forensic firearm examination indicates the pistol was the one that fired the bullet into Victor Harrow's head. Thus, the proof is evident and the presumption strong, of guilt. This Defendant needs to remain in lockup. It's where she belongs, given all the circumstances."

"One minute," Judge Prelate said, as he read through the crime lab report. It had been previously marked as "State's Exhibit 1", and he was carefully digesting its content.

Then he said, "Counsel, do you have anything further?" and looked at Thaddeus.

"Your Honor," I would ask that the court continue this hearing for one week to allow us more time to assess the crime lab report and perhaps obtain an analysis of our own."

The Judge shook his head. "Can't do that, Mister Murfee. Your motion to modify conditions of release is denied. Defendant is remanded to the custody of the Hickam County Sheriff. Mister Murfee, keep in mind you can renew the motion at any time. We're always willing to reconsider on these cases. But this isn't even a close call. The presumption here is overwhelming. Your client looks very guilty to me, as of right now this minute. We're adjourned."

His head was swimming. He hadn't expected the last battering, not from Judge Nathan R. Prelate, who he had always considered a friend. But he knew the Judge was right. It looked terrible for Erme-line right now. It looked hopeless, in fact. She shot him a look of panic as the deputy took her away. He mouthed that he would be over to talk to her.

Rulanda Barre swept up her papers and left without a word. When she reached the doors she turned. "No deals counselor. You missed the deadline."

"Got it," he said glumly. "And we don't want a deal. So don't wait around if you've got better things to do with your day."

There, he was, in 100% committed to winning this case. Now if he could only figure out some way to do that. He needed some break, some opportunity to create reasonable doubt. But he had no idea where that might come from. He slowly returned to his office.

ONCE A WEEK—SUNDAY afternoons—they brought Jaime uptown to see his mother. The deputies would take Ermeline into the attorney conference room and bring Jaime to her. They would talk and laugh and cry for an hour each time, and then would come the inevitable time for him to leave with Christine, and Ermeline would be taken, crying and sobbing, back to her cell. Wednesday evenings they also had an unofficial visit time for them when the Sheriff put a portable TV in the room and let mother and son watch some of the videos Christine brought along. Cookies and milk were provided and at least for an hour mother and child were reunited and forgot about their separation. Ermeline was extremely grateful for these visits, and she was a model prisoner. Thaddeus had purchased her a small TV, and the jailors kept her loaded with newspapers and magazines from Haines drug store. After two months of eating nothing but Silver Dome fare, the food was tasteless but filling. She was putting on weight, thanks to the lack of activity. From hustling tables eight hours a night to sitting around a jail cell, the fat was accumulating, and she hated it. Occasionally, Charlie Altiman would bring her some treat or special dish his wife had made; occasionally Thaddeus would swing by with a bag of MacDonald's burgers and fries, just for a change from the usual routine. Ermeline was grateful for it all, but she still wept for a period each day and cried herself to sleep at night. The tattooing on her breasts wasn't fading either, and that added to her worry. Try as she might in the shower room to scrub away the carnage, it wouldn't budge. It looked like she would say VICTOR the rest of her life, and that crushed her. She hadn't ever really liked Victor all that well. She didn't hate him or anything, but he was like most men who had a lot of money, he thought he was entitled, that he could buy just about anything he wanted. Who knew, she thought, maybe she would be that way too, if she suddenly won the lottery. The thought of coming into a pot of money was the furthest thing from her mind, although Thaddeus, on several occasions, had mentioned he would be filing a lawsuit for her once the criminal case was over. He didn't say who he would be suing, only that it was coming. Since the original Victor Harrow case was dismissed on Victor's death, she hadn't thought much more about being compensated for the damage to her body, much less for the hardship and horror of the incarceration and what she was living with daily, thinking about the death chamber. Even that wasn't all that frightening: but the thought of leaving Jaime without a mother was horrifying. That thought she couldn't bear, so she released that tension with tears. It was a gloomy time around the Hickam County Sheriff's Office and Jail, for everyone.

25

It was pre-trial motion day. Rulanda Barre had long ago departed for her well-appointed office in Springfield, and she returned to Orbit only to sit smugly by while Thaddeus presented his useless motions and tried to fight his way out of the paper bag he was trapped inside. She had very little to say and even less to offer by way of counter-arguments: Judge Prelate was holding up the State's side of it very nicely because the bottom line was the Defendant's motions were baseless and futile. They deserved very little notice and SAAG Barre herself gave very little notice. Her face had the look of one who was very bored with swatting away gnats and only wanted to depart their presence. They spoke only to say "Good-bye" after the court hearings. There was no more talk of plea negotiations or trying to get a better deal for Ermeline. True to her word, Rulanda Barre had withdrawn the plea offer in writing, by a letter to Thaddeus, in which she also advised that she would be seeking the death penalty and that he might like to associate more experienced counsel than he. He seriously considered this, decided she was right, and approached Ermeline with the idea. Ermeline immediately put her foot down. She wanted Thaddeus and only Thaddeus and wouldn't agree to additional counsel, even if the Judge required it.

She simply didn't trust anyone else and wouldn't work with anyone else. Thaddeus reported this in a telephone status conference the lawyers had with the Court. The Judge, thankfully, didn't push the issue. He did insist on bringing Ermeline back into court, and making a record of the fact that the court was recommending she consider the appointment of additional counsel, someone with more Capital Murder experience than Thaddeus. She angrily refused and wouldn't even look at the Judge after that. "I know my rights," she exclaimed, "and I have the right to a lawyer of my choosing, not of someone else's choosing." The deputies returned her to her cell and that was that.

ONE NOON, instead of going home and fixing lunch for the two little kids, Christine came into Thaddeus' office. She sat down across from him and waited until he looked up from the laptop screen where he was working. "What?" he said, feeling like she had been studying him.

"It's time you learn to shoot."

"Shoot? Why would I learn to shoot?" he asked. But he already knew. In a way, he was surprised it had taken her this long. Maybe she had heard the cops were about to turn their attention elsewhere, he thought.

"So you know how in case you ever need to protect yourself."

He looked hard at her. "Do you know something I don't?"

"The cops are going to move on just about any time. And the mob already tried to murder you once. You should know something about combat shooting. Keep one around the house. Keep one up here at the office. Keep one under your coat."

"I don't think so."

"Oh, did you think we were negotiating? Come with me."

He was flustered, thrown off by her demand. "Where?"

"Thayer's Sporting Goods," she said, referring to the low shingle-sided retail outlet on the west end of town. "They've got a three station shooting range. Buddy and I shoot there lots. C'mon."

Thaddeus followed her out the door. He took the stairs by use of the bannisters, his crutches under each arm. They took her car. She drove them out to Thayer's, and she asked to try a .40 caliber Glock. Mr. Thayer included two boxes of ammo when he handed her the gun. "And muffs," she said.

They went into the range and found no one else around. "All right, let me show you the basics of a semi-auto pistol. Here we go."

An hour later, they were back at the office. Several times that afternoon, he eyed the pistol-sized box that now occupied the side of his desk. He was officially the owner of a .40 caliber Glock semi-automatic pistol. What's more, he knew how to operate it. He knew how to take it apart, how to clean it, how to load it, how to work the trigger safety, and he knew the two-handed grip and pointing style of aiming along your arms. From twenty feet, he could put a three tap group into the bull's-eye every time. From thirty paces, he was almost as accurate. "Mostly," she had taught him, "you'll be shooting your assailant at five to ten feet. That's where most of your practice rounds should be fired." Then she had turned him loose. Four boxes of shells later they had returned to the office, munching Big Macs and slurping shakes. All in all, he liked the lesson. They were going to meet again Saturday morning, and Buddy was going to shoot with them. It would be crowded on Saturday, so they reserved an eight a.m. start time. Thaddeus was fascinated. He had really never known anything about guns before. Now, he was armed. He was trying out a brand new shoulder-carry holster. The gun was on the table, the holster was strapped across his back. But tonight—he would probably wear it home, with the gun, under his jacket. But would he really have the courage and willingness to shoot someone if the time ever came for that? He could only wonder.

26

There were very few pre-trial motions filed. There hadn't been a confession, so there was no motion to suppress. The search warrant had contained enough probable cause, so the court denied suppression of the gun and knife. Thaddeus made the presentation, and argued violently and loudly, but the court denied it immediately upon Thaddeus' concluding. After all, Judge Prelate had signed the search warrant himself, and he wasn't about to overturn it now. No, the search and seizure of the gun and knife were all legal and would be admitted before the jury.

The motion to suppress the crime lab reports was summarily denied. Thaddeus hadn't had enough money to have his own workup done, and so his motion to suppress was based mostly on guesswork and supposition, and the court gave it the weight it deserved: Zero. Thaddeus had considered filing a motion for change of venue, but the more he thought about it, the more he realized Ermeline's reputation in the community would only work to her good. So he decided he wouldn't want the trial in a different county even if they offered.

27

T rial began on Monday, the first week of April, on a windswept day that alternated between blowing snow and freezing rain. The snow was light and seemed more a protest than a serious event. The freezing rain came and went but never did form ice on the windows or windshields. Thaddeus was getting around with only a cane now, but he still wore the holstered gun under his coat. Morning until night. He kept it beside his recliner while he watched TV and read at night. He kept it on his bedside table. It was always loaded and ready to be fired in an instant. The deputies at the courthouse knew all about the arrangement, so they waved him through security without a question. Judge Prelate had made it very clear to them: Thaddeus could come and go at will with his gun under his coat. It was an exception to the general rule that no civilian could enter the courthouse while possessing a firearm.

The weather reminded Thaddeus of what he was up against: Snow or freezing rain, guilty or not guilty? With his cane he made it to the courtroom. Christine was close behind. She pulled a wheeled briefcase jammed with papers and pads and books on evidence. His stomach was cramped, and he needed to urinate. There was a constant feeling in his bowels of an impending explosion, but so far nothing. He knew from law school exams and the bar exam the feeling of helpless fear, and that's what he was feeling now. It was a feeling that you had done all you could to prepare, but you knew going in that even your best efforts weren't going to be good enough. Happily enough, he had made it through law school and had only had to sit for the bar exam one time, but this was his first jury trial, and this time there were no study groups, no cram courses, no memorization techniques, no hints from others who had been there before. Plus, he knew they could prove Ermeline guilty beyond a reasonable doubt without breaking much of a sweat on their side. He felt totally isolated from the world and would have traded everything he had at that moment to be waiting patiently beside a cash register for the first customer of the day in his office supply store, never knowing the feelings he was having just now. This was a terror they didn't tell you about in law school, and how could they, really? He imagined that it was the same sort of terror soldiers must feel before a battle. You had done all you could to prepare, but there was always the possibility you weren't going to make it out alive. That was exactly how he was feeling when a sudden still fell over the courtroom. The air was filled with expectancy. Someone had seen something.

At just that moment, at nine a.m., Judge Prelate's court reporter entered the courtroom from the Judge's chambers. By now, the small-auditorium was filled to overflowing with jury candidates, bystanders, and press. Several deputies milled around up front, inside the bar where only the attorneys and court officials were allowed, like they owned the place. When the court reporter entered, they scattered, most of them exiting the courtroom altogether. But their presence hadn't gone unnoticed: they had been telling the crowd, "This place belongs to us, belongs to law and order." Thaddeus furiously limped into the fenced area and made a big show of claiming the defense table. He irately laid out books and papers from one side of the table to the other and made a big production of walking around the table and claiming that space as his and his alone. At 9:05 deputy Harshman accompanied Ermeline to the table, and she took her seat beside him. Behind counsel table but in front of the bar was a wide row of upholstered captain's chairs for the attorneys while they waited their turn at the tables. Deputy Harshman helped himself to one of those chairs, directly behind Ermeline. He was letting everyone know that he was in charge of her, that she was in his custody, even though she was sitting up front with her lawyer. Rulanda Barre entered moments later with Sheriff Altiman at her side. The Sheriff was the chief investigator and would represent the law enforcement arm of the State. Thus, he would be sitting beside SAAG Barre at counsel table. She had very few books with her, just a laptop and an *Illinois Evidence* manual. Three legal pads were scattered on the table before her. Then the Judge entered, and all eyes looked his way. With a flourish of robes and his large stride he took the bench, overlooking the sea of faces. "Thank you," said Judge Prelate, as total quiet settled over the full house. "Please be seated." The Judge nodded to the bailiff Don Helzinger, who called court to order. "Oyez, oyez, oyez, the circuit court for the judicial circuit is now in session, the Honorable Nathan R. Prelate, Judge, Presiding."

"Thank you," said Judge Prelate. He surveyed counsel table and appeared satisfied with the arrangements. "Counsel," he began slowly, "are there any pre-trial matters you need to have the court take up before we begin jury selection?"

"No, Your Honor," said Rulanda Barre, quickly on her feet and looking as serious as one might look just before an execution.

"No, Your Honor," said Thaddeus, who gamely pulled himself upright and stood, one shoulder higher than the other. He wished there was *some*thing he had to bring up that might change this terrible downhill slope he was looking at. But he knew there was nothing, and he could think of no last minute tactic to spring, so he took his seat. Ermeline exhaled beside him, and he could feel her counting on him every minute they sat there.

"Very well. Ladies and Gentlemen, I will now ask the Clerk to select a jury panel by lot."

The Clerk proceeded to draw names by chance, and as those names were called, the prospective jurors took their seats in the jury box according to the number they were called.

Then the judge continued, "Those of you who are appearing today pursuant to a jury summons, you have been summoned as a prospective juror in the circuit court to render interesting and important service. Your name was drawn by lot from the combined lists of registered voters, unemployment claimants, licensed drivers, holders of Illinois Identification Cards and Illinois Disabled Person Identification Cards who reside in this county. All of those so drawn constitute the group from which jurors will be selected to hear particular cases."

Thaddeus looked at the faces in the jury box. Some he knew; most he didn't know. But counsel had been provided with background sheets on the entire jury panel, consisting of several sentences on each person who had to appear that day. He had gone over the list with Christine before court. He had gone over the list with Quentin. Last night he had gone over the list with Ilene. He felt he knew more about the panel than SAAG Barre would ever know. Some of what he knew was very helpful, most was not. He began comparing names in the jury box to names on the information sheets. Ermeline read along with him as he underlined certain factual information with his finger. "Interesting," he whispered to her, as they went quickly through the names.

The court then launched into the standard jury questions: Name, age, address, marital status, business, occupation, or profession, children, know any of the parties, know any law enforcement officials, and on and on. Then came the moment both attorneys had been pawing the ground and waiting for: the chance to ask the jurors questions themselves.

Rulanda Barre went first. "Ladies and gentlemen," she began, and an elderly gentleman in the back row immediately waved his hand.

"Present," he said weakly.

"Have any of you heard anything about this case?" she asked, ignoring the elderly man.

He sat up. "Can't say I have. Course, I don't keep up much anymore."

She let her eyes rest on him. "Did any of you know Victor Harrow?"

"Who?" the gentleman asked, as if she were speaking to him and him alone.

"Victor Harrow, the decedent."

"I don't know any decedent, no."

"The man who was murdered—did you know him?"

"No, I don't know anyone who's been murdered."

She looked frustrated and was working hard to maintain patience. "Let me ask something, and I want you to know I'm not prying here. Mister—" she found his name on her jury map. "—Mister Botticus. Do you have difficulty hearing me?"

"Not a bit. I can hear a pin drop."

"It just seemed like you weren't following my questions, that's all."

"I don't follow your questions all that well. I'm not a well man."

"And, without being specific, what is the nature of your illness?"

"Well, they tell me it's called early onset senile dementia."

Judge Prelate extended both hands across the high desk and motioned the attorneys to approach him. He whispered, "Counsel, I'm going to excuse Mr. Botticus for cause. Any objection?"

"No," Your Honor, both attorneys said in unison.

After Mister Botticus had stepped down his seat was taken by a young woman with freckles. She looked to be early thirties and was alert.

SAAG Barre continued with her questions. She asked about feelings about jury service, whether anyone had any opinions about the case, whether anyone had any strong feelings about homicide cases, whether anyone had any strong feelings or opinions about the death penalty. A few hands went up now and then but on this last question she got six responses, three of them waving dramatically to be heard. "All right," she said, "I'm going to ask each one of you individually. If you sat as a juror in this case and heard all the evidence and you believed the defendant was guilty beyond a reasonable doubt would you have any hesitation in voting guilty only because you knew the death chamber was a possible result for this defendant?"

"Objection," said Thaddeus, taking his feet. "Attempting to pre-qualify the jury."

Judge Prelate appeared thoughtful. "I don't believe it's wholly inappropriate, Mister Murfee, and I don't believe it's prejudicial. You may continue, Miss Barre."

"Would the clerk please read back the question?"

The clerk read the question again, and all eyes fastened on the juror who first had raised her hand. "All right," said SAAG Barre, "Your name is Mathilde Henna and you're the mother of three teenage boys. How would you answer my question? Any hesitation in voting guilty simply because this might be a death penalty case?"

"I don't believe the Lord wants us to judge other people," she said, and looked at the other jurors and at the gallery for support. Very few heads nodded agreement. She looked down. "I just don't think we have the right to take anyone's life for any reason. 'Judge not that ye not be judged,' and all."

"So, your religious conviction would prevent you from voting guilty, even if you believed the State had proved the defendant's guilty beyond a reasonable doubt?"

"I wouldn't say it would prevent me," Mathilde Henna said. "I just meant it would be difficult."

Great, thought Thaddeus. She's going to have to use one of her peremptory challenges to get rid of this lady. Inside, his heart lifted for joy, and he made a silent prayer of thanksgiving, though he wasn't sure he believed all that much himself.

SAAG Barre persisted, coming at it from another direction. "So, you could vote guilty, even if you knew it might result in this defendant being sent to the execution chamber?"

"Objection," said Thaddeus, again taking his feet. "Counsel is attempting to get this witness to commit, to promise. That's improper voir dire."

"Agree," said the Judge. "Miss Henna," sometimes counsel will ask you questions and I'll allow it. Sometimes I won't. This doesn't mean you've done anything wrong. But right now I'm going to instruct you that you don't have to answer counsel's last question."

Mathilde Henna shook her head. "But I want to answer. I would need to seek guidance in prayer to make my vote. I can't just decide on my own."

Great, thought Thaddeus. You just made my jury.

SAAG Barre looked down at her notes. She moved along. "Ladies and gentlemen, only the person charged with the crime knows what happened to Victor Harrow. She might not even testify. Therefore, the State has no eyewitness testimony to offer. Knowing that this is a first degree murder case, do you feel like you have to say to yourself, well the case is just too serious to decide based upon circumstantial evidence to a return a verdict of first degree murder?"

Thaddeus felt he ought to object to this question, but he couldn't formulate exactly what his objection would be. So, he decided to keep still. Along with the others in the courtroom, he waited for any hands to go up. None did, so SAAG Barre finally nodded and made her notes. Thaddeus made a note himself. He might like to come back to this when it was his turn.

She went again. "Is there anyone who just can't sit on a capital murder case—meaning a case that might result in the death penalty?"

Thaddeus shot to his feet. "Objection, asked and answered."

Judge Prelate nodded. "Counsel," he said to Attorney Barre, "You've heard from the jury on the issue of willingness to convict on a capital case. Please, move along."

She tried again, but this time slightly different. "Now, everyone on the jury is in favor of capital punishment for this offense. Is there anyone on the jury, because the nature of the offense, feels like you might be a little bit biased or prejudiced, either consciously or unconsciously, because of the type or the nature of the offense involved; is there anyone on the jury who feels that they would be in favor of a sentence other than death for homicide?"

A hand went up in back. "Ms. Henna?"

Great, thought Thaddeus, her again. Just please don't get yourself kicked off for cause. He hoped and prayed she would remain on the jury. She was totally against the death penalty, and he knew that and, while it was enough to get her kicked off by the court itself, she hadn't, so far, actually come right out and said she couldn't vote guilty on a death case. Please, don't say anymore, he silently begged.

"I've thought it over some more," Mathilde Henna said. "I could vote guilty on a death case."

Gotcha! Thought Thaddeus. Thank you!

"All right, thank you, Ms. Henna. Anyone who feels like they might be in favor of a sentence other than death on a homicide case?"

Everyone looked at everyone else. No one else was going to bite. By now, the jurors had grown more than a little curious and more were interested in making it on the jury to see what it was all about. Plus, it appeared to be an important case and, who knows? Maybe books would be written. Maybe even by one of them. Anymore, juries in the U.S. might as well have their own literary agents when they get selected to serve. They would need to be told about note taking and keeping notes separate from the books the court passed out for notes, because those books were always collected and destroyed at the end of trials. It was important to know these things.

SAAG Barre plunged ahead, knowing Ermeline's reputation in the community was spotless. "Would anyone consider, if you had the opportunity, evidence about this defendant, either good or bad, other than that arising from the incident itself?"

"Objection," said Thaddeus. "Overly broad. Too general."

"Sustained."

"Let me rephrase. If the Defendant's reputation in the community was generally good and the defendant had no prior record, would that affect how you might vote on the case, even if the State proved guilt beyond a reasonable doubt?"

"Objection. Seeks to commit the jury to a certain vote. Improper."

"Sustained. Counsel, please stay with standard voir dire."

"There has been a good deal of local pretrial publicity about this. I know, my office has the clippings and we've seen the Channel 5 news reports. Do you remember facts from any of those stories that would affect your partiality? Or could you set aside those stories and pay attention only to the facts adduced here in court."

"Objection. First, it's multiple."

"Sustained."

"And second, it violates *Mu'min versus Virginia*. The Constitution does not require the court to allow counsel to question the jurors about the contents of pretrial publicity to which they were maybe exposed. The appropriate question is whether they have such fixed opinions they couldn't be impartial, not what they remember about the news stories." He was happy with his objection; he had done his homework and knew a little more about voir dire than he had realized when he first walked in this morning. Maybe...just maybe....

"Sustained. Anything further, Miss Barre?"

She reviewed her notes—or at least appeared to review her notes. More than likely, she was trying to hide her embarrassment from having asked several improper questions, Thaddeus thought to himself. More than likely she was trying to appear thoughtful and still in charge.

"Nothing further, your honor."

"Very well. Ladies and gentlemen, we're going to take our noon recess. Please be back and in your assigned seats at one o'clock sharp. Please remember the admonition the Clerk has given you. Do not discuss the case with anyone, including with each other. Please refrain from all news accounts and TV stories about the case. If anyone approaches you and tries to discuss the case with you please notify the court immediately. Thank you; you're excused until one p.m."

Thaddeus and Ermeline put their heads together for several minutes, and then Deputy Harshman took her back to the jail for lunch. Thaddeus hurried back over to his office. He had several ideas for voir dire that he wanted to map out for when it came his turn at one o'clock.

28

Georgiana Armentrout had a system. She considered herself the lighting director, just like the credits she saw roll by in the endless movies she watched every day on AMC. For every day, around noon, she would let herself into Ermeline's deserted house and switch the lights around. One afternoon and night, she would leave on the kitchen light and the laundry room light. The next day, she would leave on a living room light and the bathroom light. Next day, she would leave on the garage light—they shone through the panes in the garage door—and the porch light. She wanted to keep it mixed up to keep prowlers away. And she always checked Ermeline's voice mail as well, following which, she would bring in the snail mail. Everything went on the kitchen table: snail mail and a white stationary pad on which she kept the voice mail messages. Soon—she hoped it would be soon—Ermeline would return home and would really need everything organized. After all, that's what good mothers did. And Georgiana Armentrout was the best—she had to be, given how she had prematurely taken away Ermeline's father in the hunting accident. More than anything, now, she always tried to make it up to her daughter.

She was deciding the afternoon/evening light show when the wall phone rang in the kitchen. She pushed her thoughts aside and picked up the receiver.

"Ermeline Ransom?" a male voice asked.

"This is her mother. How can I help you?"

"Is your daughter there?"

"She's not, but she wants me to take her messages. Please tell me the nature of the call."

"We recovered her credit card."

Credit card? thought Georgiana. What was this about a credit card. A card of Ermeline's? My goodness, what now, the poor thing.

"Her American Express card. We nabbed the person who was using it on Michigan Avenue."

"Michigan Avenue? Where are you calling from?"

"Chicago. This is Officer Nick Forenzio, Chicago PD. We've just recovered your daughter's American Express card from the woman who was using it to buy scanty clads at Macy's. Store security actually nabbed her. We booked her on possession of a stolen credit card and theft by deception. Does your daughter wish to press charges?"

"My goodness, yes." Then Georgiana had the thought of the year. "Would you give me your number where I can have her lawyer call you back?"

"Sure." The police officer slowly recited his department cell phone number to Georgiana, whereupon she read it back and he told her she had taken it down correctly.

"Well, thank you, officer—spell that name, please."

"Nick—N-I-C-K. Forenzio—F-o-R-E-N-Z-I-O. Just have your lawyer call me. We'll hold the card as evidence."

"Goodness. I'll make sure Mister Murfee hears about this. And thank you."

"Thank you, ma'am. Have a good day now."

"Thank you, again."

Georgiana sat down and drew a rectangle around the information —name and number—she had just received from the police officer. She darkened the rectangle, and then drew an arrow at either end.

Surely, Ermeline wouldn't miss this message when she got home, not with the box and the arrows.

On second thought, she decided she would call Thaddeus herself. He should probably know about this. It was probably part of his job to protect Ermeline's credit cards. Yes, that was it. She would call him right now. She knew his number by heart, and dialed it.

～

IT WAS HALF-PAST when Christine buzzed Thaddeus and asked if he had a minute. He told her to come right in. "Need coffee?" he asked when she was seated. "I'm pouring."

Christine shook her head. "Here's what I just found out. Ermeline's mother is out in my office. Seems Chicago PD has recovered a credit card belonging to her."

Thaddeus was jolted upright. "What! For real?"

"Evidently. Wanna talk to her?"

"Get her right in here, please."

Georgiana was escorted in and took a seat across from Thaddeus. Christine sat beside her, notepad poised.

The older woman searched through her purse until she found the message. It still had the officer's name and number, surrounded by a heavy black rectangle, with arrows. She passed it over to Thaddeus. "Someone stole Ermie's credit card."

"This is incredible," Thaddeus said. "When did you get this?"

"Yesterday. I wanted to come right up, but I called and you were in court."

"Thanks for coming. We'll look into this, Mrs. Armentrout."

"Whatever you can do," the woman said. "I know Ermie'll appreciate the help."

"Okay, and thanks for coming."

Christine showed her back out and thanked her again. The older woman climbed downstairs and went east across to the jail. Might as well pop in on Ermeline and say hello as long as she was uptown.

When she was gone, Thaddeus and Christine locked eyes. Finally, "You thinking what I'm thinking," he said.

"I am," she said. "Somebody was in her purse. Probably Hector, the night he stayed over."

"Exactly. And he stole her credit card."

"Question. Have you asked to see the inventory Sheriff Altiman made when he booked Ermeline in?"

"No, I haven't. Never occurred to me."

"Why don't you go over and do that," Christine said. "I think we might need to go to Chicago."

"We?"

"You're going to need me for this," she said. "I'm going down home and pick up a few things. Ask the court for time to interview a new witness that has suddenly been located. Tell Judge Prelate you need to leave court by three o'clock. We can make it to Chicago and back yet today. Judge Prelate is going to be very disapproving, and the bitch is going to pitch a hissy. Just get it done. I'll be back in one hour. We'll talk then. Oh. Do you have any money, cash?"

"About fifteen hundred. I was saving it for rent."

"Get it. Get it all. We're going to need it."

"What are we doing, Christine?" She was suddenly taking over. He wasn't sure whether he liked this. But she was becoming more the person—the soldier—he had only been told about before. Her demeanor was changing right before his eyes, and she seemed very comfortable in the role of leader.

"We are going to Chicago. We are going to find whoever was using this card."

"Oh," he said slowly. "If we can find that person—"

"We can find Hector."

"And I—" she stood and saluted, right before his eyes, "I can make him talk."

"You can?"

She looked askance at him. Her look said, are you seriously questioning my talent? "I can," she said. "Thaddeus, what did you think I was doing in Baghdad those two years?"

"I have no idea. You're not allowed to tell."

She smiled. "This much I can tell you. Everyone I was left alone to question, every prisoner, ended up spilling his guts. Fifteen minutes and they all were crying to confess."

"Okay, you're on. Let's find this little bastard. I'll keep this afternoon's voir dire very general and just eat up a couple of hours. Then —if the judge allows it—we can leave."

29

J udge Prelate made an exception. He listened and heard how desperately Thaddeus needed to interview this new witness, the one that had just been located. SAAG Barre objected and all but cursed Thaddeus, but in the end the judge allowed the evening recess to begin at three o'clock. For the next two hours— one to three— Thaddeus conducted a rather cursory voir dire. He still wasn't sure what his defense was going to be, so he didn't try to get into specifics of the case with them, never mind that that wasn't allowed anyway, everyone tried it and he would be no different. Following the day's recess, Thaddeus hurried straight over to the jail. Fifteen minutes later he was back at the office. Christine brought a workout bag into the office with her. "Parts and equipment," she said. "We're going to need some basic things. I'm ready to do my part. Now, what did you find out about the inventory?"

"I talked to Charlie. He showed me the inventory. They have her purse, but not her wallet. I talked to Ermeline. She always keeps her wallet in her purse. So somebody removed her wallet from her purse before they booked her into jail."

"Hector."

"That's what I'm thinking."

"Let's go stick some gas in the Buick and head north. I texted Buddy. He's good with the kids. They'll be fine with him tonight."

"I'll drive. Let's call the Chicago PD officer on the way. I'll bet there's more he can tell us."

"We're off."

They gassed up, got coffee at a drive-thru and headed north on I-55.

Three hours later, they were in Chicago, headed west, driving to the rendezvous with Officer Forenzio, Chicago PD. On the phone while Thaddeus drove, Christine explained about Ermeline, about Victor, and generally what they were looking for. Officer Forenzio told her that he had the name and workplace address of the woman who had been using the Amex card. Rather than giving it out over the phone, he wanted to meet with them, see some ID, and then he would give them what they wanted.

They pulled into a Dave and Buster's on the West side of the city. A police cruiser was already parked out front. It was just about six p.m. and blowing snow. The sun had been down for a couple hours already, and the lights from the adjacent freeway cast an orange tint into the sky.

Inside, they found two police officers having coffee and pie at the first booth. Names were traded and Christine and Thaddeus joined them. Thaddeus opened his wallet and displayed his bar card. Officer Forenzio studied it, studied his driver's license, and then nodded. "Okay, but let me tell you about this girl. She ain't the one you're looking for. I've run this girl in before, once for prostitution, once for possession of coke. She's a good kid, but she's gonna die if somebody don't take over."

"I can't do that," Thaddeus said.

"I know. I'm just saying. She might know the guy you're looking for and she might not. Girls like this, guys are a constant blur to them. They'll use any- and everything that comes along. A stolen credit card beef is nothing to her."

"We'll find out what we can and back off."

"She's a good kid. I think she'll honestly try to help, if you tell her the whole story like you did me. Tell her about the mom and her kid, the one charged with murder. That'll get her goin'."

"Will do," Thaddeus said. "Okay. I'm buying. Give me the check."

"Nope, can't let you do that. You catch this loser and get him out of my city and we're even. Sorry, Miss, I hate these guys."

"Hey," Christine said. "You say he's a loser, I can't disagree."

The cops smiled. Christine and Thaddeus went out to the black Buick.

"What do you say we hit the PuzzyKat Klub?"

She shook her head. "Nope. First we get a room. We'll hit the club about nine tonight, after she's dopey and feeling no pain."

"Where do we get a room?"

"Something downtown. Downtown and cheap. Our defense budget is very limited."

Thaddeus drove them back into the city. At Wacker Drive he took Madison east several blocks. "What about that?" he said, indicating a rundown looking four story hotel.

"Looks cheap enough. Let's try it."

Thad put the room on his bankcard and they checked in. Even for a run-down flophouse the room charge was over $200 for the night. Some things never change, they knew, and Chicago wasn't known for low priced anything. Christine took her workout bag up on the moaning elevator. It was a metal room key, not one of the electronic room passes. Thaddeus let them in; Christine immediately flopped on the double nearest the window. She sat up and parted the drapes with her fingers. She peered outside. Another building was close enough to reach out and touch. "View's not much," she sighed. "But we're not exactly here for the view."

Thaddeus sat on his bed. "You hungry?" They hadn't eaten since leaving Orbit. "I'm going downstairs and scout around, see what I can get us to eat."

"I would like to stretch out and try a nap, but I'm afraid of bedbugs. I'll take the easy chair and try to catch a few Z's."

"See you in a few."

He went downstairs and stood out on the sidewalk. The traffic was loud and zipping by, mostly yellow taxicabs and a few motorists who apparently hadn't gotten the news that driving in Chicago was taking your life in your hands. Much honking and tires squealing and sudden screeching stops. "Good to be in the city," he muttered and headed west.

He returned with gyros, chips, and Cokes in cans. Christine had been lightly napping in the easy chair, but she was ravenous and they gulped down the sandwiches and two bags of chips. The Cokes washed everything down. Finally, Thaddeus said he was going to try out his bed, but on top the spread. He lay down and shut his eyes and was asleep in minutes. She looked over at him when she heard the light snoring and shook her head. "Pray this place ain't buggy," she said, and closed her eyes.

She awoke him at 9:15. He had been dreaming about Ilene Crayton and the horse farm he would one day have with her. Christine's hand on his shoulder, shaking, abruptly ended his glory and brought him back to reality. Night—he could see it through the crack in the curtains. Night in Chicago, fleabag hotel, with Christine Susmann looking down at him. Work to do.

He sat up and shook his head to get clarity. "What's up first?"

"You're going to be my chauffeur tonight. You're going to drive and I'm going to make some calls. When we're done you'll be very happy."

"So what will you be doing?"

"Getting the witness statement we need."

"How?"

"Huh-uh. You're the lawyer. You can't have direct contact with the witnesses yourself. That bitch at the courthouse would like nothing better than to charge you with witness tampering. Tonight is my night. I contact the witnesses—without you."

"Oh."

"So let's get started."

They set the GPS and wound up in the parking lot of a low,

sleazy-looking building that, at one time, had probably been a fairly upscale restaurant. Now, the neighborhood had changed and the respectables had been replaced by the denizens and lounge lizards. Thaddeus placed it in PARK and stared at the white walls and roofline with purple trim and pink neons. There was a huge picture of a cat—PuzzyKat—accepting a five dollar bill from an outstretched hand. Below that it flashed GIRLS GIRLS GIRLS – ALL NUDE – BARELY LEGAL!!!.

"Crap," he said.

"Give me a hundred dollar bill out of the rent money, please."

He did as he was told. "What are you going to tell her?"

"Going to buy an address. Be right back."

And she was. She wasn't inside ten minutes until she reappeared, in no great hurry, and walked confidently to the car. In her hand she waved at him a bar tab, on the back of which was writing.

"Address," she said, and slipped it before his eyes when she was back inside the car. "Set the GPS and let's go. He'll be on the prowl in the next little while if he's not already."

"So what happened in there?"

"I found the girl, asked her about Hector. She wanted to know was I a cop. I said 'No,' and she believed me. For $100 I got the hotel *and* room number."

"How the hell did she remember all that?"

"Turns out she stayed with him for a week. Until his money ran out. Then she went back to her own place. She was coked up tonight pretty bad, and jones'n for money."

"So the money will buy her an ounce of coke."

"She wishes."

"So much for my rent money."

"A great spend, Thaddeus. It'll come back tenfold. Doesn't the Bible say tenfold?"

"Or a hundredfold, I believe."

"Well, it's worth it, whatever. Now drive on."

He slipped into traffic and obeyed the Garmin voice, going left, then straight three hundred feet, then making a U-turn and heading back, then right and then straight for a mile. While he was driving along, Christine reached behind and retrieved her fire engine red gym bag. She placed it in her lap and unzipped the top.

"What do you have in there?" he asked.

"You don't want to know."

"Now I do. What is it?"

"Not much. Firm camera, for the statement I'm going to get for you. Something I picked up from the sale barn."

"Hector's statement—you're going to record it?"

"I am," she said, and smiled. "You can use it in court."

"Probably not. It's hearsay."

"We'll worry about that later. I'm sure you'll find some way around some dumb evidentiary rule like hearsay."

"Damn."

"Trust me, Silly Boy," she laughed. "Just get me to Hector's hotel before he stuffs a wad of tissue in his underwear and goes on the prowl like some hung dude. Which, I am certain, he is not."

"How are you certain?"

"Trust me. I know this guy. I'm married to his second cousin."

"TMI. I'm sorry I asked."

"Drive on."

Garmin brought them to a hotel painted white with green window trim and a red entryway. The flashing neon said "Laura-lei Arms." Thaddeus pulled up and over the drive-in. He found an empty spot and, for the second time that night, put it in PARK while Christine gathered her bright red gym bag up over her shoulder and said she'd be back in about thirty minutes. He asked whether she needed to know anything about the statement, and she just gave him a look. "Didn't mean to insult you," he muttered as she walked around and out of the headlights.

It was cold, so he left it running but turned off the lights. He checked the time. 9:38 p.m. He was wearing his gun under his jacket, and he was glad. He would give Christine until 10:10, then he would call for police assistance because she would be in trouble if she wasn't back by then. He switched on the radio "WCGI!" the howling voice yelled through the quad speakers. The FM station then launched into a string of obnoxious hip-hop loaded with epithets against the police and against women, and Thaddeus twirled the dial. He punched it for AM and found 720 WGN and came in on the middle of a discussion about the Blackhawks' chances for a repeat Stanley Cup. He wasn't a big hockey follower—NBA was more his thing—but he wasn't all that picky right now, either. Just something to pass the time while Christine was risking life and limb to help her friend Ermeline.

He actually knew very little about Christine's prior life in the military; she said little about it whenever the topic came up. And she was death on the Middle East and what she had done there. The few times somebody had asked her about it—that Thaddeus had heard— she had abruptly changed the subject and talked about something as innocuous as Basic Training instead. He imagined Abu Ghraib or some such prison had figured into her past, but wasn't sure. And actually, it was none of his business. He liked her and liked her work and didn't really give a damn what she might have been up to in a prior life.

It was 10:10, and he was ready to dial 911 when she suddenly emerged, the same red gym bag over her shoulder, hurrying in his direction. She gave thumbs up, made a face, and jumped in. "Hit it!" she cried. "Drive, drive, drive!" He wheeled the Buick out of the slot, backed up, and slammed into DRIVE. They bounced up and over the entryway bump and veered sharply out into traffic.

"What happened?" he shouted over the clamor and honking horns coming up behind them. "Was he there?"

She laughed. Uproariously, and couldn't stop. "He was," she finally managed. "He had someone with him. Another young lady. You wouldn't believe it. I gave her a bed sheet and made her go stand in the hallway."

"What!?"

"Hector was very cooperative. Gave a very thorough, very comprehensive statement. It's all recorded and ready for you to play for the jury. And, right now, I need you to pull out your cell and dial up

Officer Forenzio. I'm putting the statement on a thumb drive and turning over a copy to him so he can put Hector on ice for us."

"What do you mean, exactly?"

"Simple. We need Hector locked up for the credit card theft so he can't leave town. If you've got a hearsay problem I want to know where we can find this guy and haul his ass into court."

"Damnation."

"Just doing my job. Now. About my raise. I know it's three months early, but we really need to talk." She giggled, a high-girlish giggle. He had never heard a more contradictory sound come out of his secretary, whom he had only known as rough-and-tumble and ready for action. "A raise!"

"You've got it. Starting Monday."

"Starting last Monday."

"Okay, last Monday."

"So, how did it work? How in heaven's name did you get him to cooperate?"

"Well...it was shocking, but he decided to help."

"What do you mean, it was shocking?"

"Oh, this." She unzipped the top of the red gym bag and withdrew a two foot baton. "Electric prod. I borrowed it from Jimmy Smitters at the sale barn. They shock the livestock with these. I mean it was like totally shocking—to Hector."

"You used that on him?" Thaddeus said with disbelief. "You shocked him?"

"Can't tell you details, Boss. But it was all legal."

"Legal according to who, the CIA?"

"Black Arts. Anyway, it's done."

"Damn it all. I'm probably done, too."

"There's nothing on the statement to indicate duress. I made sure of that."

"Coercion?" he asked. "Did you coerce his statement?"

"Nothing on the video would indicate coercion."

"Torture? What about torture?"

"Thaddeus! What do you take me for!"

"I don't know. Nobody knows what they should take you for."

She settled back against the seat. "Well, find our little cop friend and then take me for coffee. I need Starbucks like yesterday."

She laughed.

"What's funny?"

"We'll call the video the Testicle Statement."

"Don't tell me, please."

"Or we could call it Balls to the Wall."

"Damn."

"Coffee, please. I need to steady my hands."

"You've got it."

Twenty minutes later they handed off the thumb drive to Officer Nick Forenzio, who thanked them and spun around his cruiser to go get Hector. He would make sure they put him in a deep dark hole at 2700 S. California Avenue, the Cook County Jail. It was home to 12,700 men and women awaiting trial on thousands of charges, and Hector would feel right at home among his kind.

30

Early the next morning, Thaddeus brought the firm camera over to the jail and played the Hector video for Ermeline. He had watched it several times himself, all twenty-two minutes. When it was over, she sat and stared blankly at the small screen. "I was set up," she finally said. "But who would do that?"

"Unknown," Thaddeus said. "Or why. But I'm working on that."

"Do you have any leads?"

"Not really. Probably the same guys who shot me. I'm guessing it had something to do with Vic Harrow. That's the only name I can come up with."

"So when can you get me out of here?"

"Soon. Very soon."

THADDEUS HURRIED BACK to his office. He had to update Defendant's Discovery Responses by adding the name of Hector Ransom to the Defendant's witness list. He also had to disclose the existence of the recorded statement. He made the appropriate changes and put them on top the pile of papers to file and distribute when he got to court.

He still had an hour to kill when the phone rang. Christine wasn't in yet, and he didn't blame her. They hadn't made it back to Orbit until one a.m., and he knew she must have been exhausted. He answered the phone himself.

"Thaddeus Murfee," he said. "How can I help you?"

"Thad, Bruce Blongeir here."

"Hey, Bruce. What's up?"

"Look, I know we haven't really got to talk since Vic passed away, but I'm wondering. Could I run by for fifteen minutes?"

"Sure. Where are you?"

"Over at the Silver Dome. I'll hoof it right over."

"Sure, come ahead."

Why not? He hadn't really had a chance to apologize to Bruce and Marleen for filing suit against Victor—not that an apology was forthcoming, but it was a small town, and in a small town those things were just done. Marleen was Victor's daughter, and Thaddeus knew it had really hurt her when he had to sue her dad. With Bruce it was little different; he was a guy, and guys were sort of used to getting mixed up in scuffles, but with Marleen it must have hurt her, and he was definitely sorry it had to be done. All in all, of course, he would have done anything—sued anyone—to help his client, especially an innocent like Ermeline. Which put Bruce in a strange position himself. On the one hand, Victor was his father-in-law and had been very good to him, with the package store and all that. But, on the other hand, Bruce was also Ermeline's boss, and like everyone, he knew what a damn good person she was, so that must have been very difficult for him. That's probably what he wants to talk about, thought Thad. He probably wants to get it off his chest.

Bruce was dressed in his customary uniform—khakis and Oxford cloth button down, ski parka and roper boots. He came straight into Thaddeus' office like he had had been there before, and probably had, while Judge Prelate manned the office as an attorney. He sat across from Thaddeus and rubbed his temples for a minute. He was pale and looked like he had been up several nights in a row. Everyone knew he worked eighteen hour days, especially since Vic's death, and he had taken over the construction business too, but this was differ-ent. This tiredness looked like stress tired. He pushed his glasses up on his nose and thanked Thaddeus for getting him in so fast. Then he began.

"I had a call from the FBI yesterday. And I think somehow your client, Ermeline, is involved."

Thaddeus' heart jumped in his chest. Ermeline? More bad news? "How so?" he managed to say, levelly and without worry.

"Turns out Victor—is this confidential?"

"Absolutely. I'm not even taking notes."

"Turns out Victor was paying off the Governor."

"What!"

"That's right. Construction jobs. It's been going on for years."

"What?" Thaddeus' pulse was pounding, and he felt like his heart was going to explode. He was so excited he couldn't find words. Slow down, he forced himself, one thing at a time. "How do you know about this?"

Bruce leaned back. "FBI."

"FBI. You talked to them?"

"Hell, Thad, they've been in my office, going over the books."

"And? *Really?*"

"Turns out Victor was paying the Governor off every time he got a government check on jobs he'd done. At least until six months or so ago. Then he stopped. FBI thinks the Governor and his cronies might be connected to poor old Victor's death."

"You must be—"

"Lying to you? I am not. I wanted to tell you earlier, but they just called me for sure yesterday."

"What happened yesterday?"

"See, the FBI came to my office—Vic's old office. Went over the books. Traced big money to the Caymans. Yesterday, they told me the money came back every time to First National Bank of the Americas, in Chicago. Then it was picked up by Ricardo Moltinari or Johnny Bladanni—something like that. Always the same two guys."

"So how's the Governor mixed up in this?"

"Agent Pepper—the FBI agent—she says they have the Governor bugged. He's discussing the payoffs with this Moltinari guy. Something about putting Victor in a vice. And squashing his head."

"Damn! Do you have her number?"

"Better than that. I brought you her card. You can have it. I have another." Bruce pulled the embossed card from his shirt pocket. There it was: Pauline Pepper, Special Agent, Federal Bureau of Investigation, Chicago, Illinois.

At that moment Christine stuck her head in the office. "Hey. Anyone need coffee?"

"Not me," said Bruce. "I was just leaving."

"Yes, for me," said Thaddeus. "Then come in with a note pad. We've got some work to do."

He thanked Bruce, who went back to his duties at the Silver Dome Restaurant. The Silver Dome Bar wouldn't be open for another four hours. He'd be running the restaurant and package place until then. Thaddeus watched him go, and then jumped up out of his chair. He was pacing in his office and pounding his hands together when Christine returned with the coffee and notepad. "Did we win?"

"Sit down! You know what, we did just win."

"What?"

He managed to make himself sit down. "Check this out." He went on to explain what Bruce had told him, how it created reasonable doubt in Ermeline's case, and what had to come next. Soon, Christine was back at her own desk, creating a subpoena *duces tecum* for Pauline Pepper. She would be ordered to bring all of her investigative files to the circuit court in the matter of *People v. Ermeline Ransom*. The hunt was on.

31

Thaddeus eased off on the voir dire, and by noon they had a jury picked. The Clerk swore them in and Judge Prelate told SAAG to call her first witness.

"State calls Charlie Altiman," she said. Thaddeus watched her closely. He hadn't yet filed his supplemental witness disclosure list. He would wait until closing time and file that at the last minute. He was willing to give her every chance that she had given him: exactly none.

Charlie Altiman arose from counsel table—his seat beside SAAG Barre. He slowly clumped up to the witness stand, paused and swore to tell the truth when directed by Clerk. He resignedly took the witness chair. She asked him a series of leading questions: name, work address, work history, years as law enforcement officer, when he became sheriff, what his duties were, who worked for him, where his office was located, and the rest of it. Then she told him she wanted to talk about Ermeline Ransom "the Defendant." Charlie just stared at her.

"I take it you're acquainted with Ermeline Ransom?"

"Sitting right there. Next to Thad."

"I mean—did you know her before this case began?"

"Sure. I know all the Orbit kids."

"And regarding this particular case, when did you first get involved or have anything to do with Ermeline Ransom?"

"Oh, it's been awhile now. Got a call from one of my deputies. Victor Harrow was dead. One thing led to another, and I got a search warrant for Ermeline's house that same morning."

"So you felt she might have had something to do with Victor's death?" SAAG Barre shot a look at the jury on this question. Are you listening? Her look said.

"Didn't say that. I got a search warrant. That was all."

"And what did you do?"

Sheriff Altiman looked over at the jury and broke a small smile. Several jurors returned it. "I searched her house."

"And what did you find there?"

"One of the city boys found a gun and knife."

"Let me show you what's been marked State's Exhibits 42 and 43. Would this be the gun and this be the knife?" she asked, holding up the clear plastic bags in which the gun and knife had been protected while awaiting trial. She handed the two bags to the Sheriff. He turned them over and looked at the initials.

"Those aren't my initials on there. Those are Mike Smith's initials. He musta watched me pull them out of the cabinet. He must have actually found them. I've sorta forgot which one actually turned them up."

"But these items were found at Ermeline Ransom's house, correct?"

"If they're the same ones, yeah. I guess."

"You guess or they were? They were found there?"

"Yes."

"Do you know where they were?"

"Towel cabinet. Bathroom."

"Which bathroom?"

"There's only one."

"Did you ever ask Ermeline about the gun or about the knife?"

"Nope."

"No, you didn't confront her with the weapons? Why not?"

"I thought I'd leave that up to people smarter'n me."

A note of frustration crept into the Special Assistant Attorney General's voice. "And who might that be?"

"You."

"You waited for me to talk to her?"

"Or somebody. I didn't know what to ask."

"Did it occur to you to ask whether she shot Vic Harrow with that gun?"

"Never occurred to me. Ermeline's not like that."

"But you didn't rule her out as a suspect?"

"Didn't rule her out. Didn't rule her in, neither."

SAAG Barre could see this was going to be difficult. She decided to change course. "Whose fingerprints have been identified on the gun?"

"The officer that found it and Ermeline Ransom's."

"Anyone else?"

"I'm just repeating what the crime lab report says. You should have that in your file."

"And I do, Sheriff. But the jury doesn't. Do you know the cause of Victor Harrow's death."

"From what I saw at the scene, gunshot to the head."

"Have you seen the coroner's report?"

"Yes. It said Victor Harrow died of a gunshot wound to the head."

"Did it say whether the gunshot might have been self-inflicted?"

"No, but I know it wasn't."

"And how do you know that?"

"Here's where my detective work really paid off." He looked at the jury again. "The gun that shot him was found at Ermeline's house. I deduced that it wasn't self-inflicted based on that."

The jury snickered and several smiled. The Sheriff clearly didn't have any use for Rulanda Barre, and he wasn't going to help her.

Thaddeus smiled inside but managed to keep his head down, busily studying his notes. He decided to just sit back and let Sheriff Altiman have his way with her.

"Was there anything about powder burns on the victim?"

"No powder burns were found on Victor Harrow's skin. Which indicates the gun muzzle was more than three feet from him when the shot was fired."

"Why is that?"

"Any closer and the gunpowder blast would have left microscopic fragments of burned powder on Vic's skin. There wasn't any found."

"That's in the crime lab report?"

"It is."

"Your Honor, the State moves into evidence State's Exhibit 77, the ISP Crime Lab report."

The judge looked at Thaddeus. "No objection. We have been willing to stipulate all along that Victor Harrow died of a gunshot wound. Just to speed things up. But Special Assistant Attorney General Barre wanted to take the long way around. I'm just glad we're about done with it."

"Counsel, that's unnecessary," said Judge Prelate evenly. "The State must prove all elements beyond a reasonable doubt. Including cause of death. Please proceed Ms. Barre."

"Your Honor, I have nothing further," Barre said.

She proceeded to call two more incidental witnesses—fingerprint examiner and gunshot residue expert, and then she rested the State's case. Walking with his cane back to his office, Thaddeus knew she had proved the case beyond a reasonable doubt. He stopped just outside his sidewalk door and looked right and left. Looking for unknown faces had become habit now. He wished it weren't so, but he felt hunted anymore, and he was always on edge. Nobody around, so his hand relaxed on the cane. He took a deep breath of fresh April air. Soon it would be deep spring, and the robins would return and the apple trees bloom. That would all be wonderful, and he was looking forward to respite from the winter and its ice and storms. But first, he had to raise reasonable doubt. Plus, he had to survive the next gunshot. He winced. He had to raise enough reasonable doubt to walk Ermeline Ransom out of the courthouse a free woman. How he was going to do that, exactly, had never been less clear to him than it was right then.

32

They were in Skokie at the far wall of the anonymous office. Bang Bang was so furious he was sputtering. Johnny had to admit he had never seen Bang Bang go off like this before, and Johnny, who really was sociopathic so that not much scared him, realized that his own hand was shaking and that his armpits were staining his white-on-white shirt.

"—and you let me down. Shot the guy in the leg! What the hey!"

"I'll go back," Johnny said. "Just let me finish."

"Now they got your name. Whattaya mean, 'go back'?"

"Let me finish what I started. I'm gonna make sure ain't no other lawyer want nothin' to do with this case."

"You think you can, Blades? You think you can make the Bangman happy?"

Johnny's back stiffened. "I know I can. This time I'll get right up in the guy's face. Won't be no missed shot. He's dead right now."

"You talk good. The cops catch you, you gonna give anybody up?" Bang Bang asked angrily. "Or is it safe to send you down?"

"Lips are sealed. You know I don't talk. Don't even ask me that."

"Hey, I'll ask you anything I want. And you'll do what I tell you.

All right. You finish this guy off. And I don't wanna hear about no more mess!"

"You've got it, Bang Bang. You'll hear back soon. And—will I get the ten grand then?"

"Get outta here. Yes. Deal's a deal."

"Then I'm already gone."

33

Christine had prepared, filed, and issued the subpoena for Pauline Pepper, Chicago FBI. She was to appear on a grey Thursday morning when court was called to order with a loud rainstorm pattering the twenty foot windows in the ancient courtroom. The place had a musty smell, and Thaddeus realized the radiators had kicked back on. The temperature was down twenty degrees from yesterday, and the jurors were showing up back in their winter wear and scarves. Not again, he thought, as he stared out at the late, late wintry weather. Please, let spring and summer get here. And please, let me prove something with this witness that wins this terrible prosecution.

What he had to prove—rather, what he could prove through Agent Pepper, was unclear to him. He had tried the two previous days to speak to her by phone, to get a feel for her testimony, but she had refused to speak with him. Her stock response had been, "This is an ongoing investigation. It is the policy of the United States Department of Justice and the Federal Bureau of Investigation never to discuss ongoing investigations. This includes with defense lawyers, Mister Murfee. Nevertheless, I will appear in court as commanded by the court, and I will bring my investigative file. At least the file cover with the high points. Will that be all, Sir?" He was getting the same response every time he called. He even tried calling her supervisor, but that person had mysteriously disappeared from the office, and no one knew when he or she—it was never made known to him—would return. So, he was stuck. He had a witness for this morning's opening of the defense case, but he had no clue exactly what she knew and, moreover, nobody knew exactly what she would reveal. Other than what Bruce Blongeir had told him, which was that the Governor had been recorded discussing payoffs with Mister Somebody Mob Name. Some unknown. At five of nine, she still wasn't there, and he caught a peek of Judge Prelate looking out the window of his conference room, just off the courtroom. Evidently, the judge was going to wait until the last minute, to give Thaddeus as much time as possible to locate and talk to his first witness. Ermeline nudged him. "I haven't even had a chance to say hello," he smiled at her. "Sorry for the preoccupation." She told him that was okay, and asked him whether her dress was okay for court. He gave her a once-over and told her she looked fine, better than fine, great. Thaddeus had told her early that morning about the witness he had subpoenaed, but what he hadn't been able to tell her was what the witness might have to say. "We're both in the dark about that," was the way he had left it with Ermeline. Finally, the judge could wait no longer. At exactly 9 a.m. he glided out wearing his flowing black robe, glasses pushed up on his forehead as he made his way up the several steps to his throne. Quiet settled over the room. Thaddeus looked around. He didn't know what Pauline Pepper looked like, so he didn't know whether she was in the court-room or not.

"Counsel, ready to proceed?"

"Ready, Your Honor."

"Ready, Your Honor," said Thaddeus.

"Counsel—"— indicating Thaddeus, "you may call your first witness."

Thaddeus rose to his feet. Might as well play this for all it was worth. "Defense calls Special Agent Pauline Pepper." The bailiff, whose job it was to locate witnesses and seat them in the witness chair, looked around the courtroom. Seeing no one coming forth in response to the witness call, the bailiff hurried back up the long aisle to the double doors. Thaddeus could then hear him outside in the lobby, calling for the witness by name.

Sure enough, the bailiff soon returned with the witness close behind. He showed her where to stand to be sworn, although the witness was obviously an old pro and automatically raised her hand before the Clerk of the Court. She took the oath and settled comfortably into the witness chair. Thaddeus sized her up, along with the jury. She was a pleasant enough looking woman, dark hair, very little makeup, no jewelry, with nice sorority girl features, unsmiling, and clutching a blue file folder that appeared to be maybe a half-inch thick. She stared at Thaddeus, awaiting his first question.

At just that instant, just as Thaddeus was about to pose his first question to the witness, SAAG Barre spoke up. "Your Honor, the State objects to this witness. The State claims surprise."

Judge Prelate turned to the jury. "Ladies and Gentlemen, I'm going to ask the bailiff to return you to the jury room. We have a matter that needs to be taken up on the record in open court. As I've told you previously, there will be times when you'll be excused from what's being said in here. This is one of those times. Bailiff, please take the jury to the jury room."

Long pause while the jury filed out. Murmurs and complaints and sighs could be heard from them as they went out the side door. Soon, they had evacuated, and the Judge turned his attention to SAAG Barre. "Please put your objection on the record, counsel."

"Surprise, Your Honor. Pauline Pepper isn't listed in the Defendant's written disclosure. At least not until just before we started this morning, when counsel handed me his amended response to disclosure. I haven't known about this witness until that happened. Ten minutes ago."

"Counsel?" the Judge said to Thaddeus.

Thaddeus slowly drew to his feet. "Your Honor, I didn't know about this witness myself, not until yesterday. It would have been impossible for me to list her any earlier."

"Not true, Judge," Barre said, jumping to her feet. "Counsel has my number and knows where to find me in my office. He could have alerted me yesterday, when he learned about this new witness."

As they argued, the witness was still in the witness chair, slowly thumbing through the blue file folder, ignoring the proceedings. She had been around long enough that she had seen and heard everything. She even looked a trifle bored.

"Your Honor," Thaddeus said, "this witness has refused to discuss her testimony with me. I had nothing to tell Counsel about the witness. She has claimed confidentiality and secrecy imposed by the DOJ, and until I ask her questions this morning, I don't even know if she *is* a witness."

Judge Prelate frowned down at Thaddeus. "That's pretty chancy, isn't it Mister Murfee? Calling a witness whose testimony you're unsure about? Don't all the trial manuals say you should never take that chance?"

Thaddeus was exasperated; he had been feeling exactly the same way. But he couldn't come right out and say the truth, that he had no case anyway, that he was really on a fishing expedition this morning. "Your Honor, whether I told Counsel about this witness yesterday or today wouldn't have made any difference. I had nothing else to tell her but the name of the witness. That's all I know."

"But you could have let Ms. Barre do some digging of her own by letting her know yesterday," the Judge said. "I'm not sure I'm going to allow this at all."

"It shouldn't be allowed," said SAAG Barre with a hurt tone. She took her seat, not wishing to appear too pushy. Instead, she looked hurt, almost pouting, as if Thaddeus had hurt her personally.

"So what I'm going to do, Miss Barre. I'm going to give you fifteen minutes alone with the witness, in your library office. You can have the same time Thaddeus had to prepare for this witness. Maybe she'll talk to you, maybe she won't. I don't know. But you do deserve fifteen minutes with her. We'll stand in recess until 9:25, and then I want everyone back in here. Agent Pepper, do you understand?"

Agent Pepper looked up from her review of the file. "I'll be here at 9:25, Your Honor."

"Very well. The court stands in recess."

At 9:25, everyone, including the jury, had returned and been seated. Thaddeus watched the Special Agent as she took her seat. Her blank look gave no indication what, if anything, she had discussed with the Attorney General's representative. It would be very unusual for one law enforcement officer not to discuss a pending case with another law enforcement officer, so Thaddeus didn't have the highest hopes for how this was going to go, now that the witness had been sandpapered by the SAAG. Nevertheless, he had no choice but to plunge ahead.

Thaddeus continued with his case in chief.

"State your name?"

"Special Agent Pauline Pepper."

"What is your business, occupation, or profession?"

"Special Agent, Federal Bureau of Investigation."

"How long have you had that job?"

She tilted her eyes to the ceiling. "Let's see. As of yesterday, twelve years. It was my anniversary hire date yesterday."

"Well, congratulations," Thaddeus smiled.

She returned the smile; not exactly a warm smile, more in the line of a business-person-to-business-person smile of acknowledgment. A smile that said, thank you, but we're really colleagues here, not friends. Thaddeus got the message. She was cool, and she was definitely not his friend. He figured she was probably not anyone's friend, since the State hadn't called her in its case.

"And what is your rank?"

"GS-1811. General Investigation Series."

"Which means what?"

"I can carry a firearm and investigate crimes. I cannot make arrests."

"Where are you based out of?"

"Primary field office is Chicago, Illinois. My address is the Dirksen Building."

"What is your educational background?"

"College, University of Florida. Master's Degree Forensic Accounting."

"Have you done any forensic accounting in this case?"

"As a matter of fact, I have."

Thaddeus' felt his heart flip over. Finally, was he on to something here? Would it help him or hurt him? He wanted to tell Ermeline to hang on to her seat, that her future was just now coming into view. Maybe. Maybe not.

"What accounting records have you looked at?"

"I should re-phrase that. I haven't done any forensic accounting specifically related to this case, no. Nor have I been asked to do that. But I have reviewed the books and records of one Victor Harrow, whom I believe your client is charged with murdering."

"And who asked you to review Victor Harrow's records?"

"No one."

"Why did you review those records?"

"I had a suspicion of what I might find there, based on a conversation I had."

"Who did you have a conversation with?"

"Attorney Fletcher T. Franey."

"And what did Attorney Franey say to you?"

"Objection!" SAAG Barre was quickly on her feet. "Calls for hearsay."

"Business record rule exception, Your Honor," Thaddeus shot back. "Besides, the statement is not being offered for the truth of the matter asserted, only that it was said."

"This is preliminary," said Judge Prelate, with a nod at the witness. "I'm going to allow it. Please proceed."

"I'll repeat the question. What did Attorney Franey say to you?"

"That he had a telephone conference with the Attorney General of Illinois."

"What was said?"

"Same objection!"

"Overruled. Proceed, please. Objection is noted on the record."

"Franey played a recording for me. The Attorney General is asking him to look into items of property owned by Victor Harrow."

"Anything else?"

"Yes, the AG—Attorney General—instructed Franey to obtain Vic Harrow's federal income tax returns."

"Anything about that of suspicion to you?"

"Well—Attorney Franey wasn't Victor Harrow's power of attorney for income tax purposes. So it would have been illegal for him to have obtained Victor Harrow's federal income tax returns."

The hair prickled on Thaddeus' neck. Finally, a light, a curtain parted, a glimmer of hope. "Let me be sure I understand this. You're saying the Attorney General of Illinois asked Attorney Fletcher T. Franey to commit an illegal act?"

"That's what the tape recording says. I have a transcript of that conversation," she said, and removed four sheets from her file folder. She held them up, and Thaddeus quickly stood, asked permission of the court to approach, and retrieved the papers. He scanned them quickly. "Your Honor, I would submit these four sheets as Defendants' Exhibit 1."

The Judge looked at the witness. "I trust these are copies? You have others?"

"Of course."

"Very well. Any objection, Counsel?"

"Yes, Your Honor," said SAAG Barre. "First of all, it's hearsay. Second of all, it's surprise. When I had my fifteen minutes with this witness she said nothing about this supposed recorded statement. Third, it's immaterial as it doesn't make any fact in this case more or less likely."

"Is that all?"

SAAG Barre nodded. "That's all for right now. But I would like to file a written brief on this issue before Defendant's Exhibit 1 is passed to the jury."

"I don't think so," said the Judge. "Mister Murfee, please pass Defendant's Exhibit 1 to the jury. And continue with your questions. If there's more."

Thaddeus thanked the Judge and continued.

"So you say that as a result of the conversation reflected in Defendant's Exhibit 1, and as a result of your conversation with Mister Franey, you reviewed books and records of Victor Harrow?"

She nodded. "I did. Special Agent Giovanni and I went to Mister Harrow's mobile office. We were graciously allowed by Bruce Blongeir access to any records we requested."

"What records did you request?"

"I reviewed the general ledger. Agent Giovanni reviewed bank statements."

"And what did you discover, if anything, in the general ledger?"

"Objection, "said SAAG Barre, again jumping to her feet. "These records are hearsay."

"No, Your Honor," Thaddeus disagreed. "Business records exception. I can lay the foundation."

"I think there's enough foundation. Objection overruled. Please proceed with your answer, Agent Pepper."

"Thank you. You asked what I discovered in the general ledger. I found a dozen or more instances in this current year where Victor Harrow was making transfers of large amounts of cash to an account he kept in the Cayman Islands."

"Where did the money go from there?"

"First National Bank of the Americas, Chicago."

"And what happened to the money there?"

"It was withdrawn from the bank by two well-known organized crime figures. Ricardo Moltinari and Johnny Bladanni."

"Do you know where the money went from there?"

"I—we do."

"Where would that be?"

"To the Governor himself."

A group gasp went up from the jury. Judge Prelate pushed his glasses up on his forehead and blinked several times. The bailiff sat up and opened his eyes. The Clerk of the Court looked up from her screen and smiled at the people filling the courtroom. General murmurs were heard making their way among the spectators. Thaddeus paused and appeared to be examining his notes. Truth was, he was letting the damning testimony sink in. He had just created reasonable doubt, and he knew it.

"Hold it," he slowly began. "How do you know Victor Harrow's money made its way from what you have characterized as well-known mob figures, to the Governor of Illinois?"

She patted her blue folder. "I have excerpts of other conversations. The Governor and Attorney General talking. The Governor and Ricardo Moltinari talking. Money being exchanged. Names being tossed around, especially Victor Harrow's name."

"Why Victor Harrow's name?"

"Because Victor stopped paying off six months before his homicide, and the Governor and the AG were—shall we say, very upset."

"Did they want him dead?"

"They wanted him made an example of. That's as close to 'dead' as we get."

"Please hand those documents to the Clerk. I'm going to ask her to mark those as Defendant's Exhibits consecutively by conversation date and time."

The Clerk nodded. She understood, and she would see to it.

Thaddeus told the court that was all the questions he had. He figured it best to quit while he was ahead. The trial manuals *did* say that. He didn't want to push it and suddenly get an answer that convicted his client of something.

"Your witness, Counsel," the Judge said to Barre, "you may cross-examine."

Barre rose to her feet. "Now, let me shift gears a bit. Do you know anything about the arrest of my client Ermeline Ransom?"

"Vaguely."

"From your investigation, do you know anything about the gun and knife found at her residence."

"Nothing."

"So Ermeline could have shot Victor Harrow, and you wouldn't know anything about that, correct?"

"Correct."

"And in none of your recordings have you heard anything about the shooting, correct?"

"Correct."

"You're not here to tell the jury she's innocent, are you?"

"Absolutely not. I have no idea about that."

At that moment, Thaddeus could feel his defense slipping away. Ermeline was starting to sound guilty again, and he was sure the jury was having the same response to the line of questioning.

"Do you know anything about her fingerprints on the gun?"

"I do not."

"You don't know when she handled the gun, do you?"

"No."

"She could have handled the gun when she shot Victor Harrow for all you know, correct?"

"Correct."

"And in none of your recordings is there anything about fingerprints on the gun, correct?"

"Correct. I know nothing about the fingerprints."

"And with the knife, she could have used the knife to carve E-R-M in Victor's forehead, and you wouldn't know anything about that, correct?"

"That's correct."

"You're not telling the jury you have any evidence that she didn't carve him up, are you?"

"I am not. I wouldn't know that."

"That is all."

Thaddeus had his chance to re-direct, but it was flat and simply repeated what he had gone over before. At the end, he felt like Ermeline's defense had slipped away. All they had proven was that the Governor and AG had talked and that Victor had to be an example. That wasn't the same as proof that they had done it. He had been warned by Quentin Erwin, Jr.: you must prove her innocence beyond a reasonable doubt: that's the reality of what you're up against. As it stood when SA Pauline Pepper was excused from the courtroom, the Illinois governor, like governors before him, was guilty of something, but as of yet nobody even knew that for sure.

Thaddeus then asked the court for a conference in chambers. The judge agreed, and a procession followed him from the courtroom into his conference room. The participants included Thaddeus, SAAG Barre, the Clerk, the court reporter, and Ermeline. Her deputy waited just outside the glass door. Judge Prelate disappeared into his connecting office and emerged minutes later without his robe. He was dunking a tea bag into a white mug. "Sorry," he shrugged. "Only have one cup." Everyone nodded; nobody wanted anything else.

All right, said Judge Prelate, taking his place at the head of the long conference table. "Back on the record. What did you have to offer, Mister Murfee?"

"Judge, I would next like to play for the jury a video I obtained from Ermeline's ex-husband. His name is Hector Ransom."

"I know Hector," said the Judge. It was a small town. Everyone knew everyone.

"Right. Well, my paralegal and I went to Chicago the day you let us off at three. We located Hector and took his statement. I would like to play that statement for the jury."

Judge Prelate smiled. "I'm sure the Special Assistant Attorney General has something to say about that. Madam?"

SAAG Barre smiled for the first time. Now that the jury couldn't see. "Hearsay. It gives me no chance to cross-examine the witness. Totally object. I would like a copy, though, as this also is new, just like the rest of Mister Murfee's case."

"The court will have to sustain that objection. Mister Murfee the statement is hearsay, pure and simple, and the State has to be given the opportunity to cross-examine the witness. Couldn't you have asked him to come here and given an evidentiary statement? Or noticed it for his residence or place of work in Chicago?"

"Not really. He's very nomadic, Judge."

"You mean he's a ghost."

"Exactly, Your Honor, he's here one day and gone the next."

"Do you know where he is now?"

"No." He didn't want the SAAG getting to his witness and sandpapering him. He had to get there first, before Miss Barre.

"Well, that should conclude this hearing. Let the record show this evidentiary conference took place in my conference room, out of the hearing of the jury. Anything else, Counsel?"

No one had anything else, and Thaddeus left the room.

34

He discussed what had just happened with Ermeline, and when she understood that they weren't going to be allowed to play Hector's statement, her eyes filled with tears. "That's so unfair," she said. "He finally tells the truth, and the jury doesn't even get to hear it?" Thaddeus said he was sorry, but that appeared to be the end of it.

That appeared to be the end of it until he returned to his office and told Christine what had happened with the statement.

"That's why we have him locked up in jail, Thad. We can subpoena him."

"How? A subpoena isn't any good on a prisoner. The Cook County Jail would only laugh at us."

"Aha, you've misjudged me again. They will honor it if it's in a certain form."

He frowned. "What form? What am I missing?"

"Simple. We file a *writ of habeas corpus ad testificandum*. That means 'produce the body for testimony.'"

"*Habeas corpus*? For testimony."

"Damn, man. Did you pass the bar exam in this state or not? Let me draft it. I'll have it ready by the time you go back to court so you can file it and have it served on Cook County."

"Good enough. Damn. Thanks so much."

THADDEUS' next witness was Attorney Fletcher T. Franey. He laid foundation for Fletcher's role in the case. Yes, he had had a conversation with the Attorney General himself. Yes, he had done some research at the courthouse, but then suddenly the witness examination went cold: Attorney Franey, it seemed, was going to take the Fifth Amendment. It happened when Thaddeus asked him what he had discussed with the Attorney General."

Franey looked at the Judge. "Your Honor, I take the Fifth Amendment. I cannot answer that question on the grounds it may tend to incriminate me."

"Mister Franey," said the judge, "have you discussed this with your lawyer?"

"I can't afford a lawyer, Your Honor. I'm representing myself here. And I take the Fifth!"

"Very well, Counsel, you'll have to delve into a different area. The witness cannot be forced by this court to incriminate himself."

Whereupon Thaddeus broke it off. But, the damage was done. The jury now had their suspicions about Franey and his role in Victor's murder—however large or small that might be. A certain degree of doubt, however small, had been injected back into the case by Thaddeus. Franey had done what Thaddeus had wanted him to do. He excused the witness when the State had no cross-examination. It appeared the Assistant AG didn't want to get into that mess involving her boss for all the money in all the banks. She returned her attention to her notes.

Thaddeus then asked for a recess for the day, so he could procure his next witness. It was only two p.m., but the Judge grudgingly allowed it, first making Thaddeus promise that he would rest his defense the next day, that they wouldn't have to go into Friday.

35

Christine's *writ of habeas corpus ad testificandum* was filed in the Circuit Court of Hickam County, where it was immediately signed by Judge Prelate, and then it was sent by courier to Chicago, c/o Cook County Jail. By seven a.m. the next morning, two burly Cook County Sheriff's Department deputies pulled up in front of the Hickam County Jail and delivered Hector Ransom to the temporary custody of the Hickam County Sheriff, for delivery to the court when it convened at nine a.m. Simple, enough, thought Thaddeus, who would be forever grateful to Christine for the whole idea.

Court was convened, and Thaddeus called Hector Ransom as his first witness. Hector was escorted into the courtroom and down the long aisle by two deputies. He was wearing Cook County orange, flip-flops with socks, and handcuffs. When they crossed through the swinging gate they removed his handcuffs so he could take the oath. He was sworn and sat down in the witness chair, dramatically rubbing his wrists as if he might have a lawsuit against the Sheriff for brutality. His face was anything but friendly, and Thaddeus guessed he hadn't been sleeping much since being taken into custody in Chicago. Finally, he forgot about his wrists and looked around. He blinked. He looked at Ermeline who only glared at him. If looks could kill.

"State your name," Thaddeus began.

"Hector Ransom."

"Mister Ransom, what is your usual occupation?"

"Welder."

"Where do you reside?"

"Cook County Jail. Used to be Lauralei Arms Hotel in Chicago. But I been evicted from there for no rent."

"And how long have you been in the Cook County Jail?"

"Ever since you sent Christine to talk to me. Same night."

"That's been several days, then?"

Hector looked around the room. He looked at the ceiling, thinking. "I don't wanna talk about that. My public defender says I shouldn't talk about the credit card stuff."

Thaddeus looked at the jury. They were rapt, paying close attention. Good.

"What credit card stuff are you talking about?"

"I think you know that."

"But the jury doesn't know. Please tell the jury about the charges you're facing."

"Well, the cops say I took Ermeline's credit card."

"Ermeline Ransom, your ex-wife?"

"Yep. Right there beside you."

"Did you take her credit card?"

"No. I haven't seen her in over a year. How could I?"

Thaddeus looked hard at the witness. He tried to bore into him with his eyes. He could feel the anger rising in his chest, burning, like someone who has been betrayed. "You haven't seen her in over a year?"

"Nossir."

"But that's not what you told Christine, was it?"

"I don't know. I don't know what I told that. Bitch. Can I say that?"

Judge Prelate gave the witness an icy state. "You can. You are allowed to express yourself in my courtroom. It might help the jury understand who you are and what you can tell us about the case."

"Well, she come to my room. I had a date that night, and she all but broke in. Made my date wait in the hall. Naked, too."

"Did you discuss Ermeline's case with her?"

"Nope. She only asked me about the credit card. And about some gun. I told her I didn't know nothing' about no gun. Period."

"What happened then?"

"She threatened me, but I wouldn't budge. Bitch don't scare me."

"Christine Susmann you're talking about?"

"That's the one."

"My paralegal and secretary."

"If you say so."

Thaddeus stood and crossed to the Clerk's desk. He lifted the silver gun for Hector to see. "Ever seen this gun before?"

"I don't know. Probably not. I ain't much on guns."

"But it's true, is it not, that you planted this gun in Ermeline Ransom's house a few months ago?"

"Hell no. Why would I do that?"

"That's what I'd like to ask you. Why would you do that?"

"I didn't do that. I've never seen that gun before. And I bet it ain't got my fingerprints on it, am I right?"

"You are right. So you wiped your prints off the gun when you planted it, correct?"

"Hell no."

"You were wearing gloves when you handled the gun, correct?"

"Hell no."

Hector smiled. He was beginning to warm to this cat and mouse game. Thaddeus could feel the blood rising in his neck and face. He was angry and his hands clenched into fists. He would love to attack this son of a bitch and pummel him, for all the trouble and horror he'd caused Ermeline and, indirectly, Thaddeus too. Not to mention getting shot and almost dying on his front porch. Not to mention the trouble Hector had caused his own son, Jaime, who had been separated from his mother for four months now. You rotten son of a bitch, he thought. I'm going to nail your ass.

"Your Honor," Thaddeus said suddenly. "Can we take the morning recess now?"

"We may, although it's early. Let's return at ten o'clock. We're adjourned."

Thaddeus ducked out of the courtroom and limped quickly back to his office. He dragged the bum leg up the stairs with the cane. He explained to Christine how Hector was totally lying on the stand. Evidently, he had been told the recorded statement couldn't be used in court, and he was just going to make up whatever came to him at any moment. Christine became enraged and then had an idea. She told Thaddeus what she thought they should do. Thaddeus hurried back to court, a grim smile on his face. This should be fun, he thought. Let's get this done.

Christine Susmann walked quickly across the street and up the courthouse steps. She hurried inside and went through the security checkpoint. The red gym bag she was carrying went through X-ray. The deputies unzipped it and looked inside. "There's nothing here," they commented. She told them she knew that. She told them she would be filling it with her boss's legal papers when she left. They nodded they understood and let her through. She went up the double stairs and through the double doors of the Hickam County Courtroom. Court was not yet in session. She walked right up to the bar and through the swinging gate. She took a seat in the lawyers' row where she had a direct line of sight to Hector. She placed the large red bag on her lap and sat back. This should be interesting.

Judge Prelate met with two out-of-town attorneys and their client in the conference room while the morning recess proceeded. He heard the uncontested divorce they had brought for him and signed the divorce decree. Justice was once again done in Hickam County, Judge Prelate thought, with a sigh. It was a mindless, never-ending game, the divorce racket. Deep down he hated it, and he wished the legislature would take divorce out of the courts and make it a simple civil matter. File the papers with the Clerk, and the Clerk issues the divorce decree. Some days he thought otherwise, but today he was sick of it. Then it was time to convene court, and he went back to his place on the bench.

Hector Ransom was returned to the witness stand. It was only when he was seated and looking around that he first noticed Christine Susmann. And with the red bag! The same one she had brought to his room and shocked him with. The same one she had threatened to wire to his testicles if he didn't get real and get honest then and there. Sweat broke out on his forehead and his underarms were instantly clammy. Damn, he thought, who let this maniac in here! Then he couldn't control himself and his hands began to shake. She was less then fifteen feet from him. And she had the cattle prod in her bag! How in the hell had they let her into court with that!

Thaddeus began again. "Mister Ransom, during the break have you had a chance to think back over any of the questions I've asked you?"

"Yes," he said, his voice subdued and meek. "There's some stuff I need to change."

Thaddeus looked over at the jury. "Like what?"

"Miss Susmann there. I believe I might have told her I planted the gun in Ermeline's house."

A gasp shot up from the jury, and the spectators in the courtroom could be heard commenting as the information passed along the rows of gawkers. Thaddeus could feel Ermeline stiffen beside him and then release. She was instantly shaking, choking down her sobs, holding back a flood of tears. At last the truth was going to come out! At last she had hope again of seeing her little boy grow up and to be there while it happened.

"Hold it. You're now telling us you planted the gun?"

"I was drinking. It's all hazy to me. But yeah, I left the gun in her bathroom."

"In a towel closet."

"That's right."

"And how did her fingerprints get on the gun if you left it there?"

"While she was sleeping. I just placed her hand around the gun.

Like this—" he mimicked lifting and closing another's hand. The jury instantly got the idea.

"Now, Hector, I want to ask you this, and I want you to think long and hard about it. Where did you get the gun?"

"See, that's just it. These men came and found me in Louisiana. I was working there. I was minding my own business. I was trying to earn enough to pay my child support. They made me come back to Orbit, and one of them gave me the gun. They told me what to do."

"What are their names?"

"I only knew one. Johnny Bladanni. They call him the Blade."

"Johnny the Blade Bladanni?"

"That's it. He gave me the gun and said to hide it in her house. He said to get her prints on it while she was sleeping. He said to bring the $5500 back to him."

"What $5500?"

"The $5500 I used to get her to trust me. I told her I just wanted to be there Christmas morning when Jaime woke up."

"And she trusted you."

"She did. I wouldn't trust me. But she did."

"So, you participated in a conspiracy to commit murder." Thaddeus said it as a statement of fact, not as a question. He looked at the jury. They were on the edges of their chairs. Good. Time to bring down the hammer.

"When you planted the gun, did you know it had been used to murder Victor Harrow?"

"I sort of knew."

"What do you mean you sort of knew?"

"I asked them what the gun was for. I wanted to make sure they weren't going to hurt Ermeline. I still love her very much."

"Damn. Sorry, Your Honor."

"Please proceed."

"You loved her enough to help frame her for murder?"

"IF that's how you want to look at it."

"And you put the knife there too?"

"Same deal. Got her prints, hid the knife. I didn't hide them very well. I wanted them to be found."

"Those are all the questions for now."

Judge Prelate had a very troubled look on his face. His forehead was deeply furrowed, and his glasses were on his nose, where they meant business. "You may cross-examine, Miss Barre."

"Thank you," said Rulanda Barre, who swept to her feet, ready for battle. She thought she understood what had brought about Hector's sudden switch in stories, and she was going to rip right into the heart of it and expose this fraud.

"Hector, you're afraid of Christine Susmann, aren't you?"

"Yes."

"Why?"

"That bag. That's her sitting right there, and that's the same bag she used on me."

"What did you mean? She injured you with the bag?"

"She's got a cattle prod in there. She said she would use it on my balls."

"She has a cattle prod inside that red bag on her lap?"

Christine Susmann smiled and shrugged. She almost held the bag up for the court to see inside, but managed to restrain herself.

"Counsel," said Judge Prelate, "please bring the bag to the bailiff. Mister Bailiff please open the bag and inventory the contents."

Thaddeus carried the bag to the bailiff, who made quick work of unzipping it along the top. He looked inside. "Empty," he said. Judge Prelate leaned across his desk. He indicated he wanted the bailiff to lift the bag and show him the inside. The bailiff brought the bag to the Judge, who spread the top open and peered inside. "Counsel?" he said to Thaddeus. "Do you wish to have the bag marked as an exhibit?"

"I don't think that's necessary, Your Honor," but I would like to display it to the jury, let them pass it around and see it's empty. Harmless, you could say."

"Very well. You may hand the bag to the jury."

During this time SAAG Barre had taken her seat and appeared to be lost in her note-taking. "Nothing further," she managed. "No further questions."

"Counsel, may this witness be excused?"

"He may," said Thaddeus. "I'm sure he's anxious to return to jail."

"I'm sure I see Mister Erwin in the back of the courtroom. My guess is our District Attorney will have something to say about this entire scheme, perhaps bring charges against Mr. Ransom and his gang." All eyes swung to the back of the courtroom where DA Quentin Erwin, Jr. was standing right inside the doors, watching. Thaddeus had tipped him off that he wouldn't want to miss Hector's testimony when court re-convened. Quentin tossed off a small salute to the crowd and smiled. He loved the voters. He nodded. Everyone understood that new wheels were already turning right here in Orbit.

When all had settled back down, Judge Prelate said to Thaddeus, "Counsel, you may call your next witness."

"Your Honor, defense rests."

36

The jury was out just over an hour. They had wanted to hit the County up for one last lunch before they took their vote. They returned looking relaxed and ready to go home. Two members smiled at Thaddeus. One man looked intently at Ermeline and shook his head. He would later tell her that he was embarrassed for what she had been put through. He actually apologized to her.

The jury forewoman handed the verdict to the Clerk, who handed it to the Judge. He slipped his glasses down on his nose and read, and then peered over at the jury. "Ladies and gentlemen, is this your verdict?"

They all nodded in the jury box. Several mumbled "Yes."

The judge handed the verdict to the Clerk and asked her to read it. Which she did.

"We the jury duly empaneled in the above entitled cause do find the defendant—not guilty!"

Joy erupted on Ermeline's side of the room. She stood and threw her arms around Thaddeus and sobbed. He handed her several tissues, and she pressed them hard against her eyes and wept. Rulanda Barre turned to Thaddeus and said, simply, "Congrats,

Counselor. See you next time." She quickly left the courtroom. Several jurors made their way to Ermeline. They patted her shoulder, and one woman asked for a hug. Ermeline hugged and cried some more. "I just want to go home, Thad. Will you take me home?" Thaddeus said of course he would. But they would have to stop by the kindergarten on the way and pick up Jaime. Ermeline's mother Georgiana Armentrout came bursting through the swinging gate and enveloped her daughter in her loving arms. "Hate courtrooms, hate cops," she hissed. "But they got this right, this time. C'mon. Let's get you home." Thaddeus told Deputy Dale Harshman that Ermeline would drop by the jail later this week and pick up her purse and other things. Dale shook his head. Unnecessary, he told Thaddeus. We'll bring them to her house and drop them off. It's the least we can do. Christine collected up all defense legal pads, books, and other papers and snugged them inside her red gym bag. "Good for me," she said, and left for the office, a very determined smile on her face.

37

Operation Spandex might have been big news in Chicago, and it might have been big news in Springfield, but in Hickam County it hardly made a ripple. After all, this was Illinois, where corrupt governors and corrupt government officials were a way of life. They're expected to be out there, plotting and stealing and covering up and even murdering. The job of the United States Attorney for the Northern District of Illinois—the first duty at the top of every Northern District US Attorney's list—was to investigate the sitting governor and his party ties and mob ties. It's not that the ties are a surprise to anyone; it's just that the feds try to keep it toned down as much as possible, so the only people getting hurt are the people on the inside. For the most part, the little guy goes about his business and ignores the whole mess. Who knows, in four years another new face will appear as the old one is carted off to prison. Maybe the new one will be honest. Or really, maybe the new one will be less dishonest. That's about what is expected in Illinois politics, it's the most that can be hoped for.

From the relative calm of his law office, Thaddeus read the story of Operation Spandex in the online Chicago Tribune. The Governor and Attorney General had been indicted by the US Attorney, and everyone was lawyering up. Statements were being issued, and denials were flying through the air like snowflakes in January. Arrests had been made the day after Pauline Pepper testified in Hickam County in the Ermeline Ransom prosecution. The news articles didn't say that, but Thaddeus put two and two together and he wondered if calling the FBI agent and getting her admissions before the jury had accelerated the speed at which the indictments were handed down and arrests made. After all, once she testified, the buggy phones had suddenly gone dead, nobody was talking to anybody in offices or homes, and the cell phones were not ringing. The investigation was as good as over once she had spilled the beans in Hickam County Court. And Thaddeus, in some small way, was glad he had helped to bring it all to a head. The murder of Victor Harrow and the politics and greed behind that never made it into the national or statewide news reports. It was still just local news, and the trial was just a small local trial in Podunk. Nobody much outside the county gave a damn, and that was fine with Thaddeus. He had noticed, however, an uptick in new clients, and his bank account was slowly growing fatter. Hector Ransom had been indicted by Quentin Erwin, Jr.'s grand jury, along with Johnny Bladanni, for conspiracy to commit murder, attempted murder, obstruction of justice, tampering with evidence, racketeering and a whole laundry list of related charges. Johnny hadn't been arrested yet, but that would come. It would be 100 years before he again saw the light of day. Which made Thaddeus happier than anything that had happened—except, of course, Ermeline's return to her family, and her job, and her innocent way of life. She had never hurt anyone and never would. That just wasn't who she was and never had been.

38

In June he accompanied her to Quincy, where she saw Dr. Sabrina Eberhard, a dermatologist. She was an expert in tattoo removal. While Thaddeus waited outside, Dr. Eberhard examined Ermeline and made her notes. She accumulated measurements and took pictures. She estimated the layers of skin that had been penetrated by the puncture wounds and the ink. Then she called Thaddeus in for the review, once Ermeline was fully dressed and satisfied she had asked the doctor all her questions. They met in Dr. Eberhard's office, and the doctor launched into a description of medical procedures that would be done to remove the tattoos. Yes, they could be removed. Thank goodness the ink was black, which was much easier to remove than blue ink. No, the procedures wouldn't be just one or two, and they wouldn't be painless. It would be quite painful as the lasers were used to break up the ink embeds so the body's natural processes could carry away the ink globules. Ermeline was excited to hear and, at the same time, apprehensive, but her insurance would cover the procedure, and Dr. Eberhard was very reassuring. Thaddeus made his notes and asked his questions, especially about the pain and suffering. After all, he was preparing to file a lawsuit and had come along with Ermeline on a fact finding mission. He wanted to establish in his own mind how many millions of dollars in damages he would be seeking from the State.

On June 15 he shocked the workers in the Orbit County Courthouse by filing a complaint charging intentional torts against the Governor, the Attorney General, and a long list of underlings and support staff. Intentional torts meant all governmental immunity fell away. Which meant the government officials were bare, naked, and could be sued. Plus, the State self-insured program would have to pay any and all jury awards for money damages. All those whose names were known were sued. There would be more, as discovery progressed and more became known. But for now, it was enough. The lawsuit claimed a civil conspiracy orchestrated by employees of the State of Illinois and its leaders, meaning the Governor, AG, and the whole list of bagmen and helpers who had murdered Victor Harrow and tried to blame it on Ermeline Ransom. This time in the lawsuit Thaddeus had two clients: Victor Harrow's widow, and child Marleen Blongeir, were also plaintiffs, along with Ermeline. The widow and child's loved one had been murdered by employees of the State of Illinois, and they, too, were looking for payback. In the end, the suit sought one hundred million in damages. In the end, it settled one week before trial for twenty-five million for Victor's heirs and fifteen million for Ermeline Ransom. Thaddeus limited his fees to 25% because the cases had settled without trial, but he could still see he wasn't going to need to hide rent money in the office ever again. The rent would be met as long as he continued to practice law, which, who could tell? Right now he was very interested in the raising and racing of Quarter horses—the sport of Kings. And he was interested in his new hobby as well: spending as much time with Ilene Crayton as she could spare him. Which was becoming more and more as the days went by.

And the gun? Quentin Erwin asked if he still wanted to wear the gun every day. Thaddeus thought long and hard about that. The gun had become second nature when he dressed in the morning. It was the last item of dress he slipped into before shrugging into his suit coat. Its weight now went unnoticed, and its heft against his body was forgotten. He felt safe when he wore it uptown, he had to admit. No, he told Quentin, he wasn't done with the gun, not just yet.

Survival meant sleeping afternoons and evenings. He ordered a sofa-bed for the office and turned off his phone at 3 p.m. He set his cell phone alarm for 7 p.m. He would pull out the sofa bed, cover up with an Army blanket Christine loaned him, and quickly fall asleep. After seven, he would slowly awaken and stretch. One cup of coffee, then he would go by Ilene's and be home by ten. No, there was no staying over, either way, until he had settled this final "loose end" he called it. She understood but she didn't understand. Still, she had come to know he had his ways and his methods, and she was satisfied to take it slow, to let him finally feel he had tied up all loose ends. He would get home, curl up in bed, with a hot cup of coffee, by ten, eleven at the latest, and stay awake until morning. He would lie there and fight off sleep as he listened for noises. Then he would get up and prepare for work.

One morning in June, he mounted the Lifecycle. He started slowly. He took the injured leg through one painful cycle, then another. Each time it spun the full circle the pain released and diminished by a hair. Soon he realized he had ridden five minutes and hadn't passed out. The next morning he rode for seven. Then ten. Then twenty. Soon he was raising the difficulty level on the console and the sweat was beginning to roll off his body, just like before. At last he was free, wildly pedaling his imagination to the top of the Rockies and back down.

In July he left the apartment without his cane. He started to go back inside, and then thought better of it. He would try this day without the cane. If he needed it he could return. But today, just for today, he was going to balance and walk all on his own. He never needed it again. Sometimes the leg would tire late at night, and he would remember. That's just how it was, he was discovering. Life left you with memories, some good, some not so good. But, so far, he had managed to face up to them one by one, and overcome them. He had hope about tomorrow. For the first time in a long time he had hope.

He didn't know if he would continue the practice of law. He had risen to the heights he had thought he wanted before—almost, anyway. At least he had gotten close enough to the mountain top to breathe the clean air, smell the wildflowers, and see the blazing sun. Did he need to be there all the way and forever? Not anymore. Not really. At least not today.

39

The door opened without a sound. But he knew. He could hear the doorknob's inner workings unwind as it slowly released.

The Blade came at him while he was lying in bed. He watched the entry and watched him approach. It was 3:34 a.m. "Open wide," the Blade whispered. "I'm putting the first one straight down your shyster throat!" Thaddeus had known it would come in his sleep. His hand, under the pillow, came up coiled around the .40 caliber Glock. His first shot caught the Blade just off to the right of his nose. The second caught him through the right eye. Then, he got centered, and put one dead center through his forehead. A perfect three-tap in under two seconds. His hand was steady as he dialed 911. He kicked the dead invader off the end of his bed. He would change the sheets after the cops finished up. There was a plastic cover on the mattress; he had wanted as little mess as possible when it finally happened. He went to the Keurig and made a cup. He sat in the oversize recliner, clad in his boxers and a T-shirt that said Cardinals! He waited for the siren. Closer and closer it came. Then a hammering at the door.

"It's open," he shouted. "It's open."

It was always open. Finally, he could lock it and start over.

-THE END-

ALSO BY JOHN ELLSWORTH

THADDEUS MURFEE SERIES

THADDEUS MURFEE

THE DEFENDANTS

BEYOND A REASONABLE DEATH

ATTORNEY AT LARGE

CHASE, THE BAD BABY

DEFENDING TURQUOISE

THE MENTAL CASE

UNSPEAKABLE PRAYERS

THE GIRL WHO WROTE THE NEW YORK TIMES BESTSELLER

THE TRIAL LAWYER (A SMALL DEATH)

THE NEAR DEATH EXPERIENCE

SISTERS IN LAW SERIES

FRAT PARTY: SISTERS IN LAW

HELLFIRE: SISTERS IN LAW

MICHAEL GRESHAM SERIES

LIES SHE NEVER TOLD ME

THE LAWYER

SECRETS GIRLS KEEP

THE LAW PARTNERS

CARLOS THE ANT

SAKHAROV THE BEAR

ANNIE'S VERDICT

DEAD LAWYER ON AISLE 11

30 DAYS OF JUSTIS

PSYCHOLOGICAL THRILLERS

THE EMPTY PLACE AT THE TABLE

FREE BOOK FOR EMAIL SIGNUP

DISCLAIMER

This is a work of fiction. Names, characters, places, and incidents either are the by-product of the author's imagination or are used fictitiously. Any resemblance to actual persons, living or dead, events, or locales is entirely coincidental.

ABOUT THE AUTHOR

John Ellsworth 2016

USA TODAY Bestselling Author John Ellsworth practiced law in Flagstaff and Chicago. As a criminal defense attorney he became expert in defending state and federal criminal defendants. Some of that experience and knowledge led to his writing this book.

Since 2014 John has been writing legal, crime, and psychological thrillers with huge success. He has been a Kindle All-Star (Amazon's selection) many times and he has made the *USA TODAY* bestsellers' list.

Reception to John's books has been phenomenal; more than

1,000,000 have been downloaded in 40 months. All are Amazon best-sellers.

John lives in Southern California where he makes his way around his small beach town on a yellow Vespa motorscooter.

He is married and has lost count of how many grandchildren his five daughters have produced.

ellsworthbooks.com
johnellsworthbooks@gmail.com

Made in the USA
Coppell, TX
06 June 2020

27130815R10152